Praise for Megan Frazer Blakemore

P9-DIF-159

The **Firefly Code**

"An intricate mystery. . . . Will surely fascinate fans of Lois Lowry's *The Giver*." —*School Library Journal*

"Less stark than *The Giver*, this welcome addition to the dystopic utopia genre is a young cousin of Ally Condie's *Matched* and Mary Pearson's *The Adoration of Jenna Fox*." —*Kirkus Reviews*

"Will have children turning pages and thinking about important questions." —*Booklist*

"This creepy, memorable novel is a welcome addition to the relative few utopian/dystopian books for pre-YA readers. . . . An ending that will have readers eagerly anticipating the next installment." —*BCCB*

"In this gripping novel, Blakemore creates a disturbingly ordered world in which questions about friendship and family offer courageous and heartwarming testaments to the human spirit." —*Publishers Weekly*

"Fans of *The Giver* and the like will greatly enjoy this middle-grade dystopian novel." —*The Horn Book*

THE Water Castle

THE Spy Catchers of Maple Hill

the  FRIENDSHIP Riddle

The Firefly Code

Books by Megan Frazer Blakemore

The Water Castle
The Spy Catchers of Maple Hill
The Friendship Riddle
The Firefly Code
The Daybreak Bond

The Firefly Code

Megan Frazer Blakemore

BLOOMSBURY

NEW YORK LONDON OXFORD NEW DELHI SYDNEY

First published in the United States of America in May 2016
by Bloomsbury Children's Books
Paperback edition published in September 2017
www.bloomsbury.com

Bloomsbury is a registered trademark of Bloomsbury Publishing Plc

For information about permission to reproduce selections from this book, write to
Permissions, Bloomsbury Children's Books, 1385 Broadway, New York, New York 10018
Bloomsbury books may be purchased for business or promotional use. For information
on bulk purchases please contact Macmillan Corporate and Premium Sales Department at
specialmarkets@macmillan.com

The Library of Congress has cataloged the hardcover edition as follows:
Names: Blakemore, Megan Frazer, author.
Title: The Firefly code / by Megan Frazer Blakemore.
Description: New York : Bloomsbury Children's Books, 2016.
Summary: Mori and her friends live a normal life on Firefly Lane in Old Harmonie,
a utopian community where every kid knows he or she is genetically engineered to
be better and smarter, but when a strangely perfect new girl named Ilana moves
in, the friends begin to question the only world they have ever known.
Identifiers: LCCN 2015037736
ISBN 978-1-61963-636-1 (hardcover) • ISBN 978-1-61963-637-8 (e-book)
Subjects: | CYAC: Genetic engineering—Fiction. | Friendship—Fiction. | Science fiction. |
BISAC: JUVENILE FICTION/Science Fiction. | JUVENILE FICTION/Social Issues/
Friendship. | JUVENILE FICTION/Action & Adventure/General.
Classification: LCC PZ7.B574 Fi 2016 | DDC [Fic]—dc23
LC record available at http://lccn.loc.gov/2015037736

ISBN 978-1-68119-527-8 (paperback)

Book design by John Candell
Typeset by Newgen Knowledge Works (P) Ltd., Chennai, India
Printed and bound in the U.S.A. by Berryville Graphics Inc., Berryville, Virginia
4 6 8 10 9 7 5 3

To Maria Albrecht's EEE classes at the
Clinton School for Writers and Artists 2014–2015,
and to all the young writers:
Keep building your brave new worlds.

1

EVERYONE GOES TO SLEEP AT the same time on Firefly
Lane. You can watch the lights switching off around the
cul-de-sac like dominoes falling. And when the lights are off,
it's almost like the houses are empty.

That's when I like to walk around.

In the summer, sometimes I sleep in our yard in a dusty
old blue tent, so it's easy to slip out and walk through our
neighborhood by the light of the moon. The night, it robs
the houses of their color, and they look even more alike than
in the day.

I sidestep the halos from the streetlights that give off a
subtle buzz from their solar-charged batteries, and dance in
the dark spaces in between.

Each house is like a sleeping baby, nestled back on a lawn turned gray by the moon, quiet and peaceful. If I had been around fifty years ago, when Old Harmonie was formed, back in the early part of the twenty-first century, I might have done things a little differently. I might have chosen to put the houses farther apart, with more trees between them, and I would have built different styles of houses, too. But back then, they were in a rush. They did the best they could.

And maybe it's the sameness of it all that makes it feel so comfortable, like our whole community is wrapped together in a sun-warmed blanket. Maybe they knew exactly what they were doing.

I like to walk down across the tennis courts, my hand trailing along the top of the nets, then into the woods, which smell of old leaves and hypnum moss. Twigs crack beneath my feet and the glow from the streetlamps disappears and I go all the way back to the fence. It's just a demarcation. It's not meant to keep anyone out or anyone in, not really. It's not the fence that keeps us safe, it's us.

Sometimes I can see the glow of lights from Boston. I know that beyond this fence is another world, one teeming and confused. I know this from what I have learned in school and from what our parents say and from the pictures on the news that they try to shield us from. But behind this fence, it seems impossible that we could be anything but safe.

2

THE CAKE AT THEO'S THIRTEENTH was built like a set of stairs going up and up and up and twisting back on itself. Climbing the stairs in their impossible loop were tiny round bots that cycled around the cake like moons around a planet. I wondered briefly if maybe his latency had something to do with robotics—first the drones that had delivered the invitations, and now these bots. But then my mind was drawn back to the cake. Each stair was a different flavor: chocolate, vanilla, raspberry, pistachio, lemon, coconut, almond, strawberry, mocha—on and on and on. I had never known there could be so many different flavors of cake.

"How is this even possible?" I asked Benji and Julia.

"Programming those bots would actually be pretty basic," Benji said. "I could show you how if you wanted. Easy peasy."

"No, I mean all those flavors of cake!"

"I heard his mom went to, like, six different bakeries, including some on the outside," Julia said, scuffing her patent leather shoe against the ground. She wore a purple dress that was way tighter than anything my parents would ever let me wear. Its straps were skinnier than those on the tank tops she usually wore, and I could see how deeply golden her skin had already turned in the sun. I tugged on the capped sleeve on my own blue dress, dotted with tiny white flowers.

"Theo's mom never goes outside of Old Harmonie," I replied. It was an overwhelming decision, which flavor of cake to have, but I was leaning toward coconut with a little bit of the raspberry. Or maybe mango with lemon frosting.

"Right, exactly," Julia said. "But for her perfect baby's Thirteenth, anything goes." She brushed her hand over her shoulder. Normally she wore her dark hair in two tight braids, but today it was twisted into a fancy poof at the back of her head, threaded through with purple ribbons. My hair was so plain in contrast: long and straight with only a thin headband to hold it out of my eyes. We had almost the exact same shade of dark-brown hair, but that was where the similarities ended. She was tall, and I was short. She liked sports and boys and doing craft projects, and I didn't really care for any of that. I liked growing things and being out in the woods and reading books, which she could do without. But those were all just surface things, about as relevant as the color of our hair. What mattered was that we knew each other inside and out, backward and forward, and would be there for each other no matter what. That's what makes a best friend.

The party was being held in the function hall of Krita headquarters. It looked like a big red barn right down to the huge sliding doors, but no animal had ever lived there. The doors were closed, but the windows were open to let in the summer breeze while the air coolers spun the warm air until it chilled. Big glass globes hung from the high ceiling, the lights inside slowly changing their soft colors, right through the rainbow. It wasn't easy to get access to the function hall. It was mostly meant for corporate events—team-building things or quarterly meetings or celebrating new patents. Usually people held their Thirteenths in their own village at a restaurant or maybe the local library. I was hoping to have mine in the village museum. I planned to announce my latency right by the display of dinosaur bones.

I looked over at Theo, who, at that moment, was at the center of a bunch of the top administrators of the Krita Corporation. He looked small in his blue suit, smaller than the men and women who gathered around him bestowing their worldly advice on him. Even his shaggy hair, which

I had heard some of the eighth-grade girls call "swoony," made him look like a little boy. Personally, I thought his hair was ridiculous. I regularly wished for a pair of scissors so I could cut those bangs right off. They were always falling across his face, blocking out his honey-brown eyes. Not that I noticed the color of Theo Staarsgard's eyes.

"I wonder if he already knows," I said. "Do you think she's already given him his code?"

"I can tell you what Theo's genetic code is," Julia replied. "One part smarts, one part good at sports, two parts sarcasm, and nine thousand parts ego."

"I don't think there's any DNA for ego," Benji said.

"Actually," I began, but then stopped myself. No time for a nature versus nurture debate in the middle of the party, especially when there was a giant cake to contemplate. The way the bots moved around it made me think of a double helix of DNA, twisting around itself. That had to be intentional: it's on our thirteenth birthdays that we find out our genetic codes. People can either be natural, which is the old-fashioned way: with genetic material from the mom and the dad. Or they can be designed, which means that their DNA was cloned or modified, either because one of the parents had genetic or fertility problems, or because they just wanted more of a say in how their kids turned out. It doesn't really matter in the grand scheme of things—there's value in being natural and value in being designed. That's what our parents always say, anyway.

Benji tugged at his bow tie. "This cake looks amazing, but a little over-the-top for my liking. My Thirteenth is going to be a black-and-white theme. Everyone is going to dress in black and white except for me. I'm going to get an all-red suit."

"'Cause that's not over-the-top," Julia said.

"I'm going to rock it," Benji said. "And my cake will have white frosting with black, I don't know, maybe like a criss-cross pattern or like my old-school Vans sneakers, but then the inside—red velvet."

"Nice," I said. The air cooler above our head hitched and sent down a fine mist of water that caught the color-changing light and made its own tiny rainbows.

Theo broke away from the grown-ups and came over to us. "Not one word about the cake," he said.

"I was just wondering which flavor to choose is all." I looked closely at his face, trying to discern if there was anything different about him. Could he possibly have had his latency yet? What was it? Would I be able to tell? He was the first person I really knew well who had turned thirteen, and I had about a million questions for him. But Theo wasn't the kind of guy to open up and give you all the answers you wanted.

"What are you staring at, Mori? I mean really, take a holopic, it'll last longer."

"Things I do not want in my possession: a holopic of Theo," Julia said.

"I was just wondering, I mean, I was just— Did you get your code yet?"

Theo sunk down into a nearby couch. "It was bad enough talking about it with my mom."

"Sounds like a fun conversation," Benji said.

"Yeah, right?" Theo laughed. Theo didn't have a dad, just his one mom. But it didn't mean he couldn't be a natural. It just meant that whoever gave the male DNA wasn't in the picture. "She did say she was just going to choose from the donor bank, or from the genetic codes they have saved down there, but she couldn't find one that had brown eyes, mathematical aptitude, and a Scandinavian background. So, she got part of the genetic material from the bank, that's the Scandinavian side, and the rest she had them custom- ize; then she strung it all together and—well, I didn't really care to learn the details of the next part of the process."

"So does that make you designed or natural?" I asked. We weren't supposed to care. It was part of why they waited to tell us until we were thirteen, but I was still curious. I was pretty sure that I was designed. I was just a little bit too imperfect to have been the result of millions of years of nature improving itself.

"It was a natural egg mixed with custom genetics, so I guess designed? I don't know. She said it meant I was the best of both, and then she pinched my cheek. It was like the best day of her life."

I wanted to ask him what his latency was, but sometimes they make a big deal of it at the party, and I didn't want to spoil his mom's plans. Sometimes parents will put the word on a piece of paper and bake it into a cake, or show a movie of the person's life and reveal the latency at the very end.

The DJ started playing this old song, a line dance to get everyone dancing. Theo groaned, but Julia clapped her hands and dragged me out onto the dance floor. I tried to follow along with the instructions of the singer, but I always seemed to be stomping with my right foot when he was telling us to crisscross, and I had never been sure what it meant to "turn it out." So I kind of hobbled along next to Julia and Benji. I looked back over my shoulder to Theo, who was still sitting on the sofa.

Julia spun me around so that I was facing the right direction. She held my hand and I watched her feet instead of listening to the music, my glasses slipping down my nose so the world got even fuzzier. Julia was laughing, though, and Benji, too. It felt good to be there laughing with them. I was lucky to have my two best friends with me, lucky to have them as neighbors on Firefly Lane, and lucky that we all lived together in Old Harmonie.

When the music stopped, Theo and his mom were up on the stage of the function hall. He shuffled and looked at his feet. Ms. Staarsgard clasped her hands together and said, "Welcome, everyone! We are so pleased to have you all here to celebrate Theo's Thirteenth with us." She put an arm around him. She really was a beautiful woman. A handsome woman, actually. I had never understood that term, but it suited her, with her sharp jaw and long nose. Theo had that same nose.

Julia looped her elbow through mine. "Poor Theo. He looks like he's going to implode up there," she said. Then she tightened her grip around my arm. "DeShawn. Two o'clock."

I turned my head to the right to see DeShawn Harris, the light of Julia's life. He was standing with a bunch of the other high school boys, sipping a fizzy orange out of a glass bottle. He had a new watchu, a silver one that cuffed around his wrist and was embedded with tiny lights that pulsated softly, red, blue, and green. It was one of the newest models, and I knew Benji was already planning to ask his parents for one just like it.

"Don't look," she whispered. "Is he looking at me?"

"He wasn't. But maybe he is now. I can't tell because you don't want me to look."

She sighed melodramatically.

At the microphone, Ms. Staarsgard continued speaking. "As we all know, this is a big day in any young person's life. The future is about to open up, much like a satellite pulls back to show not just our small town, but the world, and the universe: bigger and bigger, on and on."

I didn't spend as much time with Ms. Staarsgard as I did with the other parents, so I had forgotten her odd way of talking.

"Krita and Old Harmonie have always been places of innovation, and in the coming years we will be going in bold new directions. It is so pleasing to me to know that Theo and his friends will not only be going along in those bold new directions, but also, in a short time, they will be leading the charge."

This was the same type of stuff the Krita executives were always saying—stuff that sounds good and important, but when you think about it, really doesn't say much at all.

Ms. Staarsgard turned and faced Theo, which made him blush even harder. "Thank you for all the joy you've given me, dear Theo. The world is opening up to you, and I cannot wait to see where you choose to go!"

The crowd clapped politely. Theo stepped toward the microphone. "Thanks, Mom. And thank you to everyone for coming." He took a deep breath. A breeze came through the open windows of the function hall and stirred the silver and blue streamers that hung from the ceiling.

"The four core values of our community are creativity, ingenuity, experimentation, and order." He tugged on the bottom of his suit coat. "These are the values that guide our decisions, and that allow us to succeed."

"Oh, geez," Julia said.

"Seriously," Benji said.

"What?" I asked. Those were the values of Krita, and they were good values. Without them, we'd be just another town, no better than the world outside. I knew Benji and Julia believed that, too. She still had her arm looped through mine, and I could feel her soft, soft skin. Julia, I was fairly certain, was a natural. Every little detail of her was just right.

"She's already decided what he's going to do when he grows up: Krita administration, just like her," Benji explained.

In the front row stood all the muckety-mucks from Krita. They wore suits and had their hair done just so. I wondered if any of them had ever even been artists or scientists. My parents were in the back sipping glasses of wine and nibbling on hors d'oeuvres with some of the other scientists. It was the scientists who did all the work of Krita, but I knew that, silly as they sometimes seemed with their fancy suits and tech gadgets, it was the executives who kept everyone's eyes on the big picture of progress. That was one of the biggest differences between inside our Kritopia of Old Harmonie and outside: inside, we never stopped experimenting and innovating, but outside they were just struggling to get by and couldn't work on making the world better.

Theo stumbled over whatever he was saying, and DeShawn laughed. Theo kept going, though. "When it came time to decide on how to reveal my latency, I decided the best thing was to keep it simple."

I felt my body tilting forward. His latency! What had he chosen?

"Because," he went on, "the bigger issue is not what the latency is, it's what you do with it. The latency I have selected is puzzles."

Puzzles—that was one of the very first latencies to be understood and released. These days it was considered a little less exciting than some of the other ones, but, thinking about it, it actually seemed to suit him.

"I chose puzzles because I think our world is a puzzle. In school we learned about the explorers in olden days who were discovering parts of our world for the first time. They didn't even really know what they would find, just that they were sure to find something as long as they were bold and struck out on the journey."

As Theo spoke, his mom mouthed the words, and I wondered how much of what he was saying he really believed.

"In more modern times, the puzzles have been in the realm of science. When we unlocked DNA, that was a great advancement that helped us to understand things like diseases so that we could live better, longer lives. And then there is the latency itself, a puzzle that was solved by my friend Mori Bloom's great-grandmother Lucy Morioka."

My gaze snapped back up toward the stage, but it felt like half the world was looking at me. My life was filled with reminders that Old Harmonie wouldn't be what it was if it hadn't been for Baba, and yet they shocked me every time. It was Baba—my great-grandmother, known to the rest of the world as Dr. Lucy Morioka—who figured out how to tweak the brain in such a way that you could release a hidden skill without damaging the mind. I could see the questions written on the audience's faces as they glanced at me: *What will you do? What will you contribute?*

"So I have to wonder, what puzzles remain? What is there left to understand, and how will it change our world? Some people think we should be happy as we are, that we have already made so many great advances that we can just keep perfecting those. But that wasn't the spirit in which Agatha Varden founded Old Harmonie. Our future lies in innovation, in puzzle solving, and I am looking forward to helping to sustain that spirit of creativity, ingenuity, experimentation, and order on which we were founded."

"She wrote it for him," Benji said. "She totally wrote it for him, right?"

Next to me, Julia nodded.

"So thank you for coming to my Thirteenth, and thank you for being a part of Old Harmonie. Enjoy the cake."

The singing started behind us and I turned to see the giant cake being wheeled toward the stage by a baker with a tall white hat. Her face was pinched with exertion. Julia hopped up next to her and helped her push the cake all the way to the edge of the stage. The timing was perfect. Just as we cooed out the final "Happy birthday to youuuuuu," they arrived in front of Theo, who bent over and blew out all thirteen candles with one healthy blow. I wondered what he wished for, if he wished for anything at all. He'd probably tell me that wishes were as silly as my trees, something you did if you couldn't make your desires happen for yourself.

The Krita people patted Ms. Staarsgard on the back and their smiles spread wide, revealing perfectly white and perfectly straight teeth, so I guess they thought he had done a good job. Benji had slipped away during the singing, and now he returned, practically dancing over to me. He held out a piece of cake—coconut with raspberry frosting, just like I'd wanted—and said, "I have the best news. Dr. Kellerman just told me. Guess what it is! Guess!" But before I could guess, he told me: "Someone is moving into Mr. Merton's house!"

3

WHEN WE GOT HOME FROM the party, I bolted upstairs to change out of my dress and the shoes that pinched my toes. Once back in my comfortable shorts and T-shirt, I grabbed my bike and rode around the neighborhood to check on my trees. Compared to the rest of Old Harmonie, Firefly Lane had been put together in a particular rush. There'd been a measles outbreak in Boston, and Krita needed to move a bunch of their employees into Old Harmonie quickly. So all the trees had been planted at the same time, in neat little rows. It's only when you get out to the edges of the forest that you have the wild old trees: oaks and pines and maples all mixed together. That's another reason why I like it out there: things were left to nature to figure it out, and nature tends to be smarter than people.

I went on and on about those trees and the need for biodiversity, until one day my dad came home with three little saplings. Just three, but at least they were three different varieties. I planted the maple out past the tennis courts, the oak tree on the edge of the forest behind our house, and the elm—a species nearly destroyed by disease ages ago, but saved in the seed bank—I planted that out front of number 9 Firefly Lane.

Just like the trees, the houses on Firefly Lane were all the same, as if they had been squeezed out by a 3-D printer and plopped down at equal intervals. Each was a different color, with different landscaping, but you could still tell they were the same, inside and out. Even if you'd never been to someone's house before, you would know just where everything was.

All of the houses were the same, that is, except for number 9, the abandoned farmhouse at the end of the cul-de-sac's loop.

Number 9 was Dr. Varden's house. It's where Old Harmonie started, not that you could tell from looking at it. Three stories tall, white with black shutters, and a sagging shingled roof. Siding boards hung off it at odd angles, and the lawn—if you could call it that—was a tangle of grass, clover, and wheaty weeds that served as a breeding ground for ticks and snakes. Though there was a jaunty red mailbox at the end of the driveway, no one lived in the house anymore. Dr. Varden was long gone, and no one else had ever moved in.

My mom said the only saving grace was that the house was set back from the road, and in the summer and spring, the leafy trees nearly obscured it. But I thought there was something noble about the way it stayed there unmoved, unchanged: it was as steady as my favorite old oak out in the forest.

I wanted desperately to get into that house, but even on a warm summer evening, the thought gave me goose bumps. I wanted to see what was left of the life that went on there before, and, more than that, to see if there were any traces of my great-grandmother. Baba, who'd died when I was five, and Dr. Varden had been friends for decades, but then Dr. Varden just left without even giving a reason why. If she had wanted to stop working, she could have gone over to the retirement high-rise that overlooked the old Quabbin Reservoir. She and Baba could have even shared an apartment. Instead, she abandoned Old Harmonie and Baba.

That was another reason I wanted to go in: to find out why Dr. Varden had left. But it was off-limits. One hundred percent. No one would go with me, and I wasn't bold enough to go alone. My dad always said I was curious enough to be creative, but timid enough to be safe. I think he meant it as a compliment.

Actually once, when I was seven, I'd walked down the driveway, all the way to the front door. There were stairs then, wooden ones, though the middle one was missing. I had put my hand on the railing and was ready to climb up when Julia started yelling my name from the street. I'd run back to her, and she told me I was just about the craziest person she had ever met, and didn't I know that place was haunted? I didn't believe in ghosts or anything, but I was still too chicken to go try again.

I stopped my bike to look at my elm, checking it for tell-tale signs of Dutch elm disease. The pointy oval leaves were all bright green and fluttered in the slight breeze, turning over to show their silvery green undersides. Each one was roughly the same shape and size, but there were tiny differences if you looked closely enough. That's the thing about nature: it doesn't offer up its secrets easily. You have to spend some time with it to really understand.

The wind picked up and as it blew past the old farm-house, the structure seemed to moan and sway. Had it been so run-down when Dr. Varden lived there? Probably not. She was a professor at MIT when she bought the farm with the old farmhouse. And then she invited friends to come and live, too, a group of artists and scientists. My great-grandmother was one of the first. She was a top neuro-scientist. Cohousing, it was called. Each person had a house, but they had shared things, too, like a field and walking trails, and a park, and a common house where they would have meals together. All the old buildings are gone, except for the common house. That's the village museum now.

Thinkers, Dr. Varden called the earliest residents of Old Harmonie. Like Baba. Always coming up with new ideas and new ways of looking at problems. Sometimes I feel like I could do that, too, like it's just below the surface and if I could only pull it out, I'd be as innovative as her. I guess that's what the latency is all about, but sometimes I worry that even with my latency released, my ideas will never be as new and revolutionary as what Baba did.

A lot of those early thinkers worked for Krita, a huge corporation, and then Krita started offering to buy people homes in the cohousing village. They said it would con- serve energy because people could carpool—this was back when people actually drove their own cars everywhere. So many people were interested that they bought another plot of land and added a whole new village. It happened quickly after that: Krita built a satellite office out in Old Harmonie, then the satellite office became the headquarters of the corporation. They bought more land. Made more villages. And by then the village that Dr. Varden started was a full- blown Utopia. It had happened naturally. If there hadn't been the measles outbreak, it probably would have kept growing at the same slow and steady pace. Once the city had been built, all that needed to happen were the rules and guidelines and everything that made it official. Krita did that.

"What are you doing?" I recognized the voice: Theo's.

"Checking my tree," I said as I turned to face him. He straddled his dirt bike. "Her name is Elma."

"Of course you named your tree."

"The maple by the tennis courts is Sappy. And the oak by my house is Annie. Like Annie Oakley. But Elma is my favorite. Don't tell the others."

He rolled his eyes, but I could see him smiling. "You shouldn't go down by that house, you know. There are snakes."

"They'll leave you alone if you leave them alone," I said. I knew this was true, but still I backed away.

"But they'll attack if you scare them."

I took a few steps back toward Elma and my bike. "Are you trying to frighten me?"

He looked past me at the house. "I've never understood why you were so obsessed with number nine. Even when we were little."

"It looks like it belongs there, don't you think? The way the driveway curves around to it, and how it's up that little knoll. Our houses, they're just dropped where it was convenient, not where they were supposed to be. I mean, aren't you curious about it at all?"

He wrinkled up his nose. "I have a nice house with whole windows and shutters that aren't ready to fall down and crush someone."

"Well, I'm curious. It was Dr. Varden's house. There could be anything in there."

"Yeah, like spiders and mice."

"You know what you should do? You should go up there with me so I can just see it for once. And if you're right about it being all old and falling down with spiders and mice, well then, I can forget about it." Even as I said it, I knew it was a lie. It would just mean I would need to find a way to get the spiders and the mice out before I could explore.

"Sure, Mori. I'll get right on that."

"Really?"

"No, not really. It's against the rules to go near there, you know that."

I did know that. And normally that would be enough for me, but not when it came to number 9. "You're not exactly the A-number-one rule follower."

"It's a stupid old house and I don't even know why they left it there."

"They had to. She made them promise not to change it or move anything inside or out. You could walk in there and it would be like a portal through time."

"Those don't exist."

"Maybe," I said. "But haven't you ever wondered what's inside? I saw pictures of the original Old Harmonie and the houses were all different then. That's the way Dr. Varden intended it. A community of individuals coming together."

"You're a real dope, you know," he told me. "Forget the tree; I think we should call *you* Sappy."

"And I'll call you Thorny," I told him.

He straightened himself up. "Thorn, I kind of like that. I am Thorn, master of Firefly Lane."

"I said Thorny, not Thorn."

"It sounds like the name of a god, don't you think? Thorn the Mighty. Thorn the Impaler."

"Thorny the Insane."

He laughed, and grabbed the handlebars of his bike. "But really, Mori, you should just stay away from that house. The great and powerful Thorn decrees it."

"Right," I said. "Anyway, you did a good job today." ·

"I got through it." He pushed his hair out of his eyes.

"I thought your speech was really good. And I liked how you just said your latency instead of making a big deal about it."

"My mom wanted to, but when I ended up choosing puzzles, I think she was a little bit disappointed I didn't go for something flashier. All my testing pointed to puzzles, except for like one little spike toward language acquisition. I think she wanted me to do that so I could talk to all the bigwigs at Krita around the world."

"I think puzzles are a perfectly respectable latency," I told him. "And your reasons for choosing it were really good, too. I mean your reasons aside from the testing."

He looked down at his shoes. "Those weren't exactly my reasons," he said. "I mean, I want to make new discoveries, but really I just like the process of solving things, of figuring them out."

"What's the difference?" I asked.

"I don't really care how it turns out. I mean, like, the 'bold new directions'—who cares?"

"Yeah, but—"

"Sure, Krita cares, and when good things happen at Krita, they help make Old Harmonie better, so I care about the outcome that way. But in the moment, that's not what I think about. I meant what I said about the core values, though, those matter—creativity, ingenuity, experimentation, order—those are all part of puzzle solving."

"What about community?" I asked.

"You know community isn't actually a core value."

"Yeah, but that's why we have those core values, to keep our community together. And part of that is the outcomes of the projects, so, I mean, it's all tied together, right?"

"I guess so." Theo shrugged. "Anyway, it's what I chose."

"Have you had it done yet?"

"Not yet. Monday."

"Oh."

"Yeah."

"Are you scared?"

He turned so he was looking right at me. "A little," he confessed.

My stomach turned. I had never known Theo to be afraid of anything. When I was little, the latency seemed so cool.

There was a hidden secret talent and it was going to be released—thanks to the work of my great-grandmother—but now I wasn't so sure. What would mine be and how would it change me? I looked at Theo, trying to memorize every bit of him so that I would know if something was different after his latency was released.

"Seriously, Mori, the stare is getting creepy." Then he flashed a grin. "Though I can understand if you can't keep your eyes off me."

I blushed, hard. "It's just that Mariah Samms called you swoony, and I'm trying to figure out what exactly it was she saw."

Now it was his turn to blush and turn away. He had milky-white skin that made it hard to hide anytime his cheeks turned pink. He regripped his handlebars. "See you tomorrow, then." He started pedaling and gave me a wave as he left. I hesitated a moment before going over and picking up my bike. "See you later, Elma." And then I rode back home, where my mom and dad were waiting for me, dinner on the table: kale noodles with fresh tomatoes.

4

THE HOUSE ACROSS FROM JULIA'S had been empty for almost four weeks, since before the end of the school year. Mr. Merton had been living there, and then he was not living. "They took him out in a van without any windows or markings or anything," Julia whispered to me as we crouched on her lawn watching the gardeners who worked in Mr. Merton's yard.

"Did they have a sheet over him?" I asked.

"Yep. And the people who carried him out, they wore jumpsuits, like those gardeners, only all white instead of blue. And they had these weird black sunglasses that covered the whole top half of their heads."

"Creepy," Benji said.

"Seriously creepy," she agreed.

The gardeners were pulling out the oversize and ratty rhododendron that had grown so high it covered Mr. Merton's first-floor window and reached for the second. It was giving them a lot of trouble.

"Theo's getting his latency today," I said.

"It's weird that it's puzzles, right?" Benji asked. "I thought for sure it would be one of the neuro-physicals. You know, hand-eye coordination or something."

"He already has all that," I said.

"Wouldn't it be funny if it were artistic? My sister's was being able to draw anything she sees. You know, visual replication? It's pretty cool, actually. Once I nail my ollie, I'm going to have her draw me doing it. Better than a holopic."

That type of artistic ability was one of the earliest latencies unleashed. Baba had gotten the idea after she met a man who could draw whole cityscapes after flying over the city just once. I thought that would be pretty useful in terms of drawing all the plants and animals around Old Harmonie, but with my eye, I didn't think my testing would recommend any of the artistic latencies.

"Theo's mom would never let him do something so impractical, though," Benji went on. "I really thought she would try to get him to do something political. Like people skills."

"It has to exist in there somewhere for them to pull it out," Julia said. "They can't magically make it appear. Like, remember the time he told Dr. Kellerman that the fourth-grade curriculum made him want to eat his shorts?"

"I thought that was pretty funny, actually," I said. "It was just that he said it to Dr. Kellerman that was the problem—I don't think I've ever seen him crack a smile. That was Theo's mistake."

Julia laughed and said, "I thought Dr. Kellerman was going to spontaneously combust."

"Still," I said. "Maybe he does have that kind of diplomacy in him. Deep down."

"Like bottom of an ocean cavern down," Julia said.

"Diplomacy would really be more like a dampening, don't you think?" Benji asked. "Like dampening saying the first thing that comes to your mind."

"Maybe," I said. But that wasn't really what I was getting at. When Baba first developed the latency, people couldn't pick. Whatever the skill was remained a mystery until after the procedure. Then the scientists figured out how to predict the skill with testing. And after that they developed a way to use testing to determine the most likely skills, and then target that very specific part of the brain. It seemed a lot less magical that way. "Sometimes I wish it were still like the old days. You know, when it was all a big surprise and you had no idea what might be hidden inside of you."

"No way," Benji said. "I mean, what if it was something totally worthless? Like that remembering the dates thing?

Who cares if it rained on Tuesday, August fourth, 2015? Now we don't get any of those boring latencies, and we can have useful ones."

"Sure," I said. "I guess."

Across the street, one of the gardeners let out a string of words that would have had any of us grounded for weeks. The roots of the rhododendron reached down so far and were so tangled that the two gardeners ended up pulling out axes and hacking away at them.

"You'd think a laser cutter could do it," Benji said. "Just zap right through it. I bet I could design something that could scoop it right out of the earth. Or just vaporize it. Or maybe turn it into instant compost?" I could see the wheels turning in his brain. "Compost would be best, of course, but vaporizing it would be sick."

They were a crew from outside of Old Harmonie, not Krita employees. Their truck said "Somerville," a name that sounded as sweet and beautiful as an August peach. "I wonder what it's like in Somerville," I said. "You know, I bet Somerville would be just about the nicest place you could go outside of Old Harmonie. I bet it's not as bad as some of the other places out there."

"Summer-what?" Benji asked.

"Somerville," I said, and pointed at the white work pickup. It was an old truck, with a steering wheel and everything. I'd even noticed the man who drove it drop keys in his pocket when he got out. So strange. Out there they waste a lot of energy with single-user vehicles—not like the smart technology of our solar-powered KritaCars that monitor their own efficiency so they generate more power than they use.

"We are not going to try to hitch a ride to Somerville or anywhere else," Julia said. "I swear, I will throw my body down in front of that truck and let it drive right over me before I would let you do that, Mori."

"Well, of course I don't really mean it," I said. I pulled off my glasses to clean them. They'd been acting funny, like the retina cam wasn't transmitting quite right, which would mean another trip to the ophthalmologist for me.

"You'd have to go through the decontamination showers when you came back in," Julia reminded me. Those showers were our shared nightmare: you had to take off all your clothes and walk through and allegedly no one could see you, but still—you never knew.

"And you'd feel guilty out there," Benji said. "You'd give people all your money and your snacks and probably even your shoes."

"I'm not saying I actually want to go—I mean, of course not. We all know what it's like out there. I'm just saying that the town has a pretty name."

But Julia still put herself in between me and the truck as if there were actually a danger of me running and climbing in, as if I were doing anything more than just talking. She shifted the band of her watchu around her wrist.

We were so focused on Mr. Merton's old house that we almost missed the KritaCar as it putted up the road. It drove along the straight part of Firefly Lane, right between us and the gardeners, then pulled into Theo's driveway, which was at the top of the circular part of our street. Theo's mom got out, followed by his nanny. Together they helped Theo from the car. He wore his regular clothes—basketball shorts and a T-shirt—but he also had a cotton cap on his head, the kind babies wear in the hospital. Was it covering up a bandage? I shivered, and goose bumps popped up on my arms and legs even though we were still sitting in full sun.

"Do you think he's okay?" Julia asked.

The KritaCar backed out of the driveway, then wound its way past us, empty as a ghost ship.

"Theo!" Benji called.

Theo turned his head, but it was like he didn't even see us. His mom waved to us, and his nanny led him inside and shut the door.

5

WHEN I WAS BORN, THE retina on my right eye hadn't formed correctly: it was missing a lot of the rods and cones that let people see, so they gave me an artificial one. It took up a big chunk of my 30 percent enhancements allotment, the amount a person can be changed from how they are born. A retina is a tiny thing, obviously not a huge portion of my body by mass or area or volume or any of those measurements. But its complexity and its necessity—that's what makes it count more in my allotment. I'm not entirely sure how they figure it all out, but there are formulas and equations designed in the ethics department.

Now I wear glasses with a tiny camera that transmits information to a receptor cell in my brain, and that sends a signal to my optic nerve. Without them on, I get a headache, since my left eye can't figure out why my right eye isn't working anymore. Once I'm fully grown, I can get a different system, one that's all internal and I won't need to wear the glasses, but really, they aren't so bad. In earlier versions, they were huge and covered your whole face like a visor on a helmet.

With my glasses acting up, I needed to go to my doctor, so Mom and I got on the bus with Dad and rode into Center Harmonie. It left Firefly Lane and passed through Nashoba Village, past the library, guarded over by two stone owls with steely looks, and past the museum in the old common house. From Nashoba, we took a twisting road through some woods, and then the bus eased onto the main road in line with the other buses so we became a train snaking our way through to Center Harmonie.

Center Harmonie was different from our village. The buildings were tall and made of metal and glass, with shiny surfaces that bent and tilted at dramatic angles. To me it looked like a bad dream, and I always felt my chest tighten when we got in the city, something that didn't help with my checkups.

The bus stopped in front of headquarters, and pretty much everyone got out except Mom and me. Dad gave us kisses on our cheeks and said we should stop by for lunch in the cafeteria when we were done. That was one thing I liked about the city: at the cafeteria you could get whatever you wanted to eat. They even made this sorbet out of coconuts and mint and raspberries that tasted just like summer.

The doors of the bus shut themselves, and it pulled back out onto Main Street. There were people walking together, holding meetings in coffee shops. Everyone had an office, but not everyone used theirs. Mom always did, since she liked the calm and order of her fertility lab. Dad was an epidemiologist, but he sometimes liked to work outside on the village green, as long as he wasn't working with specimens, of course.

Dr. Cartwright's office was a few blocks away from the main Krita building. She was the one who had fixed my eye in the first place, and she'd been the one to check on me ever since. I liked her. She always dressed very fashionably with pointy-toed shoes and perfectly applied lipstick.

In the exam room, a helper bot buzzed to life on the counter in front of me. "Good morning, Mori! Good morning, Dr. Bloom." Mom nodded at it, and the black eyes on its white orb of a face blinked in response. "How are you feeling today?"

"Fine," I replied. A green light flashed where its ear would be as it scanned me. "Your blood pressure is good, though your heart rate is slightly elevated. Are you feeling nervous?"

"A little, I guess."

"I'll let Dr. Cartwright know."

"Okay," I said. I twisted my watchu on my wrist. It was still loose enough that I wouldn't get fitted for a new one for another year at least. Why had I chosen that pink band? Julia had chosen a sophisticated deep purple for hers.

"Good. Our records indicate that you are here for a check of your prosthetic?"

"It's not a prosthetic," Mom said. "It's an integrated system."

The helper bot swiveled to face Mom. "I hear your concern."

Mom rolled her eyes.

"Things are just a little fuzzy sometimes," I said.

"Noted. I will alert Dr. Cartwright that you are ready to see her."

And with a hum, the helper bot powered down.

"I can't get used to those," Mom said with a shudder.

The door opened then, and in came Dr. Cartwright wearing a slim polka-dotted skirt and a blouse with a flouncy bow. All I could think about was how that bow would be a disaster if you were eating soup. Dr. Cartwright took the glasses off my face and placed them in a special box lined with a soft cloth. "We can replace those lenses while you're here. Dodo picked up a slight weakening in your left eye, so we can also add a prescription there."

"A weakening?" Mom's body leaned toward mine.

"Nothing to be concerned about. Totally normal. If it gets worse we can laser it, and it's not even a measurable adjustment."

I felt Mom's body relax. She was always worried about my using up all of my 30 percent. It's one of the oldest rules in Old Harmonie: everyone in Krita is allowed enhancements of their baseline talents up to 30 percent, but not more. There are two different kinds: therapies and enhancements. Therapies are medical: they fix a deficiency. Like my retina. Enhancements make something stronger, whether it needs to be or not. Like sometimes people will get enhancements to make them taller, or to have better lung capacity. It's all physical, not like the latency, which is more mental and isn't a part of the 30 percent calculation.

Even though there are two categories, the line between a therapy and an enhancement is pretty blurry. When my retina surgery is finally done I'll have better than 20/20 vision, so is that a therapy or an enhancement? "It's not to put a limit on anyone," Baba had said about her 30 percent rule. "Humans grow and change through struggle. If we solve all of our problems, how can we ever evolve? How will we ever know our own humanity?" I knew my mom agreed with that, too, but she says it's different when it's your own child who needs help. I think that we have rules for a reason, and they should be the same for everyone. Still, I didn't like the way she wrung her hands whenever we came to Dr. Cartwright's, so it was good news that a prescription, or even the laser surgery, didn't count in the computation.

"Now just lie back and relax while I run some tests."

The tests consisted of her running different images through the system, first just sparks of light, then an apple on a table or an old-fashioned eye chart that I had to read, but then more complicated things, like a dog running across a field at sunset. I had to tell her what I saw, and Dodo, the helper bot, recorded it all. It always made me feel a little queasy, but when Dr. Cartwright said, "All done; not so bad, right?" I nodded in agreement.

"She's looking good. We can probably go a year before we check her, but we're definitely going to want to check her after her latency release," Dr. Cartwright said. "Sometimes those functions interfere with the eye work, especially if it's artistic."

"Mori's latency isn't artistic, that's for sure."

"Thanks, Mom." My artwork wasn't terrible. I mean, she had my drawings up all over the house, didn't she? She took my best plant drawings and put them in simple white frames.

Dr. Cartwright lowered her tablet. "Do you know what it's going to be?"

"Mori's testing has shown—and of course we noticed, too—that she's got a real knack for details, for history, and for planning, so we're looking at the logic-based latencies, though we haven't ruled out any of the puzzles, especially spatial skills."

"The retina is definitely connected to the spatial understanding, so let's be sure to check her, okay?"

"Do we need to talk about this now? It's almost a year away," I said.

Dr. Cartwright grinned. "Of course, Mori. And as for now, you are looking great. Remember, this adjustment might give you a headache for a couple days, so take it easy." I held out my hand and she pressed a button on my watchu to upload her report onto my data set. Our watchus act as mini-repositories for us, storing our files and checking our basic body functions once a day. Plus they tell time. "Any questions?" she asked.

I shook my head. She was right. The change was enough of a difference that it made me a little shaky, like being on the merry-go-round in the park. "Can we go see Dad now?" I asked. "I really want some of that sorbet."

Dr. Cartwright and Mom both smiled. Adults have this way of smiling at kids like we are all glowing gold. It's weird, but I guess it does feel pretty good.

6

THERE WAS A VASE OF flowers waiting for me when we got home. *I hope your eye appointment went well* was written on the card. It wasn't signed, but I recognized the shaky cursive as Theo's. I glanced at my mom. She shrugged, then leaned in. "Boys are weird."

"Really weird," I replied.

"You should put them up in your room," she told me.

"Maybe," I said. But I left them on the counter and raced to Julia's. She was out back in her pool. I sat on the edge, my feet hanging down into the water. "Theo sent me flowers."

She splashed over to me. "This morning he came over and asked me to play tennis with him. It was like something out of an old movie. He was so polite and asked me, 'Would you care for lemonade or water, Julia?'"

"You don't think—" I began.

Julia grabbed on to the edge of the pool. "It was only yesterday that he got it—"

"It couldn't be a coincidence."

Our words tumbled over each other's. "Maybe he's just feeling tired."

"Or maybe they gave him a mood enhancer or something."

"Maybe it's permanent?"

"Maybe they released the wrong thing? I mean, like, maybe he really did have this polite guy hiding out inside of him and—"

"They didn't release the wrong thing. That just doesn't happen." Julia dunked underwater, then popped back up. "His mom came and found him and told him he needed to go home to rest."

"His mom took two days off work?"

"I know, right? And then a KritaCar came and got them."

My stomach started twisting. "Do you think he's okay?"

"Oh, Mori, he's fine. It's just his latency. It's no big deal."

I wished Benji were there so we could ask him how it had been with his sister.

"Come on," Julia said. "Change into your suit. The water feels great."

"I need to check on my trees," I told her.

"The whole point of trees is that you don't need to check on them."

"I don't think that's the whole point of them."

"Whatever," Julia said. Then a teasing smile flashed across her lips. "What kind of flowers did he send you?"

"Gerber daisies," I said. "You know, the big kind."

"You sure they weren't roses?"

I blushed. "They were Gerber daisies. Red and pink and—"

"Red and pink, huh? Theo's got a crush," she sang. "Theo's got a crush!"

"Watch out, Julia. I just might send those flowers on to DeShawn. I can copy your handwriting exactly, remember."

Her smile faltered. "You wouldn't!"

"Maybe yes, maybe no."

"Mori!"

I crouched down next to the pool and held out my pinkie. "I pinkie-swear I will never, ever reveal your undying love of DeShawn Harris, not even if I am kidnapped and tortured by pirates."

She hooked her pinkie through mine. "Cool. Come back after you check on those trees."

I grabbed my bike from her driveway and rode out onto Firefly Lane. The gardeners were back at the house across the street. They'd put a thick hedge all around the property and now were planting two rosebushes at the end of the front walk, the flowers still in tight buds but visibly bright red at the tips. The gardeners were sweating. I thought for a moment that I ought to offer them a glass of water or something. That's what a nice person would do, and my friends were always telling me I was the nicest. But that would mean talking to them up close, passing a glass to them. I wasn't sure I'd be able to make the words come out of my mouth. And anyway, it wouldn't be entirely safe, I didn't think. They'd been through the decontamination process, of course, but the problem with out there is that nothing was regulated or monitored. A whole new disease might have cropped up and no one would even know it, or a new bacteria, or a new type of insect—anything, really. And our decontamination system wouldn't even know to look for it or how to destroy it.

So instead I pedaled on around the block to check on the maple first. Then I cruised over to the bottom of the cul-de-sac. Elma looked okay, but I found myself staring at old number 9. The way it tilted to the side seemed jaunty, almost like an invitation.

I biked the long way back home, past the playground, where I saw Theo sitting on a swing, totally still. He wasn't even using his foot to rock himself back and forth. I put my bike in the rack and walked over to him. He didn't seem to notice me, so I said, "Hi, Theo."

He looked up. There were dark circles under his eyes, the kind Benji got when his allergies flared up before his seasonal dose of antihistamines: shiny and almost purple.

"Thanks for the flowers," I told him.

"Don't thank me," he said to the ground. "Thank the pain meds they gave me."

"Okay, thank you, pain meds. It was very nice of you to give me flowers." I tried to make my voice sound pleasant but mostly I was wondering why Theo had to have pain medicine at all. "Are you feeling better now?" I asked.

"No, Mori, I'm not." His voice was heavy with anger. He tilted his head up to me and his hair fell back; I could see his eyes, but they weren't the warm honey brown I was used to. They seemed iced over like solid amber. "My head hurts like someone is driving an ice pick through my nostrils and up into my brain, and your cheery chirping is like a dog whistle right in my ear. Over and over and over again."

My throat closed in on itself. Theo was quick with put-downs, it's true, but usually they were one-liners, and almost never aimed at me. "I see. Well, then. I guess . . . I guess I'll just go home. Do you want me to tell your mom—"

He held up his hand and flapped it like a bird's beak. "Stop talking, Mori. Please, for once."

So I did. I got back on my bike and rode home, where I took the flowers he had given me and dumped them into the compost, note and all.

7

MOM PULLED THE CASSEROLE OUT of the small Jetsonator oven on our counter. I wasn't allowed to use it yet, but it wasn't like cooking was hard. You got the tray out of the refrigerator, put it in the oven, and pushed the GO button. Sometimes Dad actually combined ingredients and came up with his own concoctions, but it was better when we had the ready-made meals from the delivery service.

"Huh," Mom said.

"What?" I asked from my perch on the red stool by the counter. I was stacking toothpicks to make a tree skeleton. I thought if I had a tissue I could color it green with a marker, then tear it up to make leaves. It was better than thinking about stupid Theo and his stupid head.

"I could've sworn it said sweet potato and black beans, but this is distinctly green, wouldn't you say?"

"Green as Kentucky bluegrass."

"It'll be a mystery," she said, and scooped out some of the casserole onto each of our plates while I took salads from the refrigerator, unwrapped and dumped them onto salad plates, then dropped the compostable containers into the bin.

Dad joined us at the dining room table, and we were in the middle of a fun guessing game about what our dinner was—

"I taste kale and red bliss potatoes—"

"And dill. Definitely dill."

"Are those sweet peppers?"

—when the conversation took a decided right turn.

"Theo dropped off flowers for Mori," Mom said to Dad.

Dad put down his fork and knife. "Theo Staarsgard?"

"No, Dad, the other Theo." My voice sounded clipped. "Anyway, it wasn't really him."

"Oh? Who was it?" Mom asked. "Julia didn't do it as a joke, did she?"

"No, it was him. But it was only because they have him on pain medication because his head hurts so much after his latency."

Dad smiled and said, "Hey, now, don't sell yourself short."

"He told me himself, Dad. He told me to thank the medicine, not him. Why did he even need medication?"

Neither of them spoke. It was like they were playing rock, paper, scissors with their eyes to see who would have to answer this question. Mom lost. "The latency is a completely standard and simple procedure. Some people, though, just experience some discomfort. It's like with your retina—when you get it adjusted and you get a headache—the latency can do the same thing."

"It wasn't discomfort. He said it was like someone was stabbing him up the nose."

"He might have been exaggerating a little bit," Dad said. "Listen, I remember after mine, I got to lie in bed and just listen to music, relax. I felt a little woozy, but after a couple of days, I was good as new. Better than new."

"Why hasn't anyone told me it could hurt?"

"We don't want to worry you," Mom said. "And for most people it doesn't hurt. But you're right. We should be talking to you more about this. You're coming up on thirteen, and that can be a confusing time."

"It's almost a year away," I said, trying to backtrack.

"It's time to start preparing, though. To start thinking about your latency. It's a big choice. Nothing is set in stone, and you have a say."

"But I don't have any idea what it should be!" I heard the hitch in my voice. On top of this new revelation that the latency might be painful was the continued pressure of making such a big, big choice.

"I know we've talked a lot about the latency because of Baba's role in its development, but that was always in the abstract," Mom said. Baba had been studying with a neuroscientist in Wisconsin who was investigating sudden savant syndrome—people who, after an injury, developed amazing abilities. Like someone would get hit on the head and *boom*—they could memorize long strings of numbers. Or they were in a car accident and *wham*—musical genius. That was Baba's biggest contribution to Old Harmonie. Baba realized there was a way to cause the talent to be released without the accompanying damage to the rest of the brain. "You know about why the latency is so important, and her role in it." She sprinkled salt onto her salad. "But I know it's different when we're actually talking about you."

"Do you understand what's going to happen?" Dad asked.

"Yes. You're going to set free my inner genius."

Dad laughed, and Mom said, "Well, we're going to do our best. And we'll probably do some dampening, too."

Dampening was like the opposite of the latency. If you had some dangerous qualities, your parents could dampen them. They could do that at any time. Julia's parents did it to her once. She was a little too competitive, so they dialed it down so that she wouldn't hurt any of her friends—or herself—by pushing too hard. She said it felt like having your head swirled around in the clothes washer. "Have you ever dampened me?" I dragged a green leaf out of the casserole.

"No," Mom said. "We haven't ever had to." Dampening was mostly done to keep kids safe and to help them succeed. Like if they were distracted a lot, parents might dampen their scattered attention when they started school so they could focus—but not too much to inhibit creativity. It was all a delicate balance, one of the challenges of being a parent, Mom always said.

"Though we certainly considered it when you were two and it seemed the only word you knew was 'why?' You always have been curious," Dad said.

"But not too curious," Mom said.

"Yes. You are the baby bear of curiosity," Dad said.

"The Three Little Bears" was probably the first story that any kid in Old Harmonie heard. Moderation was key— not too hot, not too cold, just right. That's what kept Old Harmonie going.

"Does everyone have a latency released?"

"Oh, Mori, don't let Theo scare you."

"No, I mean, does everyone have some hidden genius that needs to be set free?"

Mom's body relaxed and Dad chuckled. "Oh, honey," she said. That wasn't what I had meant, either. I didn't really know what my latency should be, but I assumed I had *something*. Mom clapped her hands together and said, "We should make a list of potential latencies." She was up from the chair and back with her tablet paper. It was new, and she was quite proud of it. It looked just like regular lined paper, but everything she wrote was fed to her central drive. She wrote *Mori's Latencies* at the top and then drew a square around the words. She tapped her pen on the pad. No one said anything.

"Maybe it makes more sense to think about the skills you are already showing," Dad said.

"Right," Mom said. "Your testing shows a real aptitude for both logical and creative thinking, especially when it comes to details. And of course we've noticed your kindness."

"That's not a skill," I told them.

All of this was making me feel about as low as the tides in the demonstration pools in Center Harmonie. Lower. Like the weird sluggy-snail thing that clung to the glass of the tanks.

"Okay, let's do this," Mom said. "Let's start with the big categories. We've got memory, music, art, puzzles and logic, mathematics, language, neuro-physical, and mechanical and spatial skills. How about we start with memory?"

There were different kinds of memory. Some people, you could tell them a date, and they would tell you what day of the week it was and the weather and everything that happened to them on that day. But then there were people whose memory release was more about holding knowledge in their head, usually about a specific topic. To be able to have a whole encyclopedia of plants and animals in my head would be pretty cool. "I'd like specialized memory. For plants and maybe animals."

This earned me another exchanged look between my parents. "Specialized memory isn't usually recommended," Mom said.

"Why not? Those were some of the first patients that Baba was working with when she developed the latency."

"Sometimes the topic—well, first you have to have the ability latent in you, and that can actually be really hard to determine. It's still one of the things people are working on, but, well, do you remember Annie Wilcow's son?" Mom asked, turning to Dad. "He was showing a memory latency on his testing, and they thought it was for coding, but it turns out it was just random strings of numbers. If they had meaning, he couldn't remember them. So his whole latency was totally wasted."

"Even if it works, it's kind of a waste," Dad said.

"Why?" I asked.

"I know you like plants now, but it might change," Dad said. "If I'd done specialized memory, it would have been for space exploration—which was on its last legs then, by the way, and now, well, that's all kaput, isn't it?"

"You could've been a historian," I said.

"We're not saying it has to lead directly to your job here," Mom said.

"But you should be thinking of your future."

"What were yours?" I asked.

Mom rubbed her temples. "Well, mine was visual memory. A good choice, since now I can see the long lines of genetic code and remember them and move them around easily in my head. It makes the work so much faster."

"Mine was a puzzle latency: logical thinking. How one thing leads to another like loops on a chain," Dad said.

"So you can predict how a disease might go," I said.

"Right."

"Let's put that on my list."

Mom wrote it down. "I think we should put visual memory for you, too. It's really an all-around useful skill."

"Fine," I said. It was true that having a visual memory where I could store images of all the plants—images I could never draw accurately—would be useful. But I didn't want my latency to mean more work on my eye. My retina cam and glasses were great, but Dr. Cartwright had said if we went in that direction, I'd need more care taken with my eye. No, thank you.

Sometimes I wondered if my latency was something that hadn't even shown itself yet. Something I had never tried or something I had tried and not been very good at. I thought of my drawings upstairs, how the lines were always shaky even when I held a leaf down and traced it. Or music. Maybe I was a glorious musician in the making, on some instrument I had never even seen, like a lyre or a didgeridoo, and all I needed was for the doctors to alter the right neural pathways to bring out the skill. Or maybe my latency would let me be the person who finally figured out how to put the vaccines we need right into our genes. That's where thinking about the latency got overwhelming. The possibilities branched out like vines.

"I think we can skip arts and music," Mom said. "Anything under mathematics?"

I shook my head.

"Remember, it's not only computations."

"I'm just not interested."

"How about mechanical reasoning? You like to build things."

I rubbed my eyes beneath my glasses.

"Someone's getting sleepy," Dad said.

"That's probably enough for tonight. We've got a list started. We still have a lot of time, but a year can go by quickly," she said. "I just want to be prepared."

I frowned.

Mom ruffled my hair. "You know, why don't we clean up, and then maybe we can watch a show?"

"Can we have cookies?" I asked. There'd been cookie dough in our delivery that day. Mom had tried to hide it when she unpacked the cooler the deliver bot had left on the front steps, but I had seen it.

Mom hesitated.

"Come on," Dad said. "I haven't had any sugar today."

"We had ice cream at the cafeteria," Mom said.

"That was coconut sorbet," I said. "It was practically a health food."

Mom relented and she even let me scoop out the dough onto the tray—I made them double the size she would have—and together we fed the tray through the oven. We ate them still warm as we sat on the couch. "You know, Mori," she said, a bit of melted chocolate on her lip, "just take a little time and think about all you could do with an improved visual memory, how that would change your life. I don't want you to rule it out because of your eye."

My mouth was full of cookie. "Mmm-hmm," I said. It wasn't a lie, exactly. She thought I was talking about her suggestion; I was expressing my delight in the cookie. She reached out and tucked my hair behind my ear, which jostled my glasses, but I didn't even complain. It took a split second for them to refocus and it looked like for just that moment, Mom was worried about something. But when the world was crisp again, she was smiling. "I love you, Mori."

"I love you, too, Mom."

"More than all the dandelions in Snowdrop field."

"More than all the raindrops in the sea."

She smiled, and I looked down at a magazine on the table. When I looked back up at her, it was there again, a flicker of worry, but only for a second, like when you're flipping past stations on the television.

8

WE SAT ON JULIA'S LAWN all morning, watching the house across the street so we wouldn't miss the arrival of our new neighbor. Benji assured us he had it on good authority that it was move-in day.

"Good authority from who?" Theo demanded.

"Dr. Kellerman told me," Benji said.

"Busybody," Theo muttered. I tried to look at him without staring. He'd been glowering since he'd come out of the house that morning.

"But he's usually right," Julia said. Then she turned to me. "If the new boy is cute, we have to promise right now that we won't fight over him."

"You really think it will be a boy?" Benji asked.

Julia smiled. "Fifty-fifty chance, right?"

"I promise I will never, ever fight with you over a boy," I told her. "DeShawn Harris could rip his actual heart from his chest and hand it to me, and I'd just pass it right on to you."

"I think that is the most disgusting thing you've ever said in your entire life, Mori, but I appreciate it."

"Focus!" Benji said. "They could be here any minute!"

It was nearly noon before the moving van arrived, and workers unloaded box after box, but there was no sign of the family. Finally, after Theo swore he was going to pass out from hunger, and Benji was nearly reduced to a puddle of anticipation, a KritaCar pulled up. The door slid open and a man stepped out. He was tall and his black hair reached for the sky, making him seem even taller. He was dressed more fashionably than any parent we knew: white pants that fell to his mid-calf and prismatic-lensed glasses that wrapped around his face, shielding his eyes.

"I'll probably look like that when I'm older," Benji said. But Benji's brown skin was sallow, like sand, where the man's skin glowed like the sun through autumn leaves. Benji kept his tightly curled hair cropped close to his head, and then there was also the matter of height: Benji had always been the smallest boy in our class. Even I had grown taller than him that spring. I'd stayed the same height all winter when the natural world lay dormant beneath our feet. When the trees popped out their budded leaves, and the crocuses and daffodils shot up from the ground, I grew three inches. My bones and joints ached, and each morning Mom would rub a salve of warm oil over my skin. "Growing pains," she said with a sigh, a soft smile, and a shake of her head. It was the same look she reserved for the baby raccoons that emerged beneath our porch each spring.

"Maybe there are *no* kids." Julia sighed, staring at the car in the driveway across the street.

As if to confirm this fear, out stepped an equally fashionable and beautiful woman: she wore a long, sleeveless dress that flowed down to her ankles and a chain of heavy, chunky beads around her neck. Her hair was twisted up into an elaborate bun, which seemed so glamorous compared to the short, practical haircuts the moms on our street wore. No way these two were parents.

We all sank back. There was a morning of summer vacation wasted.

But then the man knocked on the back window.

"It could be a dog," Julia said.

It wasn't a dog.

A girl stepped out of the car, tall like her father—her legs seemed to sprout out of her shorts—her hair pulled back into a ponytail full of curls. She stretched her lithe arms above her head and leaned her body from side to side.

"This is what I'm writing about in my journal tonight." Benji sighed.

"She's not a what, she's a who," I said. But I knew that I, too, would note the arrival of this new, wholly unbelievable family when I sat down to write in my journal, but the entry would be mostly questions: Where did they move here from? Were they from another Kritopia or outside? It had to be someplace amazing, so what would they make of our little neighborhood? We had to write in our journals every night; it was supposed to help if we ever had memory loss. They could use recordings and our journal entries to reupload our own past into our hippocampus. It seemed so far-fetched that we would lose our memories, and unless something truly spectacular happened, I usually rushed through it. This girl was worth writing about. She spun around and appeared to look right at us. Benji raised up his hand in a wave, even though the bush was between us and her. She bent her body back into the car, retrieved her backpack, then headed into the house.

A dull silence overcame us. Like a Thirteenth party where suddenly the guest of honor just disappeared.

"Good grief," Theo finally said. "At least now we can go get something to eat."

Before we could stand up, we heard the *clip, clip, clip* of fancy shoes on the pavement. "What are you children doing hiding behind the shrubbery? Didn't you see we have a new family joining our neighborhood?" Ms. Staarsgard stood on Julia's driveway wearing one of her typical business suits: bright blue with a skirt that looked difficult to walk in. She had thick-rimmed sunglasses that barely covered her eyes, but were so dark you couldn't even be sure she *had* eyes. "We're going over to introduce ourselves. Come on, children. Theo!"

There wasn't a single one of us who was about to argue with Ms. Staarsgard. We stood up, and I brushed my dirty hands off on my shirt, which only left a smudge on the white cotton.

Ms. Staarsgard was a couple strides ahead of us as we made our way across the street. "We are so lucky to have a house open up just when this family needed one."

"I bet Mr. Merton didn't feel lucky," Theo muttered.

Ms. Staarsgard turned to look back over her shoulder. "You all are about to make a new, dear friend. Someday you will understand how exciting this moment is."

"Oh, I understand, Ms. Staarsgard," Benji said. "I was hoping for another boy, but I bet this girl will be great, too."

"You have no idea," Ms. Staarsgard said, more to herself than us. She took her sunglasses off, folded them, and tucked them into the breast pocket of her suit. Then she knocked two sharp raps on the front door of Mr. Merton's old house.

After a moment in which none of us spoke, the door opened and revealed the two parents, but not the girl. Ms. Staarsgard extended her hand, and when the man took it, she wrapped her other hand around his, too, and shook firmly. "Hello!" she said cheerily. "I'm Tova Staarsgard and I live just across the way. I know you are very busy, but I wanted to come right over and introduce myself."

"Thank you," the woman said. "I'm Meryl Naughton, and this is my husband, Greg."

"We could not be happier that you have moved in. We've heard so much about you and your special, special girl. I've brought some of the neighborhood children over to meet her. You'll find they are very bright—perfect playmates for your precious one."

Ms. Staarsgard had to butter people up as part of her job—greasing the wheels, Dad called it—but I thought she might be laying it on a bit thick with a "precious" plus two "specials." I mean, was any kid that magnificent?

"I thought all the children in Old Harmonie were very bright. Isn't that the design?" When Meryl Naughton spoke, the right side of her mouth twitched up into a half grin. Up close I could see that her hair was the orange-brown color of an end-of-season chrysanthemum. Her cheeks were paler than the rest of the skin on her face, and dusted over with fat freckles.

"Oh, but these children are exceptionally so." She reached back and grabbed Theo. "My son, Theo, just had his Thirteenth and has done his latency already. Puzzles."

Theo tried to squirm free of his mother's grasp, but she held tight, her perfectly painted red fingernails tucking into his skin.

"Good to know if we need some help with a thousand-piece jigsaw puzzle," Greg Naughton said. "As a matter of fact, we just got one of the Eiffel Tower that is quite a doozy!"

Ms. Staarsgard laughed. "How clever! But of course his mind is meant for greater puzzles than that. All these children are. Including yours. We are forging ahead here on Firefly Lane—leading the charge of progress."

Theo finally managed to get loose from his mother, and he came back and stood next to me. His cheeks were red and I knew his mother was embarrassing him with her KritaCorp talk.

"We also have an eye to our past. Did I mention that Mori here is a great-granddaughter of Lucy Morioka, a founder and a dear friend of Dr. Varden. Yes, the children of Firefly Lane are very appropriate playmates for the proper development of your child."

The way she said it made me feel like I was a prescription being offered up by a doctor. Then she patted my head and made me feel like a dog. Julia looked over at me and mouthed the word "playmates" to me. I just shrugged. Ms. Staarsgard had her strange ways.

"I'm sure they will be. She's sleeping right now, but I'm sure she will be happy to meet them soon."

"Not fully adjusted yet?" Ms. Staarsgard asked, and I wondered just what it was this girl needed to be adjusted to.

"It was a long journey. She's tired."

"Oh, I'm sure of that. We're just so excited to meet her, to see what she's all about. We—these children, that is—have been waiting a long time to meet their new playmate."

"Like a thousand years," Benji said.

Ms. Staarsgard turned to look at him. "Sometimes change is a long time coming, Benji, but once it arrives, the impact can be immense, wouldn't you say?"

"I guess," he replied.

Ms. Staarsgard turned back to the Naughtons. "Now, if there are ever any problems, you will call me. Immediately." Her voice dropped an octave on that last word.

Meryl Naughton looked over Ms. Staarsgard at my friends and me. "I don't see how this charming group could lead our little one astray."

Ms. Staarsgard only pursed her lips and then, after a moment, said, "We just wouldn't want an unfortunate outcome, would we?"

"No," Meryl Naughton said. "We wouldn't."

Julia raised her eyebrows at me, and I knew she was thinking the same thing I was: adults are so strange. But then Greg Naughton gave us a warm smile and said, "It was so lovely to meet you all. We're sure Ilana is just going to love you!"

Ilana. I didn't think I had ever met anyone named Ilana.

"Right, then," Ms. Staarsgard said. "I'm sure you have unpacking and settling in to do. It was lovely to meet you, and welcome to the neighborhood." She spun around and ushered us down the path like a mother duck pushing her babies along with her wings.

Once we were back across the street, she turned to us and smiled. She put one hand on Theo's shoulder and one on mine. "I hope, in time, you will all realize what a great day today is."

"Mom, it's just, like, one new girl. It's not like we've solved the storm surge problem or something."

Her smile faltered, but then she said, "Come on, kiddos, I've had Clara whip up some tofu peanut satay for lunch, and we even have some cherries for dessert!"

"Is there any of that cake left, Ms. Staarsgard?" I asked.

"For you, little Mori, of course!"

So we all headed over to Theo's. I looked back over my shoulder toward the Naughtons' house. I thought maybe I saw a flicker of the curtain in the upstairs window but decided that was just my mind playing tricks on me, trying to make the girl appear.

But she didn't appear, not for two more days.

Two days is a long time to theorize.

Theo, Julia, Benji, and I met at Julia's that second day in her pool. I swapped my glasses out for my prescription goggles so I could see in the water and clung to three pool noodles to keep myself afloat while we talked.

"I saw her leave the house early yesterday morning. Running. Toward Center Harmonie." Julia pushed a strand of wet hair out of her face. She floated on an inner tube, her bum hanging down into the water. "She was gone a long time. It was like a training run. She could be getting ready for the Olympics. Track and field or the marathon. She's that good."

Mom said the Olympics used to be held in one city, a different one every four years, all over the world. Now each country has its own team and, while they compete at the same time, each of them is in a local facility. You can watch it all on television, and they make it look like they are running or swimming or whatever right next to one another.

"Was she faster than you?" Benji asked from the side of the pool. He hardly ever came in the water with us. He said he didn't like to muss up his hair, but I think the chlorine made his asthma worse.

"No," Julia said, then spun herself around in a spiral. "No one is faster than me."

"So you think," Benji said, still smiling at her.

"Witness protection program," Theo said. "Clearly. They dropped her and her family here, and they're trying to make it seem all casual, but instead they're just drawing attention to themselves." He was acting more normal today. But even that was unsettling. Just what had happened over the course of this week to make his mood fly from place to place like a bird warning others of a coming predator?

"My sister says she's a narc," Benji said.

"What's a narc?" I asked.

"They work for the government, like undercover, and go into schools and figure out if kids are doing drugs or building bombs or anything," Benji explained. His older sister gave us the real deal on everything.

"No one's building bombs or doing drugs here," I said.

But still the stories spilled out, each one more wild than the next.

"I don't think she's a narc. Or in witness protection, or any of those other crazy ideas," I said. "She's just a girl. She's just a girl and I think it's pretty crummy that we haven't gone back and asked her to play with us. Maybe she's shy and is afraid to come over and see us."

"Maybe," Julia said. "Or maybe she just doesn't want to make friends."

But I was already swimming to the pool's stairs. I tossed the noodles onto the pool deck and climbed out. I put my clothes on right on top of my wet bathing suit.

"Where are you going?" Benji asked.

"To see her," I told them.

As I coasted over on my bike, dripping wet and standing on the pedals, I thought about my friends' theories about the new girl: narc, witness protection, actor researching a part, reporter writing about the youth of Old Harmonie.

All those theories we had, we never came close to the truth.

The truth, it turns out, was far too fantastical and strange for it to ever have occurred to us, let alone for us to defend or debate it.

It was in us all the time, and we never saw it.

The truth.

It's not always as real as it appears.

9

I SHOULD HAVE GONE HOME to change before I went to Ilana's house. But anger and fear that I would chicken out carried me all the way to her doorstep. My swimsuit had soaked through my clothes, and my hair dripped down, leaving little splashes on her doorstep. I pressed the bell all the same.

A moment later her mother answered. Her dress swirled with colors that dizzied me. "Why, hello there. It seems a wave has splashed a mermaid onto my front step."

"I was swimming," I said. And then, "Hi. It's a pleasure to meet you. I'm Mori."

"I know who you are. We met the other day, remember?" Her voice sounded like sweet honey. She smelled like it, too. "Come on in."

"I'm all wet," I said.

"I can see that," she replied.

"I'm here to see, um, Ilana."

"So I assumed." A faint smile played on her lips. Was she teasing me? "Tell you what, you go around back, and I'll send Ilana out to you." She pointed to a slate-tiled path that led to their yard. It was full of roses, bright and blooming. When Mr. Merton owned the house, the landscaping had been sparse and dying. In fact, some of the other grown-ups had offered to fix it up for him, but he'd refused. Now here it was in full bloom.

I looked at the lawn furniture: some chairs around a glass-topped table and one chaise longue. Then there was a swing set. Would Ilana think we were too old for swing sets? But surely this had not belonged to Mr. Merton.

I sat on the edge of the chaise longue.

Ilana came out, her flip-flops flapping, and sat down on one of the swings. "Hi," she said. "I'm Ilana."

"Mori," I said. "I mean, I'm Mori. I live around on the other side of the cul-de-sac."

Kicking off her shoes, she started pumping the swing, going higher and higher. I watched her floating above me, then shuttling back away. When I'd first glimpsed her, I thought she looked like a movie star, but now she looked like an athlete. I could see all her muscles moving beneath her coppery skin. And her eyes—shocking green blue and flashing bright above her lightly freckled cheekbones. She looked like the girls in the teen magazines that Benji's sister subscribed to, mailed each month from the Kritopia outside of New York City. Only more so—more glowing, more real, more healthy, more *present*. If I ever fell down, she could bend over and right me without much effort at all. It helped that she was a full six inches taller than me, even taller than Julia, maybe even as tall as Theo.

Natural. One hundred percent natural. The way she moved, the way she shined, she had to be.

"Where'd you move here from?" I asked.

"California." Her voice drifted down to me.

"California? You mean you were in Calliope?"

"Calliope?" She paused in her pumping, her legs still straight out in front of her even as she swung backward. "Right, yes, Calliope. The Kritopia in Northern California."

She pumped herself back up higher and higher. I didn't know what else to say. This had been a terrible idea. I should have at least brought someone along with me to help make conversation.

Just as quickly as she started swinging, she stopped, letting her feet slide through the grass below the swing. "So what's cool around here, anyway?"

I wasn't sure what she would think was cool. I wasn't sure if there was anything cool at all. "I can show you," I said. "Do you have a bike?"

She walked around the house and pulled a red ten-speed from the shed. "Right on. Let's go."

We rode slowly around the block, away from Julia's house. I pointed out where Benji lived. "He's really nice. You'll like him."

She grinned, and it was like she turned on the sun and shined it right on me. "I'm sure I will."

I pointed out my house as we passed it, then pedaled up to the driveway of number 9.

"Who lives there?" she asked, squinting back at the house.

"No one. Not anymore, anyway. It's Dr. Varden's old house."

Ilana closed her eyes for a second. "Dr. Varden. Yes. Founder of Old Harmonie. What's inside?"

"Don't know. We've never gone in," I told her. "I want to see what she left behind, but no one will come with me."

"Really?"

"We're not supposed to go in there. It's against the rules."

"Says who?" she asked.

"Well, our parents, for starters. But I bet it's amazing inside. They can't move the house," I explained. "Or change it in any way. That was part of the deal Dr. Varden made when Krita took over. Otherwise I bet it would be a museum or something."

"And you've never been inside?" she asked. She looked at the house, not at me.

"Never." I shivered a little, and hoped she wouldn't see—I didn't want her to think I was silly for being afraid of a house.

"Huh." Then she looked back at me. "Interesting."

"Let me show you something else. Something even cooler."

We rode down to the park and left our bikes in the rack.

"Do you play?" she asked, nodding her head toward the tennis courts.

"Not really," I said. "I mean, I have played, but I don't like it very much. Mostly I play with Julia, and she's so . . ."

"So what?" Ilana asked.

"She's just a little competitive is all." I felt my stomach flip-flop. Julia was probably already fuming about me leaving her behind to go off with Ilana, and now I was bad-mouthing her before the two had even met. "Anyway, the courts are getting old and the ball bounces funny."

As we laced around the courts, I heard some of the littler kids squealing on the playground. "It's nice here," she said. "Real homey. We didn't have parks like this in Calliope—there was a lot more concrete. We could smell the ocean though, sometimes; that was nice."

With a quick glance over my shoulder, I led her a few steps into the woods. Then I hesitated. The only friend I had ever brought in with me was Julia. I'd shown her the field of squishy green hypnum moss that seemed to me to be the world's most luxurious bed. I showed her the mint leaves we could eat, and my special tree. She had been perfectly pleasant, and had even helped me to sketch a rare purple clematis that we found. But she never asked to come back with me, and it had become my solitary place.

"Everything okay?" Ilana asked. Her face was wide and open, with crinkles around her eyes from her smile.

I didn't know what I would do if Ilana thought the woods were dumb or boring—definitely not cool. I took a deep breath. "Yep. This way."

The woods weren't strictly off-limits, but not many people ventured into them. We didn't have to go very far before it felt like a new world. The sounds of Firefly Lane faded, and soon it was just our feet cracking twigs, birds calling to one another, and the occasional squirrel trilling out a warning to his family. "Did you have forests in Calliope?" I asked.

She shook her head. "Not like this."

"It's my favorite place. No one else really understands. They think it's just dark and damp. But—"

"It's like we went through an invisible door to another realm. Like in a dream, you know? I had a dream once where I was in these deep dark woods, and it was foggy, but then I broke out into a sunny clearing. There were all these little animals and I could talk to them—you probably think this is really silly."

"No!" I said. "It's not silly at all. I have dreams like that, too."

"I thought you might."

A smile spread over my face, and I felt as warm as a rock in the sun. "I'm documenting it," I told her. "I have—well, it's not done yet, but I'm putting together a book. I draw all the plants and animals I see, and then I write their scientific name and their common name and where I saw it and how much of it there is. That sort of thing."

"That's a really great idea," she said. "You can't truly understand a place until you study it."

"I'm not a very good artist, though."

I bent over and picked up a pinecone, its edges white with sap. Pinecones are a perfect example of the patterns of nature. The spirals of the scales work according to the Fibonacci sequence to create the golden ratio. My mom explained it to me once, carefully numbering all of the scales of a pinecone we'd found. Nature has all these patterns and internal logic. It doesn't make mistakes.

I tossed the pinecone to her and she caught it. "Smell it," I said. "I bet you didn't have that in Calliope."

"Only from a spray can." She laughed. "But you know, it still feels familiar. Like I've smelled it before. For real."

"I have a theory about that," I said. "You know, when something feels familiar even though it's new to you. I think that means it was meant to be a part of you. Like you and the pinecones—you were meant to be in this part of the world."

"I like that."

I showed her all of my favorite places in the forest before leading her to the oak tree that had split and grown so there was a perfect crook for sitting—big enough for both of us, it turned out. "We could have a picnic in this tree," she said, leaning back and looking up at the sky through the breaks in the leaves. "We could *live* here."

"Sometimes," I confessed, "I come out here and pretend this is a totally separate world. My world. And I think about how I would build a shelter and gather food and all of that. I've even thought about building a tree house out here. It wouldn't just be in the nook of the tree, but around the split trunk so the tree was a part of the house. We could have two little beds and windows all around."

"Does your world have a name?"

I shook my head.

"Well, if we're going to build our own realm out here, we should name it," she said.

"Biologists always use Latin names—like the scientific name is in Latin."

"Do you know the Latin name for the woods?"

I shook my head. "My name means 'forest' in Japanese. But I don't want to name this place after me."

"Why not?"

A gray squirrel tossed down a nut, then scampered down the tree trunk. "It just doesn't seem right to name a place after yourself. That's what conquerors do. We're just borrowing this spot for a bit."

"Okay then, how about this: What kind of a tree is this?" she asked.

"An oak," I told her.

"And we're at the edge of the oak, so Oakedge."

"That's perfect!" I said, then repeated the name. "Oakedge."

"Welcome to the Village of Oakedge," Ilana said. "So, if we are going to move out here, we are going to need a source of food."

I didn't know if we were playing a game or if Ilana really wanted to move out into the woods with me, but I didn't especially care. Just thinking about it made me giddy, and even if it couldn't really happen, it was nice to imagine a place that grew up out of the natural world, where you wouldn't need something like a latency because everything and everyone would be perfect just the way it was.

"You want to taste something great?" I hopped down and led her a bit farther into the woods, to a patch of low plants with deep green leaves. "Chew," I said as I handed her a leaf.

"Mint!" she replied.

I chewed my own leaf, then paused. Normally I was by myself and just spit it out when I was through, but I wasn't sure I could do that in front of her. But then she spit hers out and said, "What else can we eat?"

So I spit mine out and said, "Sometimes I bring a field guide, but I don't quite trust myself with the mushrooms or berries."

"That's smart," she said.

Which was nice, instead of being told it was too dangerous to be out here alone or that I was being foolish for even thinking of foraging in the woods for food.

My vision blurred, and I took my glasses off and wiped them.

"Those are some fancy glasses," she said.

"It's for an artificial retina. I was born without one, so I've got this chip—anyway, they keep getting dirty and blurry."

"In Oakedge your vision is perfect," she said. "It's our world, so we get to make the rules."

"Yes. Out here my vision is perfect. And I am strong and I can scramble up the trees."

"And we can fly from limb to limb like flying squirrels."

"Or swing like monkeys!" I agreed. "Hey, how much of your thirty percent have you used?"

She turned back to me. "Thirty percent of what?"

"Your enhancements?"

Ilana's gaze shifted away from me to something off in the distance that seemed to be nothing at all. I heard a chipmunk a short distance away, clicking and squeaking about his nuts. A woodpecker drilled into a tree.

"Six percent," she finally said.

"Lucky," I told her. "I'm already at twenty-seven. What about your latency? Do you know what you want to do for yours?"

"I haven't really thought about it yet."

"Really? I think about it all the time. My mom really wants me to do visual memory, and I will probably do something memory related, just not visual, because, you know." I tapped my glasses. "But I sometimes like to think I have a musician or an artist hiding inside of me. And other times . . ."

"Yeah?" she prompted.

"Sometimes I think about not getting a latency done at all." I tasted the words as I tested them out, paid attention to how they sounded and also how they felt. I wasn't sure I really meant what I said, but it gave me a little rush to say it. Like I really did have a choice in the matter. "What do you think about that?"

"I'm sure my parents will come up with the best choice for me."

Her voice sounded far away, like she was slip, slip, slipping down a cliff and away from me. I didn't want that to happen.

"Come on," I said. She followed right behind me as we made our way up an embankment and through to the oldest part of the forest, where the trees were tall, with thick trunks, and the ground was laden with leaves, pine needles, and broken-off branches. "Here." We were at the fence. A vine of some sort started at our feet and laced its way up between the chain links.

"What is it?"

"It's our fence. The outside barrier of Old Harmonie." I'd never brought anyone else out here. Julia would come if I asked her, but she had no interest in the fence or what was beyond. Theo would say I was being dopey again. Benji would only wonder if he could design a better fence, one that changed colors or played music—or turned into a skate ramp.

"What's out there?" she asked.

"The rest of the world. That way is Boston."

"Have you ever been?"

"To Boston? No, of course not."

"Why not?"

"Well, it's just, you know, it's so crowded and it floods all the time and so many people are sick. They don't really take care of themselves so much out there. I mean, I'm sure some of them want to, but they don't have a lot of resources."

She stared east. "What do you mean?"

"Well, like they don't have as much stuff to help with problems or the people who know how to fix things out there." I actually wasn't sure what I meant. That's just one of the things we'd always been told.

She looped her fingers through the fence. "It's a pretty weak fence," she said, shaking it back and forth.

"It's all we need," I told her. "We all work together here, and keep our eyes open. We keep each other safe." I wondered if I shouldn't have brought her out here after all. Maybe she didn't really understand the strange feeling that came over me when I looked out at the outside world.

"Thanks, Mori," she said. "Thanks for showing me the woods and the fence. Thanks for letting me into Oakedge."

"You're welcome."

Our hips bumped together as we walked back toward the tree. We climbed up into it, the space just right for the two of us, and we surveyed the world in front of us. All of the smells of the forest came up to meet us, the smells of things growing and alive. I could forget about Theo and his latency and his strange mood swings. I could forget about the choice I would have to make about my own latency. I'd always felt calm out here. Now, standing next to Ilana in the tree, it felt like home.

10

IN THE MORNING, I RODE toward Julia's house like I did most summer mornings. She was already over at Theo's, though. Theo's house was at the top of the circle of the cul-de-sac, right where the straight road split into two to make the circle, giving him an ever-so-slightly-bigger lot, which afforded an ever-so-slightly-larger driveway. He'd put up two basketball hoops there and called it his mini-court. They were playing one-on-one, and I slowed down to watch Julia sink what, on the small court, was a three-point shot, nothing but net. She saw me and waved. I waved back but didn't stop riding by on my banana-seat bike.

As if she had expected me, Ilana stepped out her front door as I coasted onto her driveway. "Come on," I said. "I want you to meet everyone."

I hadn't realized that Julia and Theo had followed me, and were waiting out in the middle of Firefly Lane with Benji, who rocked his skateboard back and forth under one foot. For Christmas Benji had received a brand-new skateboard, along with a helmet and pads for his knees, elbows, and wrists. He'd carried that skateboard around all winter and started peppering his speech with old-school skater slang. *"That pizza looks totally gnarly, bro."* Julia doubted that anyone, anywhere, ever had spoken like that, and our parents could neither confirm nor deny it.

It took about a million years to walk down her driveway and over to my gang of friends. I pushed my bike between us as we walked. "Are they nice?" she whispered to me.

"Very," I said. "Most of the time, anyway."

"Will we let them see Oakedge?"

I peeked at her from the corner of my eyes. "Maybe."

When we finally came up to them, I said, "Everyone, this is Ilana. Ilana, this is Theo, Benji, and Julia."

"Wanna play?" It was Theo who asked, his voice lower and more gravelly than usual, as if he had swallowed a handful of pebbles. For a second I thought maybe it was another remnant of his latency, but then he held the basketball on the palms of his hands, offering it to her as a tribute, and I realized it was just Ilana affecting him the way she affected me.

She nodded her head and her dark corkscrew curls shimmered like a waterfall over her shoulders. I twisted my own plain hair around my fingers. When I'd first met her, her hair looked chestnut brown, but now I could see hints of red. Each strand was a different, perfect shade: natural.

My parents said they didn't like that word, that all children were special whether they were conceived naturally or designed in a lab or some combination, like Theo, but what other word could describe Ilana?

"Welcome," Benji said. "Firefly Lane is the most fun cul-de-sac in Nashoba. You're lucky. Cul-de-sac. That's a funny word, isn't it? I've never really thought about it, but it is a funny word. Three words, actually, I guess."

Julia pressed her foot on top of his like it was a button to turn him off.

"Like the dog?" Ilana asked.

"What dog?" Benji replied.

"The one on TV," she said matter-of-factly.

I glanced over at Julia, and she just shrugged.

Ilana smiled. "I think that's a great name, and I bet you're right that this is a fantastic cul-de-sac to live on."

Benji beamed.

"Anyway, I would love to play basketball. I'm pretty decent."

I thought I saw Julia smirk.

"Well, then," Theo said. "Why don't you take Benji and Mori on your side, and Julia and I will team up."

We started walking back toward Theo's house. "Ilana moved here from California," I told them. It felt good to be the one who actually knew Ilana, knew what was going on before everyone else for once. I could even feel my chest puffing up and myself walking taller.

"Right," she said. "My folks worked at the office out there."

"How'd you even get here?" Julia asked.

"Plane," she said, as if it was the most natural thing in the world. As if air travel weren't highly restricted—only people with lots of money and lots of influence could afford it. Her parents must have been way up the ladder at Krita, then— higher, even, than Theo's mom.

"Right," I said. "I've never been on a plane. Is it nice?"

"I guess," she said. Then she turned and flashed her smile at me. I would practice and practice for weeks and still couldn't get my whole face to shine like hers did when she smiled. "They gave me dinner on a tray with a different section for each kind of food. Chicken, potatoes, and carrots. Real carrots. And for dessert there was ice cream with whipped cream, and they put a little toy plane in it so it was like the whipped cream was the fluffy clouds and the plane was us."

"Big whoop," Julia said.

"I think it sounds amazing," Benji said. He was positively beside himself. "You're really from California? Were there palm trees?"

"A few," Ilana said.

Benji sighed. "What I wouldn't give to see a palm tree."

"You have a palm tree in your living room," Theo told him.

"A real palm tree," Benji replied. "One planted and growing in the ground, not a pot."

"What's it like there?" I asked. "Is it set up the same way, with villages and a center and everything?" I had heard that the other Kritopias were set up differently.

She hesitated. "Yes." Another pause. "Sort of. The coastal landscape of California is beautiful, but more wide open than the Eastern Utopia. The villages are situated like links on a chain, divided by walls."

"Walls?"

"There's no forest to separate the neighborhoods, so we have walls."

I looked out over the lush green trees that formed a barrier between Nashoba and the villages on either side. A wall would be so much sadder. "But it's not the fences that keep us safe. It's us. Their planners mustn't have been as good," I said. "Our planners were the originals, you know? The ones from Harvard and MIT and all the tech companies around Boston."

Ilana smiled. "Northern California wasn't exactly lacking in the brain trust."

"I would have at least covered the walls in vines. Bamboo, maybe. Then you could cultivate it for fibers."

"They could have used you out there," Ilana said.

I grinned.

"Mori's going to make the world a more beautiful place," Julia said, looping her arm through mine.

"Oh, yes," Theo said. "One tree at a time. Did you meet Elma yet?"

"Elma?"

"That's one of Mori's trees," Theo said. He grinned over at me. "She names them."

Ilana turned to me. "I think that's lovely."

I turned to Theo and stuck my tongue out at him.

"Sappy," he said back.

"Thorny," I said to him. He pushed his bangs out of his eyes, and it felt like nothing at all had changed in him.

It was a lot of information to take in. Whenever I'd thought about any of our sister Kritopias—Calliope in California, Citroen in Florida, and Wrightsville near Chicago—I'd figured they were maybe a little different, but still beautiful. But here was Ilana telling us the world there was quite different from our own.

Theo still had the basketball, and he started dribbling it as soon as he got onto the court. "We'll take this side, you guys get that net. No body fouls, have to pass at least once before each basket, no cherry picking—the usual."

"Got it," Ilana said. She bent over and tugged up her socks so they reached straight up to her knees. It didn't make her legs look any less long. I wanted to do something to prepare, too, so I bent over and retied my shoe. When I stood up, the ball was flying at me. I caught it, and immediately stepped forward once, then again.

"Traveling!" Julia yelled.

"I didn't know we'd started," I said.

"No worries," Ilana said. "We'll get them."

I threw the ball to Julia, who dribbled to the left, then faked around Benji. Theo was running up the court. She passed to him and he sunk the shot. "Two to nothing," Julia called out. She passed the ball to Ilana.

Ilana stood still for a moment, surveying the court. Then she nodded, as if she'd come to a decision. She started dribbling slowly, walking instead of running. Theo hesitated, then came at her. Without looking at me, she called my name, and soared the ball up into the sky. It landed right in front of me, and I caught it on the first bounce. This time I started dribbling. I wasn't very good at it, but I made it a few yards before Julia was on me. I grabbed the ball to my chest, then pivoted. Benji was heading my way. I passed the ball to him, and he rushed toward the basket. "Shoot!" Ilana called. So he did. It hit the backboard and bounced off, but Ilana was there to catch it and toss it right in. It seemed effortless to her. She high-fived Benji, then rushed over and high-fived me.

We went back and forth for a few points, but then Ilana took control of the situation. It felt like she knew how Benji and I were going to play even if we didn't know ourselves. She threw the ball where we were going to be right before we arrived. We were already up by six when I found myself under the basket. "Mori!" she called. I turned and the ball was in my hands. "Shoot! Shoot!" So I did. A clumsy layup, not at all the form that Julia had taught me, but still the ball soared, hit the rim, and danced around and around and around before slipping down for another two points.

I clapped my hands and jumped up and down. "I never score! Never ever!"

Ilana threw her arm around my neck. "Stick with me, kid, and you'll be a baller in no time."

"Nice shot, Mori," Theo said.

"All my coaching is paying off!" Julia added.

On the next play, Ilana stole the ball away from Julia. Julia was learning, though. Instead of going straight toward Ilana, she headed toward Benji. Theo was covering me, and Julia figured, rightly, that Ilana would throw to Benji. Just as Benji caught the ball, Julia checked him with her elbow. "Foul!" Benji cried. "That was totally a foul!"

"It was an accident," Julia said. But I wasn't so sure. She didn't normally run at people with her elbows out.

"Either way, I get my foul shots."

Benji stood on the line that Theo had painted the previous fall. He bounced the ball a few times. "Should I do a
trick shot? Backward and between my legs?"

"Just shoot, numb nuts," Theo said.

So Benji did. It was an impressive shot, actually, a gorgeous parabolic arch that flew so high up into the sky, I lost
it for a minute in the glare of the sun.

Then it fell down right into Mr. Quist's backyard.

"Oh, no," Theo groaned.

"You just sent the ball into the land of no return," Julia
told him.

"I'll get it," Ilana said.

"You can't," I said. "Mr. Quist has told us a million times
to stay away from his yard. From his house. From his
everything."

"I'll just pop over the fence."

"Over the fence? Are you kidding?" Julia asked.

But Ilana was already scrambling up the tree at the end
of the driveway.

"Forget it," I called up to her.

"Really," Julia said. "I can ask my dad to get it when he
gets back from his power walk."

"No." She grunted. "I can get it. I just have to figure out
how to get down on the other side without messing up the
garden." She edged out on one branch while holding the
branch above her. Her sneakers seemed fixed to the lower

branch, but she wobbled back and forth. The fence was six and a half feet tall, precisely. Theo's neighbor, a single man named Meldrick Quist, valued his privacy, and his prized cucumbers, and said that this height blocked the view of passersby—in other words, Theo—while still delivering the proper level of sun to his vegetables.

"I'm taller," Theo said.

"Barely," she said back. "And I doubt you can balance this well." She shimmied to the right a little and tugged on the branch.

"Just swing down and grab it, why don't you?" Julia asked.

"If I could just get out a little farther—"

It's like we saw her falling before she actually started. Next to me, Benji gasped, and Theo lurched forward. Ilana's left arm pinwheeled in the air as if she were grasping, grasping for a handhold that would never come. Then her left foot kicked out.

She tumbled forward, out of sight, away from us. The cacophony of sounds echoed back to us: thump, crash, the cry of a cat, another crash. Nothing from Ilana. Theo ran forward, scrambling up the fence.

Six and a half feet. Straight down. Was that enough to break an arm?

I turned toward Julia's house, ready to run and call for an ambulance.

"Unbelievable," Theo said.

I turned to see him grasping the edge of the fence, peering over. Sticking up above his head was the basketball, clasped tightly in Ilana's hands.

⚲

Ilana had landed right on a patch of Mr. Quist's cucumbers, and she returned to our side of the fence covered in goopy seeds. Mr. Quist wasn't home, so we decided to leave him a note, though Benji advocated for playing innocent. "Easy for you to say," Theo told him. "You live on the other side of the cul-de-sac."

Theo got a piece of paper and a pen from inside and put them in front of me. "Why me?" I asked.

"You have the neatest handwriting."

"And you're the kindest," Benji said.

"And you probably feel the worst about this," Julia added.

I took the pen.

Dear Mr. Quist,

Due to a tragic basketball accident, one of our members found themselves deposited rather violently into your cucumber patch.

"Shouldn't it be herself?" Theo asked.

"I'm trying to maintain anonymity."

We are very sorry for this accident. We know that your cucumbers are irreplaceable, but perhaps we can offer some sort of service in reparation. There are five of us and we are hard workers and not usually as clumsy as this accident might make you think.

Sincerely,

"Who's going to sign it?" Benji asked.

"We're all going to sign it," I said.

"All of us? I don't even like playing basketball," Benji said.

"It was your ridiculous showboating that sent the ball over the fence," Theo said. "Trying to impress the new girl."

"I wasn't showboating," Benji said.

"I can't believe you're all afraid of Mr. Quist," I said, shaking my head, the pen still over the paper. "If I sign it, you all need to sign it."

"I'm not signing a letter for a crime I didn't commit," Julia insisted.

"It was a group effort," I said. "We are a marauding band of criminals now."

"Maybe we don't need to sign it at all," Benji suggested.

I shook my head and signed the letter

The Firefly Five

11

BEFORE WE REPORTED TO MR. Quist's the next morning, Ilana and I hiked out to Oakedge. We hadn't meant to stay so long, but we'd been lying on our backs, staring up through the leaves and talking about what type of shelter to build—I wanted to build a frame out of sticks and cover it in canvas, like my tent, but Ilana wanted to make a lean-to completely out of branches so it couldn't be seen, even from above. The next thing we knew, it was nine thirty.

"Where have you been?" Julia demanded when we got to Theo's. She sat on a basketball under the net on Theo's mini-court. "We were supposed to meet here at nine o'clock." Benji and Theo stood behind her, and it felt a little like coming up to a queen and her soldiers.

"Sorry," I said.

"And you left poor Theo here with Mr. Quist ready to strike at any moment."

"Whoa, there. Poor Theo nothing," Theo replied.

I knew Julia had to be really mad if she was going to profess sympathy for Theo. And I supposed we could have asked her into the woods with us, but it still felt like a special, fragile thing between me and Ilana; and anyway, she probably would have suggested building the shelter out of something solid and practical like stones.

"Let's march to our doom," Benji said.

Mr. Quist was waiting for us. He had his hands on his hips, which were encircled by a gardening apron. "The Firefly Five, I presume. I was wondering when you would show up."

"We're sorry," I said.

"I've never felt so much like poor old Mr. McGregor, his garden assaulted by Peter Rabbit and Benjamin Bunny."

Benji kicked up his skateboard. "I'm no bunny," he mumbled.

"That's right. A no-bunny nobody," Mr. Quist said.

"Hey," Julia said, flicking a braid over her shoulder.

"It was an accident," Theo said.

"I thought I'd made things clear with your family." Mr. Quist was scowling, but when I looked at him, his eyes were turned up like he was smiling, and they twinkled a bit.

"We were just playing basketball and—"

"It went over the fence—"

"And we didn't want to bother your cat—"

"Or you, so—"

"It was me." Ilana stepped forward. "If you want to know, the basketball went over the fence, and I was trying to drop myself down without disturbing your garden, but I slipped and I'm afraid I landed on your cucumbers. And a few other things."

Mr. Quist rubbed his hand across his forehead. "At least one of you I can understand." He pulled out a small notebook, no bigger than his hand. "Here are my calculations. You destroyed three cucumber vines and two summer squash. These seeds were planted in late winter, and I have spent one to two hours a day on the garden. One point five hours a day for approximately one hundred twenty days give us one hundred eighty hours, and we'll say you owe me one-tenth of that, so that's approximately eighteen hours of work that you owe me. I don't care if one of you Firing Five does it—"

"It's the," Benji began, but then stopped, and no one stepped up to correct Mr. Quist.

He went on as if Benji hadn't spoken at all. "—or if you divide it up amongst yourselves. But you will complete eighteen hours of work, and they will be logged here. I am the keeper of the log. Got it?"

"Got it," I said.

"Good. She who speaks first gets the first task." He held out a small rake-like thing. "You're going to be planting mustard in that bed over there."

I started to giggle. I couldn't help it. Benji giggled next to me. Mr. Quist sighed and looked up to the heavens. "Where do you think mustard comes from?"

I knew enough not to say from the delivery service.

"Mustard the condiment is made from mustard seeds. Mustard seeds grow on mustard plants. You can also eat the greens. You are going to plant mustard seeds." He pointed to a raised bed.

"But I thought you just said you make mustard out of mustard seeds?" Benji asked.

"Honest to goodness, what do they even teach you in school? Each mustard seed will grow a mustard plant, which in turn will have several flowers and hundreds of seeds. It's simple multiplication. Do you at least learn that in your backward academies?"

"In third grade," Benji said. "Sometimes in second if you're smart about math, like Julia."

"I'm sure she's a genius." He turned to Theo. "You look like you're built for spreading compost. And you two workhorses," he said to Julia and Ilana. "The retaining wall needs repair. The bricks are there. Figure it out."

And with that, he was gone back inside.

"He's calculating it wrong," Julia grumbled.

"What do you mean?"

"It was fuzzy math. Estimations here. Rounding there. He should have added up all the work he's done, divided by the number of plants, and then given us the proportional amount. We didn't destroy one-tenth of his garden."

"You going to tell him that, Julia?" Theo asked.

I had my tiny rake, and I was turning over the dirt in the raised bed. A ladybug landed right on my knee.

"Ladybugs aren't all girls," I whispered to Benji, who was coming along behind me, digging tiny holes and dropping seeds. "They don't even all have spots."

"Mm-hmm," Benji said.

I looked over at Ilana and Julia, who were stacking bricks that had fallen off the retaining wall. They didn't use any cement or anything, and I wondered if it would just fall again.

By the afternoon, only Ilana and I were left. They all had reasons: Julia had her art lesson, Benji's mom picked him up for an asthma checkup, and then Theo's nanny called him home. Still, it kind of felt like they were flaking off from us, leaving Ilana and me behind the way we had left them.

My hands had dirt in all the creases and under my nails. "I guess we should have worn gloves," Ilana said, looking at her own dirty hands.

I rubbed my finger over a callus. "I kind of like it."

"This is good preparation. Maybe we could grow our own little garden in Oakedge."

Mr. Quist came back out to check on us. "Twenty minutes left, girls."

"Why do you even do this?" Ilana asked him. "Why don't you just get the vegetables delivered?"

"You have cucumbers in your delivery yesterday?"

"Yes."

"And tomatoes?"

"Yes."

"Did you ever consider where they came from?"

I glanced over at Ilana. "I knew they were grown, but I didn't know it was right here."

"Not all of the vegetables, but in the summer, I do my part. We can't just import all of our food. It's not safe and it's not sustainable. I've been telling the people at Krita for years that we need our own farms."

"My parents say the same thing, that we should have local food. They say it's better that way. More natural."

Mr. Quist stopped moving and regarded Ilana carefully, the way the nurses looked me over at a checkup. A little bird flew down from the fence between Mr. Quist's house and Theo's. It hopped right up to Ilana and pecked at the ground at her feet before looking up, seemingly startled to see her human face. "Is that what your parents tell you?" Mr. Quist asked her.

"Yes." Ilana furrowed her brow. "They even go out of Old Harmonie to get food."

"So do I from time to time."

"Is that your job?" I asked. "Are you in agriculture?"

"I'm retired."

"What was your job?"

"I worked in the Idea Box."

"Really?" I asked. "That is so cool!" If you worked in the Idea Box, you spent all day coming up with any sort of idea and trying to make it work. Hacking, they sometimes called it. They'd come up with a problem and then hack it—just spitting out any old crazy solution to see what would do the trick. The more creative, the better. Some of the stuff went nowhere—most of it, actually—but some of it led to great innovations. Like our watchus; they came out of the Idea Box when people wanted a way to track their body's vital signs over time in natural settings—plus be able to tell what time it was without looking at a phone.

"Cooler than other positions, I suppose." He plucked a dying leaf from one of the plants. "You're the one who planted those trees, right?"

"Yes. I thought the plants could use more variety, to avoid diseases and all."

He smiled then. "Precisely."

"We've been thinking of starting our own garden, actually," Ilana said. "Do you have any seeds?"

Mr. Quist hesitated, then said, "I can do you one better. Come by later this week and I'll have some seedlings prepared."

"The place we have in mind is kind of shaded," I said.

"I'll choose some that can do well without a lot of sun." He turned his head to the side. "You'll share the bounty with me, won't you?"

"Of course," I said.

"All right, then." He clapped his hands together. "You've done good work. The ledger is clean."

"But we didn't do the full eighteen hours," I said. "Even with all of us working—"

Ilana elbowed me in the side. "Thank you for this lesson," she said to Mr. Quist, and she tugged me away from the garden.

12

ILANA INVITED ME OVER FOR dinner. I spent twenty
minutes in my bedroom figuring out what to wear. Her
mother was the picture of glamour, and her father—I had
never seen a more handsome man.

They must be artists, I decided, trying to picture my
mother in the sleeveless dresses I'd seen Ilana's mother
wearing. In the air-cooled offices of Krita, my mother would
shiver and shake and then put on a sensible cardigan. So
far I had not seen either of Ilana's parents boarding the
bus to the village or to Center Harmonie. Artists often
worked at home or outside. *En plein air,* Julia had said
about the art lessons she took from a woman over in Oneida
Village. Sometimes I would stop my bike outside of Felicia

Winthrop's house, number 27 Firefly Lane, and listen to her practice her violin. It was times like that I really wished there was a test that would tell me that hiding deep inside of me was a musical ability that could be released by my latency and that I, too, could play notes that danced out and around the neighborhood.

I knew that out in Calliope they had the film actors and pop musicians, and their work was beamed all around the world both within and without the Kritopia system. So maybe Ilana's parents had been part of that world, the pop art world, but decided to move east and refocus on more classical work. That would make a lot of sense. It would certainly explain the breezily confident way they all walked around.

Which made the problem of deciding what to wear that much worse. In the end I wore my green Capri pants with a black shirt that had a funny little lace collar that I had always hated but thought maybe it would look sophisticated or cute or something other than like myself.

Ilana was sitting on her front steps waiting for me when I arrived.

"Hi," I said, feeling shy all of a sudden.

"Hi," she said back. She scratched at a long scrape on her calf.

"When did you get that?" I asked.

"Sometime when we were in the garden, I guess. I came home, and there it was. Pretty cool, huh?" She picked at it. "I really can't remember ever getting anything like this before."

I wrinkled my nose.

"Well, no, wait, I think when I was seven I fell off my bike and needed stitches."

"You don't remember needing stitches?"

"You know how pain is. It messes with your memories." I thought of Theo. He'd been a bit more normal lately, and I wondered if his head still hurt or if he even remembered how he'd acted just after his latency.

She stood up and strode around to the back of her house, so I followed her. This time I sat on one of the swings. She climbed up the slide and on top of the monkey bars, where she sat with her legs hanging down. "I wonder what kind of seedlings Mr. Quist is going to give us," I said.

"I hope there are lots of berries. I really like berries."

"Me too. I was wondering, though, if we were allowed to plant a real garden in the woods."

"I'll review the regulations," she said.

I laughed.

"What?"

"It's just a funny way to say it. Anyway, it's not an actual regulation, probably."

"You haven't read the regulations?"

"Well, not cover to cover." Everyone had a thick copy of the *Kritopia Guidebook for Old Harmonie* in their house, but no one had ever sat down and read the whole thing. "I've read the part about the history, and some of the philosophy. I think that's interesting. But I haven't gotten into the nitty-gritty rules or anything."

"Who's talking funny now?"

"What?"

"Nitty-gritty? You sound like my grandma Aggie."

"'Nitty-gritty' is not a grandmother phrase. 'Fiddlesticks' is a grandmother phrase."

"Oh, fiddlesticks!" Ilana cried out. "I have forgotten to review the nitty-gritty of the regulations!"

I began pumping the swing. "Oh, fiddlesticks! You've gotten far higher than me!"

"Oh, fiddlesticks!" Ilana said as she stood up on the monkey bars. "I'm falling to my doom."

And then she was.

Falling.

No, not falling.

Flying.

And then, before I could even yell her name, she landed on her feet, crouched down with one hand on the ground like a superhero in a movie.

All of this before my brain had a chance to figure it out. It was like the camera couldn't resolve the image.

"Ilana!"

But she was laughing. "It's hardly a jump at all," she said.

"Ilana," I said again, quieter this time.

"Oh, fiddlesticks," Ilana said. "I fear I've upset my friend Mori." She put a hand on my shoulder. "I didn't mean to scare you. It was just a game."

I shook my head. "You could've been hurt. Badly. You could've broken an arm or a leg or cracked your skull open."

"It's only two point seven meters high. I've jumped off of there a million times. Or at least a hundred."

"It doesn't matter," I said. "You shouldn't do things like that." But all the while I was wondering why I was so upset. I had seen Theo and Julia do things much crazier than that before. And me. I had done things like that once, when I was very little. I remember Julia and me pumping higher, and higher, and higher, then seeing who could jump the farthest. She usually won, but I didn't mind, because it felt like I was an eagle soaring on a thermal. Now, though, just the thought of it made me sick to my stomach. I could see every possible bad scenario.

"Is it time for dinner yet?"

"Sure. Let's go inside."

She started walking toward the sliding door at the back of the house, but then she stopped and turned so that we were staring right at each other. She looked down at me, and I tilted my head up so that I was staring right into her aquamarine eyes. "I'd never do anything to scare you on purpose. And I won't ever do that again."

As soon as we stepped inside her cool house, I heard her parents' laughter coming from the kitchen. Ilana stopped. "My parents are different," she said.

"I know," I practically sighed.

"No. Different."

"Everyone thinks their parents are weird," I said. "Even Benji, and his are the nicest."

"I didn't say weird. I said different."

"Are there, like, things I shouldn't say or do?" Julia's mother didn't like people to use nonspecific words. *It physically pains her*, Julia said. Whenever you were around her you had to be careful not to say "stuff" or "things," or even "dirt" instead of "soil," or "germs" instead of "microbes." We usually tried to only go over there when it was her dad's day at home.

"No, not that. It's just that, back in California, sometimes they made my friends uncomfortable."

"Because they're so beautiful?"

Ilana looked me over. "Did you get dressed up to come here?"

I looked down at my outfit. *This old thing?* I wanted to say. Instead I croaked out, "Maybe."

She tugged on one of her curls, then let it boing back up. "This is exactly what I mean. They're just people, you know."

"But you have to admit they are especially attractive people. Like you."

"That's just how we're constructed," she said.

I didn't want to get into an argument with her about how outsides do influence our perceptions, even if they shouldn't. And I didn't want to talk to her about how probably she wasn't even constructed at all. Beauty like that had to come from nature. I said, "I'll be fine."

I wasn't.

Ilana's father's eyes looked like green marbles, clear and shiny. They took in my full measure, warmly, pulling the good to the surface like a magnet. He took my hand in both of his and shook it while saying, "Thank you so much for being such a welcoming friend to Ilana."

"Your eyes are very green, Dr. Naughton. I mean, Mr. Naughton. Or—"

He laughed, warm as sunshine. "It is doctor, but call me Greg. And my lovely wife is Meryl."

Ilana huffed and tugged me into the dining room. It had an old wooden table, stained dark with nicks and scratches. There was a brightly colored runner down the middle, with two large bowls of fruit. In between the bowls was a plate of cheeses. I glanced over my shoulder at Ilana. "See," she mouthed.

"You don't—" I began. "I mean, I've never seen something like this from the delivery service."

"Don't worry, it's all local," Ilana's mother assured me. "Over in Fruitlands they have a terrific dairy farm, and then in Point Loma there's a goat farm. That's blue goat cheese. And then we visited a berry farm in Stow—"

"No, not Stow," Ilana's dad said. "It was in Harvard."

"Wait, you left Old Harmonie? For strawberries?" I knew people went outside of the gates for things they needed sometimes, but for something as simple as strawberries? That seemed like an unnecessary risk.

Ilana's mom laughed. "That's where the best ones are."

"We get strawberries here," I said, still trying to work through what they were telling me: that they had been willing to take the risk of going outside of Old Harmonie—not to mention the indignity of decontamination—just to get strawberries.

Ilana's mom wrinkled her nose. "A shadow of strawberries, maybe. Not the real deal."

"Did you go?" I asked Ilana.

She shook her head, then picked up a strawberry and took a bite.

Ilana's dad pointed to the cheese tray. "You really need to try the blue goat cheese. It's to die for."

"I'm not supposed to eat anything with mold in it."

Ilana's dad raised his eyebrows, and her mom gave a tinkling laugh. "I guess you'd better stick to the cheddar, then," she said as she lowered herself into a chair with arms that curved around and seemed to hug her. She hooked one leg over one of the arms, grabbed a bunch of grapes, and began popping them into her mouth.

"I need to wash my hands," I said.

"Of course," Meryl replied. "You, too, Ilana."

Ilana scrunched up her face but followed me into the kitchen. "Wash your hands?"

"I always wash my hands before I eat. Everyone does." I switched on the tap.

"What's on them? Is everyone extra dirty here?"

I felt myself blushing, so I jammed my hands under the warm water and scrubbed hard with the pumice soap they had. "No, of course not. It's just, you know, there are germs, things you can't see—microbes."

"We don't have that problem in Calliope."

"Maybe it's everyone in Calliope who's dirty," I muttered, then stepped out of the way so she could wash her own hands.

When we came back into the room, Ilana's father was pouring wine into two glasses. Ilana's mom sliced off a thin bit of the cheese with the green vein. "So," she said. "Tell me your story."

"My story?"

"Yes. The story of Mori."

"Mom," Ilana said. "Not everyone has a story."

Her mom laughed and said, "Well, that's a horrible thing to say about a guest." She turned back to me.

"Um, well, I was born here."

"Not here?" her mom asked, pointing at the floor.

"No." I laughed. "At the clinic in the village."

"Not in the hospital in Center Harmonie?"

I shook my head. "My mom said they almost didn't make it there since I was born early and I came so fast."

Ilana's parents exchanged a look and I wondered if this was the type of information that was supposed to stay in a family. "Anyway, I grew up here. My parents both work in the center. My mom is a fertility specialist, and my dad works in epidemiology. Not like you."

"Like us?" Ilana's father asked. He sat down on a bench on the far side of the table, and gestured for me to sit down, too. I took a seat and Ilana filled a plate with fruit and cheddar for me. She took a huge piece of the blue cheese for herself.

"You know, artists and all."

Ilana's mom laughed again. I don't think I'd ever heard my mother laugh that much. "We're not artists."

"Not exactly," her dad said.

"I work in robotics," her mom said. She tucked a stray strand of hair behind her ear. "Artificial intelligence, mostly."

"Like the teaching modules?" I asked.

"Well, not that project, exactly. My work is a little more sophisticated."

"And I'm in materials research," Greg said.

Benji's dad worked in materials research, too. He used to bring home goopy polymers for us to play with when we were little.

"I'm sorry. I just thought—"

"I love that you think we're artists," Ilana's father said as he plucked a grape from a bunch. "You still haven't told us your story."

"Maybe Ilana is right," I said. "I don't know that I have a story."

"Well, where are you happiest?"

I started to say with my friends, but that wasn't entirely true. "Outside. At night. In the summer. Sometimes my dad pitches a tent for me in the yard and I sleep there. I like to walk out in the moonlight."

Ilana's mom was peeling an orange with bright skin and purple-red fruit. A blood orange; my brain pulled the name out of its deeper memory banks. "Well, now. There you go. Mori the night-walker."

13

WHEN I WOKE THE NEXT morning, a little later than usual, I slipped my glasses on and waited for the room to come into focus. "Mori!" my mom called up the stairs. "Ilana's here to see you."

I clomped downstairs still in my pajamas, my hair a tangled snarl at the back of my head. Ilana was standing in our front hallway wearing orange shorts and a T-shirt with thin stripes. I rubbed my eyes under my glasses.

"What are you doing today?" she asked.

"Um, the same thing we do every day. Hang out. Maybe go swimming."

"No!" she said. "We are going to Center Harmonie. We're going to the museum. Hurry up or we'll miss the bus."

"To the museum? With who? Is one of your parents bringing us?"

"No, we'll just take the bus, and then we can take a KritaCar home, or go hang out in the park or the central offices until the buses head home."

I reached a finger up beneath my glasses and wiped some crust away. The museum was one of my favorite places to go, but I'd never gone anywhere on the bus alone.

Ilana stepped closer to me. "Listen," she whispered. "They have a whole section on edible plants—"

"I know," I said, feeling myself starting to wake up. "The botany exhibit is my favorite part of the whole museum!"

"We need to educate ourselves. So come on, get dressed."

"I need to ask my parents."

She frowned. "Really?"

"Yes." I laughed. "I can't just hop on the bus and head into the city. Geez. Come on, they're in the kitchen." I was going to have to come up with a good story to convince them to let us go, a really good reason why we needed to go to that museum.

Mom was dressed in her work clothes, but Dad had on shorts and a polo shirt and his leather sandals. They were drinking coffee at the kitchen table. "Ilana and I want to take an educational trip to the museum. The Old Harmonie Museum. We can take the bus with you, Mom, and then we can meet you to take the bus home or a KritaCar."

Dad started laughing. "You have it all planned out, don't you."

"Not bad for first thing in the morning, right?" Ilana asked. She flashed her brightest smile.

Mom took a sip from her coffee. "What do you want to see there?"

"I want to show Ilana the botany exhibit, and also about our history here, since she's new. Also, I thought maybe going to the museum and learning about all the things we have done here in Old Harmonie could give me a better idea of what I might want for my latency."

"Well, now, that's laying it on a bit thick, wouldn't you say?" Dad asked.

I tried to smile like Ilana. "We really do need to pursue all options."

The sun streamed through our picture window, and the grass outside was a bright, bright green. It really was a lovely day. Maybe that's what swayed my usually cautious mother. She turned to Ilana. "You'll watch her the whole time?"

"Of course," Ilana said.

"And report back immediately if anything happens? I can give you our numbers."

"Mom, she's not my babysitter. She's my friend."

"I'm just covering all the bases."

"Bases covered," Ilana said.

Mom sighed, then did her crinkly-eyed sad-happy smile. "Fine. But you've got ten minutes to get out the door. I'll find a protein bar and some fruit for you. Now go get dressed and get that bird's nest out of your hair."

Ilana and I clasped hands and ran upstairs.

We held hands the whole time on the KritaBus, too, giggling together. Ms. Staarsgard was in the front of the bus with the other executives, and she turned and looked back at us. I thought she would shake her head, or put her finger to her lips to shush us, but she just smiled and returned to her conversation with the other administrators. The grownups are always telling us that distinctions don't matter, but you couldn't tell that from the way they split themselves up: executives at the front, scientists—grouping themselves by specialty—taking up most of the middle, and the handful of artists in the back with us.

After the drop-off at KritaCorp, the bus rounded a curve and stopped. Ilana and I tumbled into the garden outside of the Old Harmonie Museum of Our History and Our Future. The building was made up of two tall towers that twisted together and were connected by footbridges: a double helix. One strand was our past, and the other was our future, which had rotating exhibits of the latest research being done at Krita. I thought it was just perfect, the way it showed how important both the past and the future were, and how they were tied to each other.

I still couldn't believe that my mom had let us ride the bus into the city on our own (well, sort of on our own—she rode in the middle of the bus on her way to work), and that we would be allowed to take a KritaCar home, all by ourselves. The woman at the welcome desk raised an eyebrow, but then waved us in.

I brought Ilana to the indoor botanical garden first. It was warm compared to the air-cooled main hall. "They have a sample of every kind of plant that ever grew in this area. Ones that are still alive, and ones that are extinct." I had spent ages in here, sketching the plants before carefully labeling them. We went all through the exhibit, looking at the plants and trying to decide which ones we had seen out at Oakedge, and which of those we could eat.

"Come on," she said once we had seen all of the plants. "What else is cool to see here?"

We came out of the exhibit on the other side, into the hall of flags. There was a huge flag to represent the heritage of each of the original founders of Old Harmonie, and smaller ones for the newcomers. I knew exactly where the Japanese and Scottish flags could be found, across from each other in the hall. The Scottish flag was blue with a white *X* across it, and the Japanese flag had a red circle on the white background; they were among the more simple ones, and I liked that. "Which ones are yours?" I asked.

She seemed perplexed. "Can I choose whichever one I want?"

"No." I laughed. "Those are mine." I pointed. "Japan and Scotland."

"How do you know?" She looked me up and down.

"Well, my dad's heritage is Scottish and my mom's is Japanese."

"They came from there? Your dad doesn't have an accent, and anyway, I thought your great-grandmother was a founder."

"She was. I don't mean that's where they came here from, but that's where they trace their heritage back to, and so that's what I am."

"You're not thirteen yet." She frowned. "Isn't that when you find out your genetic makeup here?"

"That's just your genetics. It's not who you are."

I looked at her closely. When you turned thirteen, you learned your exact genetic code: what you shared with your parents, what came from other people, what was cloned, and what was completely manufactured. You would think that if you looked like your parents, it must mean you were natural, but some parents designed babies to look like them. It didn't always work, though. Sometimes it seemed the parents were the only ones who saw the similarities. Like, my mom and I both have epicanthic folds, but her eyes are small and wide set, and mine are so absurdly big they seem to take up half my face. My dad swears that my nose comes right off the Scottish Highlands, which I suppose means that in Scotland everyone has noses shaped like sharp axes, pointing out to smell the sea air. That's how I know I'm designed. You can pick and choose all the parts you want—a certain shape of eye, a certain sized body—but it doesn't always come out exactly as planned.

And everyone's genetics were so mixed up after so many generations, we were all a bit of everything anyway. Maybe that's why Ilana was hard to guess about. Like a lot of people, her skin was brown, and so was her hair—brown and red and sometimes even orange. It had big bouncy curls that never got frizzy. Her eyes were that magnificent green blue of a troubled ocean. She was especially tall, with long limbs. When she smiled, two little dimples appeared.

"Of course it's who you are," she said. "Each one of us is unique because of our specific genetics. You can't just make up a history."

I twisted my hands together. "We're all made up of lots of different pieces. Some folks probably couldn't trace back all the threads if they wanted to, you know, if you keep going back and back, it would just end in the gene bank. So it's what gets passed along by your family—your culture—that really matters. Don't your parents ever talk about it?"

With all the genetic borrowing and manufacturing, the history passed down from person to person was what really counted. That's why each family held it so close. My mom had a sake set from Japan even though she didn't drink alcohol—four ceramic cups and a bottle all on a square plate. They sat on a shelf in the living room. Dad had a kilt with the family tartan. They valued these things, I knew, because neither of them had ever been to Japan or Scotland, and they probably never would.

Ilana was quiet. The tip of her tongue was on the point of her top lip. Behind us I heard familiar clipped footsteps. When I turned around, Ms. Staarsgard was walking right toward us, so I didn't have much time to think how strange it was that Ilana hadn't known her heritage as quickly and easily as she would know her age.

"I wondered where you two children were headed this morning. I don't think I've ever heard so much giggling on the KritaBus. Do you like our museum, Ilana?"

Ilana said, "Sure, it's cool."

"Indeed it is. I'm here to see the Animals and Artificial Intelligence exhibit. I've taken a particular interest in Bio-Tech-Intelligence. I presume you have, too, Ilana." She stared right at Ilana, as if I weren't even there.

"*I* certainly have, Ms. Staarsgard," I told her, though I didn't admit my sudden interest had been spurred on by a desire to impress Ilana's parents. The next time I was invited over, I would not make the mistake of telling them there was absolutely nothing of note about me.

Ilana just shrugged. "I get an awful lot of that at home."

"I wish you would accompany me. It's an eye-opening exhibit. Our museum staff has really outdone themselves this time."

"Sure, okay," Ilana said. I think we both realized we didn't have a choice.

"Come along, then, girls." She started walking at an amazing pace given the skinny heels on her shoes. I supposed Animal-AI was one of the bold new directions she liked to talk about, and she was in a hurry to show it off to our newest resident.

As she approached a glass door, it slid open onto one of the footbridges. We were several stories up and could see out over the city to the villages beyond, each one at the end of the spoke of a wheel, with Center Harmonie as the hub. "Firefly Lane is that way," I told her, pointing west.

"I trust you and your family have adjusted well to life on our little cul-de-sac?" Ms. Staarsgard asked.

"Yep," Ilana said. "The kids are real nice."

"Of course they are. I know my Theo can be a bit rough around the edges, but he has a good heart. They all do."

I wondered if Ms. Staarsgard even realized she was making me feel invisible.

She opened the door to the future section of the museum and we were greeted by a beast. I rocked back and Ilana caught me. Ms. Staarsgard laughed, which at least told me she knew I was there. "Oh, don't mind Koko II. He's perfectly harmless."

Koko II was a metal gorilla, almost ten feet tall. His heavy lidded eyes were closed, and his fists were balled on his lap.

"Koko II was one of our first forays into human-other communication. Of course you know the story of the original Koko, right?"

I shook my head.

"Really? Such a charming story. There was a gorilla in a zoo and they taught her sign language. It was proof that animals really had thoughts and a desire to communicate them. Anyway, Dr. Varden must have been feeling whimsical that day, because when she first started work on this project, she decided to honor Koko with a gorilla bot. He could speak about two hundred fifty words and hold conversations about basic things like the weather."

"With only two hundred fifty words?" I asked.

"That is the average number of words used by humans, believe it or not. Koko II was the basis for our chat bots and our helper bots, of course. We've exported those helper bots all over the world. A simple invention, but it's funded countless projects."

"Can he still talk?" Ilana asked.

"No, he's not much more than a sculpture, I'm afraid. As the technology improved, he was abandoned. They found him down in a box in the storage area marked simply 'Gorilla.'

They weren't sure what they were going to find when they opened it." She laughed. "Come along, then, and let's see the good stuff."

Ilana looked over at me and raised her eyebrows. A morning with Ms. Staarsgard had not exactly been our plan.

"She tried several other projects based around animals. There were the robotic dolphins that learned speech from live dolphins; that was a study on language acquisition, too. Then she did something with robobees that focused on individual bots working as one. You see, what Dr. Varden realized," Ms. Staarsgard said as she led us up to a case showing a taxidermied dog with a camera attached to its head, "was that if we ever wanted to have true artificial intelligence, we needed to start with animals, whose intelligence is of course lesser than ours, then work up to AI that mimicked human intelligence. So this dog, Benji—"

"I told you Benji was a dog's name!" Ilana said.

"This dog," Ms. Staarsgard went on, "was equipped with a camera that recorded his every move. Dr. Varden and her team—including your great-grandmother—they studied the footage and realized that the meandering that dogs do, it serves a purpose. It's searching for the edges of a territory, and any given dangers. They were able to mimic that and put it into bots that could explore, say, a bombing site, or a structure after a fire."

"That's really cool," I said.

"Of course, a lot of our robotics and artificial intelligence is about biomimicry: taking the advantages of animals and putting them into robotics. And that's where co-physicality started as well—with animals. Look over here."

This time she brought us over to an area with a wall about waist high. When we looked down, there was a maze with mice running through it. The mice wore tiny little helmets. "Oh!" I said. "They are so cute!"

"Cute, maybe, but definitely teachable. The helmets are connected to their brains, and also to sensors on the door. When they think about the door opening, it opens."

"Whoa!" Ilana said. "You guys totally gave those mice psychic powers."

"Was this what Benji was working on for his internship in sixth grade?"

Ms. Staarsgard shook her head. "Benji was working in a lab a few floors down from this sort of thing. But I imagine that one day he will bring us leaps and bounds past this, to things we can't even imagine yet. You are all charging forward in bold new directions."

"Sure," I said glumly, still not sure what my bold new directions were.

"Unfortunately, this project did not culminate as we expected. What the mice learned, it seemed, they could not unlearn. When they got to a door, they would just stare at it and think instead of pushing it open."

"So what happened to the project?" I asked.

"When a project's outcomes fail to warrant the expenditures, we cancel it. Of course, these mice playmates got a second life here!" She laughed, and I realized that her laugh sounded the exact same every time.

"My great-grandmother said that failure was a chance to learn," I said.

I didn't remember much about Baba—I had been so young when she had died—but I did remember her teaching me to tie my shoes. My fingers had seemed like broken pencils as I tried to make the loops and twists. I'd lift my hands away and there would be the laces, flat and flopping next to my shoes. "Don't worry, little Mori," she'd said. "What did you do that time, and what went wrong?" When I'd told her I didn't know, she told me to pay better attention. "When you can understand why you failed, you can learn more than if you succeeded." Which had seemed a strange lesson when all I wanted was to get my sneakers tied so I could go outside and play with my friends. As if she'd sensed my frustration, she'd leaned forward and slowly, slowly demonstrated tying the shoes again while saying, "Sometimes the things I tell you, I tell you so you will remember them your whole life. So you'll have them to fall back on."

"Pardon me?" Ms. Staarsgard asked.

"I said that my great-grandmother told me that you could learn more from a failure than from a success. So instead of canceling the project, maybe the scientists should've had a chance to try to, you know, work backward and see what went wrong."

"Your great-grandmother and her friends were very idealistic. You know, when Dr. Varden started this place, it was just for their hobbies. For fooling around. If at first you don't succeed, try, try again is all very well and good in that context, but Krita can't waste precious resources."

"But," I began, feeling flustered. "If they had a chance to figure it out, maybe they would succeed."

Ms. Staarsgard smiled at me. "Theo does say you are a sweet girl." Ilana elbowed me and grinned, but Ms. Staarsgard kept talking. "I don't expect you to understand the financial situation of a corporation like Krita. In fact, we shield you children from such matters. When projects don't succeed, they are drawing resources from projects that could be life-altering. Do you understand?"

"I guess, but—"

She sighed. "Let me put it to you this way: Do you like our neighborhood?"

"Of course."

"Do you like your home and having your food arrive and your school and your time with your friends?"

"Yes."

"Krita takes care of all that for you. We've taken what Dr. Varden and your great-grandmother started and made it even better. Krita is able to take care of you because we have successful advances and inventions that we can monetize."

"What about the Idea Box?" I asked.

It seemed like she was trying not to roll her eyes at me. "A vestige of past times that occasionally yields high results. Fortunately, the cost-benefit evens out in the end." She looked down at her watchu, a tiny one on a slim silver-and-gold band. "I'm afraid I'm neglecting my duties and must return to KritaCorp. It was so lovely to spend this time with you two children." And then she clipped away.

Ilana and I walked around a corner and saw an old photograph, blown up to life size, of Dr. Varden and my great-grandmother. In the picture the two women stood side by side in a field. Behind them in the mid-distance was number 9, standing straight and tall. My great-grandmother had her hand up on her forehead, shielding her eyes from the sun, which cast her face in shadow. Dr. Varden was clearer. She stared right at the camera, her lips stretched into a smile that twinkled all the way up to her eyes. She was tall and strong-looking, with dark hair that fell to her shoulders.

"You look like your great-grandmother," Ilana said.

"Yeah," I said. "Everyone says so." I sniffed. "I still don't think Ms. Staarsgard was right about shutting down projects. I mean, that's not how science works, don't you think?"

"Sure. Your baba and Dr. Varden must have gotten up to some great work. That's what I don't understand. How she could have built all this and just left."

"When she went, she broke Baba's heart," I told her. "That's what my mom always says."

"Were they a couple?"

"I don't think so. They weren't married. A friend can break your heart, too." I stepped closer to the picture. In the glass, I could see the reflection of Ilana and me next to Dr. Varden and Baba. "But one's thing for sure: something must have gone really wrong for her to leave. She wouldn't abandon a project because the outcomes weren't meeting expenditures or whatever Ms. Staarsgard said. And you know where the answers are?" I asked. I pointed at the photograph, right at number 9. "If we could get in there, I bet we could find out about the projects she was working on. And why she left."

"You know, old houses like that, they usually had a basement with a bulkhead door. It was metal, but it would sit on wood. If that's rotted out at all, I bet we could get in that way."

"You really think so?" I asked. My heart beat faster, and I couldn't tell if it was fear or excitement that was making it race.

"There's only one way to find out," she said.

14

"OH, LOOK WHO'S DECIDED TO grace us with their presence," Julia said when Ilana and I rode up onto her driveway.

I flinched but didn't say anything. Ilana spoke for both of us: "We're going over to number nine and wanted to see who would come with us."

Theo shook his head. "Not you, too."

"I've never let a grown-over path stop me before," she said. "Coming?"

None of them agreed, but they all followed us. Even Julia, though she hung behind until the last possible moment.

"Wait," Benji said when we stopped our bikes at the end of the driveway. "Did you mean go *to* number nine or *into* number nine? Because I don't think Mori has given you all the relevant information."

"Like what?" Ilana asked.

"It's against the rules," Benji told her.

"I told her it was not exactly allowed," I said.

"It's *definitely* not allowed. Forbidden. Verboten. Ix-nay on the going in-yay," Benji said.

"I think we should go in. Don't you, Mori?" Ilana asked.

I nodded eagerly as a puppy, and, while I was disappointed in myself for acting so dopey in front of her, it was outweighed by the fact that she wanted to go into number 9. With me.

"You're crazy," Julia said. "There's a reason it's against the rules."

"We *think* there's a reason," I said. "Julia, come on. This really matters to me."

"But why?" she asked.

"Because Dr. Varden was Baba's best friend. And she just left. She didn't say good-bye or anything. She was just gone. I need to know why."

"But you don't know if you're going to find an answer in there," Julia said. "We can go to the library, to the archives. I'll go with you—"

"No," I said. The word popped out of my mouth, but I meant it with full force. I didn't normally go against my friends, and I never broke the rules, but today I was going to. "They always talk about how great Dr. Varden was, all of her wonderful contributions, but they never say why she left. I want to find out, and I want to find out now. So I'm going in with Ilana. You can come or not."

Julia didn't say anything, but her hands twisted back and forth on the handles of her bike. "We're coming with you," she finally said.

"We are?" Benji said.

The house tilted over to the left, as if leaning on the air to take a rest. A shutter by an upstairs window hung at an off-kilter angle. The stairs were completely missing from the front door.

"Come on, then," I said.

"I'm just working it out," Theo said. He stared at the front of the house. "I wish we had a house plan so we could figure out the safest way to get in there."

"We'll have to go around back," Ilana told the others. "Mori and I think there's likely to be a bulkhead back there."

She dropped her bike in the middle of the driveway, and we all did the same.

"What about you, Ilana?" Theo asked. "What do you think you're going to find in there?"

"I'm with Mori. I want to know more about Dr. Varden and why she left," she said. "My question is, why haven't you gone in before? Curiosity is highly valued here, isn't it?"

"My dad says I'm just curious enough for creativity, but timid enough to be safe," I said as I sidestepped an anthill.

"There's no danger here," Ilana said, surveying the land and house in front of her.

"I've heard Dr. Varden is still in there," Benji said.

"Like living as a hermit?" Ilana asked.

"No. Her body. Still in her bed."

"Ew," Julia said. "She'd be all decomposed."

"That's the kicker—she isn't. She invented something so she's in total stasis. She's in there in her granny nightgown, looking for all the world like she's sleeping, but in reality she's as dead as a doornail."

"Dead as a what?" Ilana asked, her brow furrowed like ripples in a stream.

"Doornail," Benji said.

"What's a doornail?" Ilana asked. "Is it like a nail in a door? Because a nail isn't alive, so how can it be dead?"

Julia sighed and asked Benji, "Who told you about her being in bed and the invention and everything?"

"DeShawn," Benji said. "He swore that he and some of the other guys snuck in there, and went upstairs, and there she was in bed, just waiting for science to get to the point where they can cure whatever strange disease she has, and then she'll be reanimated."

"He was messing with you, numb nuts," Theo said. "No way she's still in there, let alone in stasis."

I was feeling pretty good. I was co-leading this expedition into number 9, a place I had always wanted to see. Ilana was at my side. I could finally be on the verge of finding out why Dr. Varden had left Old Harmonie—and my great-grandmother—behind. In fact, we really were like Dr. Varden and Baba, back at the beginning, striking out into the great unknown.

Then there was a buzzing sound, low and fierce, all around me. "Ow!" I cried as something pinched me on my ankle. Then again, and again, on my knees, my arms. The buzzing surrounded me, and I saw that it was bees. Hundreds of them.

Thousands.

Tiny flashes of black-and-yellow anger that darted at my arms, my face, my eyes. I squinted against the assault.

Were they in my ears?

My ears?

Through the roar I heard Benji call out in pain, and Julia, too.

It was like they were cocooning me. I would be interred in their bodies. Through the haze of them all, I saw Ilana, so clearly, so still. A bee landed on her arm. She watched it sting her, then brushed it away with a sly smile.

But no.

That must have been some sort of vision brought on by the pain, the swelling, the loss of oxygen as my throat tightened.

It was Theo who pulled me off the nest of yellow jackets. I'd stepped right on it, so enthralled I'd been in my own fantasy, I hadn't even seen it.

Julia said he carried me all the way to the bikes and put me on my seat. He was about to get on behind me, but Ilana pushed him out of the way. She sat behind me and pedaled us home.

"You've never seen someone ride so fast. They say adrenaline takes over and you can do superhuman things, but this, this was amazing."

Mom, whose turn it was to have a day off, called an ambulance. They came and shoved a tube down my throat before they even put me on a stretcher.

One hundred seventeen stings. That's what the nurses told me.

I was lucky to be alive.

So now I owed Theo my life. And Ilana. But mostly Theo, I think, for acting first. That's what Julia said, and my mom and dad, too. "Thank goodness for Theo," they said over and over and over again.

Julia told me it would have almost been romantic if it had been anyone but Theo.

She had been stung nine times, and Benji five. Theo got twenty-seven stings, mostly on his arms. There were still red bumps when I saw him three days later. Mom and Dad sent me over to his house with snickerdoodles, of all the embarrassing things, to thank him.

"We told them we were out behind the old tennis court," he said. "Looking for a lost ball."

"I know," I said. I had picked up that much in the hospital.

He paused the game he was playing on the television. It was a mix of squares, triangles, and diamonds in all different colors, and it looked like he was fitting them together in complex patterns. Normally we weren't allowed to have screen time during the day, so I figured it had to be something to do with his latency. He was slumped back onto the couch. His mother had decorated the house in Scandinavian style, and the lightly padded couch didn't seem particularly comfortable, but he managed to recline all over it.

"Did Ilana come to see you?" Theo asked.

I shook my head. Everyone else had. Even Theo, but I'd been sleeping. Or pretending to be.

"There's something about her," he said, rubbing the bridge of his nose. "Something just a little off, you know?"

"No, I don't know." I could feel my lower lip pushing out. But I could still picture that one yellow jacket, how it hadn't even bothered her.

He looked over at me. "You don't think there's anything weird about her at all?"

"No," I said firmly.

His hair fell into his eyes, which had dark circles under them. "All right then," he said. "I'm glad you're okay and thanks for the cookies."

"You're welcome," I said.

"You can go now," he told me.

"Right," I said. Blushing.

"It's just that you look like you have chicken pox or something, all those red dots. It's making me nervous."

"Your arms, too," I said, pointing. "And three on your face."

He glanced down at his arms, then right back at the screen. "I don't notice them on myself. Anyway, I'll see you tomorrow, maybe."

His nanny, Clara, walked me out. She said, "They say that boys are mean to you when they like you."

I found myself blushing even harder.

"You listen to me, Mori. You wait until they are old enough to know to treat you well. Or they'll think they can always get away with treating you like that." She shook her head as she spoke.

"I'll do that. Thanks."

It was good advice, I thought as I walked down his driveway.

I looked toward Ilana's house. She had saved me too, but my dad hadn't made her snickerdoodles or sent me over with thanks.

I knew which room was hers because it was right where my room would be. She was up there, looking down at me, so I waved. She waved back. I hesitated before turning and heading up the street to my own house. Maybe she would come out. Maybe she would see how I was doing, or even apologize, though it wasn't her fault that stupid old me had walked onto a yellow jacket nest. She didn't move from the window, though, and I felt her eyes watching me the whole walk home.

15

"I WAS WAITING," ILANA SAID when she showed up on my doorstep. "I was waiting until I saw you out and about and that you were okay. You are okay, aren't you?"

I readjusted my glasses on my face. The left lens had a little smear, but I waited to wipe it. "I'm fine. I kind of wondered why you didn't visit, though."

"Well, like I said, I was waiting. My parents thought you might not want too many people around. Anyway, I'm not so great at lying, and I heard that Theo told them we were all out by the tennis courts."

"Yeah, he did."

"But also, I was busy. Come on."

"Where?"

"Oakedge."

We climbed onto our bikes and rode around the cul-de-sac. I shuddered a little as we rode past number 9, but there was still a part of me that wanted to see inside. She shoved her bike into the rack at the park, and I put mine next to hers, then we slipped past the playground and the tennis courts and out into the woods. She took me just past the tree with the crook in it to a small clearing where the sun dappled the ground. "Ta-da!" she exclaimed. There was a patch of earth that had been turned over so the deep, dark brown of it was showing. Planted in it were twelve small seedlings. "We've got some of those mustard greens that Mr. Quist was talking about—he had some already going in his greenhouse. And then he gave us some sweet peas, and some chard. I don't know if we'll get enough sun back here, but I tried to do them in this clearing. What do you think?"

"I can't believe you really did it," I said, smiling.

"You're not mad I did it without you, are you?"

"No," I said. "Gardening is more than just planting."

"Right. It rained a little the night before last, and the ground is still damp, so I don't think we need to water them. Mr. Quist said something about fertilizers or compost. He said he'd give us some. I think the crabby old man thing is just an act."

I squatted down, leaned over, and sniffed. I couldn't smell the plants yet, just the earthy soil, but that was a good enough start. "Did you tell everyone else?"

She sat down at the edge of the garden. "I didn't really see anyone after the first day. I ran into Benji. Otherwise they've mostly been over at Julia's or Theo's."

"You could've gone over," I said.

She shrugged.

"Do you . . . ," I began. "I mean, are you happy here?"

"Sure." She grinned at me. "This is great." She spread her arms wide and I knew she meant Oakedge and the whole forest around it. As if it agreed with her, a chickadee called across the clearing, and another one trilled back.

"Well, yeah, this is great," I said. "But my other friends—"

"Benji is real nice," she said. She brushed a curl off of her forehead.

"But Julia and Theo—"

"Oh, Theo's just a little prickly."

"Thorny," I said.

"Right. And Julia, well . . ."

"Well, what?" I asked.

Ilana got the far-off look she sometimes got. Not like she was looking into the distance, but into a whole other world. She said, "Jealousy is natural in girls our age."

I laughed. I didn't mean to, but it just bubbled out of me. It felt like someone releasing the gas from an experiment that was about to blow.

"What?"

"You do speak awfully formally sometimes."

She spun around so she was facing me. "I guess I'm just saying that I understand why she might not like me so much."

"Did they make you feel like you shouldn't hang out with them without me?"

"No biggie," she replied. She reached over and patted down the dirt around one of the chard plants. "I still want to get some berries."

"It's stupid if they left you out. The yellow jackets weren't your fault."

She looked back at me. "I was the one who said we should go into the house. If it hadn't been for me, you wouldn't have been stung."

"But *I* was the one who told you about number nine, how I always wanted to go in there. At the museum, I was practically begging." I looked down at the dirt. It really was a lovely shade of brown, and if it weren't so cold, it might feel nice to just sink down in it. People did that sometimes. They took mud baths to clean all the toxins out of their skin. I bet that would feel good on my stings. I lifted my eyes. Ilana was still staring right at me. We both knew it wasn't the yellow jackets that had Julia mad at us. I cleared my throat. "She's been my best friend my whole life. But I guess people can have different kinds of friends. Different kinds of best friends."

"Of course," Ilana said.

"Did you have a best friend back in Calliope?" I asked. I hadn't ever thought of that before, that she might have had a whole group of friends she had left behind.

Ilana looked down at the ground and scratched around her ear. "Yeah!" she said with a big smile. "Yeah, her name was Emily. Emily Wixham. We did everything together."

"Like what?" I asked. I felt a hint of jealousy creeping into my chest.

"Oh, you know, we went to this fake beach they built us and just played there. And sometimes we'd go running or we'd play volleyball or tetherball—things like that."

"Do you miss her?"

"Sure. But we write to each other. And she's real busy this summer. She's turning thirteen and getting her latency and all, so—" Then she looked at me and I guess the jealousy was showing, because she said, "Hey, you're my best friend now."

"And you're mine, too. You and Julia."

She held out her hand, palm up, to me. "My mom told me that people used to do this thing called blood sisters. They would cut a little bit of their finger or their palm, and then blend the blood together. Then they'd promise to be blood sisters forever."

My stomach turned. "That is so unsanitary!"

"She also said they would spit on their hands to make a promise."

"Are you asking me to do that? Because I can promise to be friends forever, but I don't want to cut myself, and I only spit when I'm brushing my teeth. Or eating mint leaves."

She laughed. I loved her laugh. It was full and hearty and sounded like leaves rustling before a storm. "No, silly. But we could have our own promise. An Oakedge promise." She reached over and snapped off a leaf from a mint plant just outside of our garden. Then she tore it in half. "Here, take one bite of this half." I did as she said, and she took a bite of hers. "Now switch," she said, holding out the remaining bit of her half of the leaf to me. I traded with her, and we each chewed the second half. "By the power of these mint leaves, I, Ilana Naughton, and Mori Bloom are forever sisters, the daughters of Oakedge. Now you say it."

"By the power of these mint leaves, I, Mori Bloom, and Ilana Naughton are forever sisters, the daughters of Oakedge."

"Now you have to swallow your leaf."

I swallowed hard to make it go down. It scratched as it traveled down my throat.

"Perfect," she said.

"Perfect," I agreed.

She held out her hand. I extended my hand back and placed it in her palm. She gave a squeeze and I squeezed back and we sat like that in silence, just listening to the birds and the squirrels and the branches in the breeze.

She leaned back and I lay next to her so we were looking up through the veil of leaves from the oak tree. The sun shone through them so it was hard to tell what was the leaves and what was the space between: it was just a beautiful blue-and-green pattern, like Ilana's dappled eyes.

"They're going to be wondering where we are," I said.

She was quiet for a moment, just looking up at the trees, but then she nodded, and hopped to her feet in one easy motion. She reached her hand down to me and pulled me up. In a blink, she started running through the forest back toward the park just fast enough so that I could keep up.

As we rounded the bottom of the cul-de-sac, she slowed and then stopped in front of number 9. "See those boxes back there?" She pointed to some wooden boxes that sprouted up, crooked, out of the tall grass. "They're beehives."

I felt my body go stiff.

"Honeybees," she said. "They aren't mean like yellow jackets; and anyway, I doubt there are any still living there. But if Dr. Varden kept bees, she probably had a garden. I bet we could find all sorts of stuff in her house. Tools and maybe old seeds and everything."

She started down the driveway.

"We can't go without everyone else," I said.

"Why not? I thought we weren't telling them about Oakedge yet."

"We're not." I was still a little scared after the last time, but more than that, I wanted to put our group back together. Maybe if we had some good memories together, we really could all be friends, even Julia and Ilana. "But we are the Firefly Five," I said. "We started this number nine adventure together, and we should finish it together, too."

"Okay," she said, and started pedaling up the street.

Theo was against the idea, of course. "Are you crazy? Mori almost died last time."

"I didn't almost die," I said for the millionth time.

"You *almost* almost died," Benji said.

"Mori wants to go in," Ilana said. "And Mori is my friend. Isn't she yours?"

Julia turned her head away. Theo kicked at the ground. "Mori talks to inchworms and she likes to make up stories about bikes that can fly, but you don't see me attaching wings to my bike, do you? And that's because I actually want Mori to live to see her thirteenth birthday. That's what a friend does."

"I don't need anyone to protect me," I said.

Theo didn't even bother to reply.

"I want to see what Dr. Varden left behind. There has to be some clue in there about why she left. Anyway, there's no reason for them to keep this from us. It's as much ours as anyone else's."

"Well, yeah, except that she's still in there, remember?" Benji said.

Ilana was undeterred. "You don't have to come with us, but Mori and I are going. Right, Mori?"

"Right," I agreed.

We might as well have dared them.

Walking through the grass, I kept my eyes down, looking for another yellow jacket nest.

We were just passing the side of the house when Theo grabbed my arm. A thin black snake slithered in front of us. "Black racer," he whispered. "Not poisonous, but vicious."

I knew. My parents had made sure I knew about any and all potential dangers in our neighborhood. Black racer snakes. Poisonous red berries. Standing water.

Ilana, who was up ahead of us, turned back. "What is it?"

"Nothing," Theo called before I could tell her about the snake. Where there was one, there could be more, and I didn't want one to attack her. They were defensive fighters, like most animals. But if she stumbled over one, it would bite and bite and bite until she retreated.

Which, I suppose, could have happened to me if Theo hadn't stopped me.

Julia and Benji caught up as the snake disappeared from sight.

"I do not like this place," Benji said.

"Me neither," Julia agreed. "And that's without even believing that Dr. Varden's body is still in there."

"But you aren't a hundred percent sure, right?" Benji asked.

"Guys, just think about it," I said. "There could be all sorts of cool stuff in there."

When we got around back, we saw wooden trellises covered over with vines that were heavy with grapes. Raised gardens put out a tangle of vegetables, cucumber blooms climbing over the first hints of tomatoes. Mr. Quist would love to see this: all of these plants surviving on their own. Beyond them, there was a set of four wooden boxes that were grown over with white-yellow wax. "What are those?" Benji asked.

"Honeybee hives," Ilana replied.

She headed straight for the bulkhead door. There was a lock on the door, but the wood that it sat on was all rotted out. Ilana tugged at it, and it moved. With Theo's help, she pulled it all the way off.

The scent of the basement rushed out to meet us—dank and alive. It smelled like the soil in our garden in Oakedge, mixed with the musty boxes of Baba's that Mom kept stored in the eaves of our house.

"Maybe we shouldn't," Benji said. "Isn't this like breaking in? Isn't that illegal?"

"No one lives here," Ilana said.

"No one alive, anyway," Benji said.

"No one lives here," Ilana said again. "Who's going to care?" She pulled a flashlight out of her backpack and shined it down the stairs.

Theo went first. He had a big metal flashlight that cast a narrow band of golden light down the stairs. I stayed close behind him. As we descended, I realized that he had a sweet-spicy smell to him, like cinnamon, only all his own. I wondered how I could have known someone my whole life, practically, and not realized that about him.

We stopped at the bottom of the stairs, a tight little circle of us. Theo, Ilana, and Julia shined their flashlights all around. The walls were lined with shelves, and the shelves were full of cloudy jars. Benji stepped forward and put his hand on one. "Are those eyeballs?" he squeaked.

"Don't be an idiot," Theo said.

"Then what are they?" Julia asked.

"Canning," I said. Everyone turned to look at me. I moved closer to the shelves and squinted in the faint light. "Green beans." I pointed. "Pickles, carrots, tomatoes."

"In those jars?" Julia asked.

"People used to do that," I said. "They'd grow extra and then can them to get through the winter. Baba told me about it. Now it seems like too much work, that's what she said."

"And the eyeballs?" Benji asked.

Ilana pointed her flashlight right at them. "They look like eggs," she said.

This was something else my great-grandmother had told me about, before she died. "Pickled eggs. Baba said they were delicious, but she didn't know how to make them."

"Ugh," Julia said. "That sounds disgusting."

"These ones look like they melted." Benji picked up a smaller jar filled with clouded golden liquid.

"Honey," Ilana said.

"Really?" Benji struggled to twist open the lid. "I love honey." He jammed his finger right in and pulled it out, covered in the sticky stuff, and pressed it into his mouth.

"Wait! You don't know how old that is," Julia said.

"Honey doesn't go bad," I told her.

Julia narrowed her eyes as I scooped my finger in. It was cool and smooth, and in my mouth it tasted like eating a warm sunny day, nothing like the super-sweet stuff we had in our condiments station, filled by the deliver bot each week.

Theo took the jar from Benji and took a taste himself. His eyes grew wide before shutting halfway. He looked like he did when we were kids, when he was still chubby and goofy.

We passed the jar around, and even Julia took a taste. "There are shelves and shelves of it," Benji said. "This is amazing. There's enough for all of Firefly Lane, maybe even the village."

"We can't tell anyone about this, numb nuts," Theo said.

"He's right," Julia agreed. "This has to be our secret. Our honey hangout."

"The Firefly Five at the Honey Hangout," Benji said. "Sounds like a funny TV show."

I glanced over at Julia. She didn't tell Benji we weren't the Firefly Five anymore, and I figured that was a good sign.

"Come on, there's more to see," Ilana said. We made our way farther into the basement. It got cooler as we moved, and I found myself inching closer to Julia and Theo. Theo's hand brushed against mine, and I thought he might try to hold it, and I wondered what I would do if he did. Instead he switched his flashlight into that hand and veered off toward a stack of boxes.

I found a table full of notebooks with speckled black-and-white covers. Each one had a month and a year written on the front in slanted cursive. I opened one to a page toward the middle of the book. At the top of the page was a sketch of green grass, flowering trees, and a small garden. Each plant was labeled. It looked familiar and I realized it was the backyard of number 9. *Pollen and nectar galore, but still the bees suffer*, it said. *Brood nest still small. Many bee mummies on bottom board.*

"I think it's notes about the bees," I said. I kept flipping through. My eyes were drawn to the careful sketches that looked the way my own drawings did in my head, before I actually tried to get them down on paper. Other pages were nearly filled with words, all in that slanted script. It was hard to read in the dark of the basement, but I was able to pick out some sections written in a heavier hand:

> *Today I lunched with the Krita executives (Me? A lady who lunches?) and then to cleanse my palate, I checked on the hives. It was a beautiful day out on the farm, with a soft breeze coming from the west.*

It was a bit like the journals we had to keep, and I realized that's what I was holding: Dr. Varden's journal. She was much more detailed than I ever was, especially about the bees:

> *Many bees with pollen under their wings, a pretty shade of bright sunshine yellow. Queen Bee was seen on second frame of middle box. Appears healthy. Brood pattern is consistent and complete.*
> *More Krita workers coming from Boston. Krita building even faster than these bees. Ugly little pillbox houses. My Firefly Lane is still safe from it, at least.*

I flipped through the pages of the journal and read more while my friends chatted around me. The taste of honey was

still on my lips. Then I saw Baba's name, and my heart gal-
loped away.

*The hive must survive. And so we say good-bye
to Queen Victoria and hello to Queen Elizabeth.
Lucy tells me it's sentimental of me to name them,
and she is right. But perhaps there is more of that
in me than I or anyone else suspects. Perhaps that
is why I cling so hard to my vision of this place and
resist the changes of the Krita board. But then,
perhaps I ought to take a hint from Queen Victoria
and abdicate my little throne.*

On and on I read until I felt like I knew these bees and the
person who cared for them. Dr. Varden had always seemed
like a person from a time I could never connect to, as far
away as Mae Jemison or Marie Curie. But these books made
her real, someone I could touch.

*The honeybees serve a purpose. Without
pollinators, up to 90% of plant life would be lost—
including much of the food we eat.
Humans? The necessity for our species is less
clear. I'll work to save the bees.*

She talked about how bee colonies had collapsed in
the winter of 2006 and 2007, back when there was no Old

Harmonie, only Dr. Varden's farm. They simply vanished. Beekeepers checked their hives in the spring, and instead of finding a warm mass of buzzing bees, they found nothing. No bees. No corpses. Gone.

It is still not certain what caused the Colony Collapse of aught six and aught seven. Most likely it was not one thing, but many: the combined deleterious effects of stressed colonies, pesticides (including the ones used to fight off the mites that attack our bees), the mites themselves, limited diets in the agricultural industry, pathogens—a dangerous cocktail overflowing.
And so it goes,
and so it goes,
and so we go.

"What'ch'ya got there?" Ilana asked, peeking over my shoulder. I saw Julia on the other side of the room, digging through a box of old clothes.

"It's a journal, I think. Mostly about bees, but other stuff, too."

"Cool."

"I think so, too," I said. "Maybe it has the answers I'm looking for."

"This is just the tip of the iceberg," Ilana said. "We should go upstairs."

A rickety set of old wooden stairs led upward. It was right when Ilana put her hand on the banister that we heard a robotic wailing noise coming from outside: high then low, high then low. Each village had a siren on top of its tallest building. When it rang, it meant get to shelter right away.

"A safe-in-place drill?" Julia asked.

No one knew. "We're sheltered here," I said.

"We can't stay here," Benji said. "Everyone will be looking for us. Mori's house is closest. Let's go!"

We hurried out of the house. Ilana and Theo put the bulkhead back on, though at a crooked angle. We didn't think anyone would notice. Back on our bikes, we raced home.

16

DAD WAS WAITING AT THE door for me. He threw it open and ushered us all in. "We were in the woods," I lied.

"The closest house," he said. "Why didn't you go to the Russerts'?"

The closest house to number 9 was actually the Collins family, who had somehow managed to get an exception to the two-child rule, and had two sets of twins under five. As we'd raced by, Mrs. Collins was running across the yard with a toddler under each arm.

"Oh," was all I could think to say.

"Oh, indeed," Dad replied. "Go on inside until we know what this is all about. I'll let your parents know where you are."

"It's not a drill?" Julia asked.

"No, Julia, it's not a drill."

"It's funny how the houses are all the same," Ilana mused.

"They aren't that way in California?" I asked.

"California?" she said, looking confused. "No, I suppose they aren't."

"Are you okay?" Benji asked.

Ilana looked upward, as if into her brain, then shook her head. "Yeah. I'm fine. Sorry. We had a lot of these at Calliope. Lockdowns, we called them. Sometimes they'd last for days."

"Days?" Benji asked.

"You got good food?" Theo asked me.

"Some," I said.

"We're not going to be here for days," Julia said.

"And anyway, isn't it better to be together?" I asked. "I mean, Theo, really, you want to spend all that time with your nanny? Or Benji, with your sister?" We made our way toward the back of the house. "You know, I can't even remember the reasons for the siren," I said. We had learned them way back in first or second grade.

"Weather, Outbreak, Outsiders, Other," Benji said. "WOOO! How could you forget?"

"I hope it's weather," Julia said. "That could pass quickly."

"Right," I said. "Like maybe a tornado." We had never had a tornado, but I'd read that the sky turned green. They had them a lot in the Wrightsville Kritopia, where they'd sweep across the flat landscape. I wondered what it would feel like to see the sky the color of pale pea soup. Our sky, though, was bright blue and dotted with puffy white clouds. "But I don't think it's weather."

"Did you take that from the house?" Julia asked.

I had forgotten that I still had the notebook in my hand. I'd ridden all the way home with it tucked into my armpit. "I didn't mean to," I said. But I had, hadn't I? I'd wanted a chance to read more. "I'll put it back the next time we go."

"Why would we go again?" Julia asked.

"Why wouldn't we?" Ilana replied.

"We have to get out of here first." Julia sniffed. "I mean, you might want to stay here forever, but some of us have other stuff to do."

Dad poked his head into the kitchen. "It's all of Old Harmonie," he said. "Your mom sent a message that the siren sounded at the corporation, too. But there's nothing to worry about."

My friends shifted next to me. None of them were going to challenge my father. "All of Old Harmonie is under lockdown, and we shouldn't worry?" I asked.

"Lockdown?" He shook his head. "It's just a precaution. If it were serious, we'd have more instructions."

"Right," Benji said. "Just a precaution. Let's make the best of it. What'd you do during all those lockdowns, Ilana?"

"Oh, you know, play games. Cards."

"We have cards," I said. "Let me get them." I dug through a drawer on a sideboard and found an old beat-up deck of cards with pictures from each of the Kritopias on them. My friends had sat down around the kitchen table. "What should we play?" I asked, tapping the deck against the table-top. "War? Go Fish?"

"How about Snap?" Ilana suggested.

"I don't know that game," I said.

"It must be a fabulous Calliope game," Julia said.

I handed the deck to Ilana, who began to shuffle.

"I've been called in," Dad said, peeking his head back into the room.

"Outbreak," Theo said, nodding his head so his thick hair flopped into his eyes, and he had to push it back with the heel of his hand like a toddler.

Diseases could spread quickly. Back twenty or thirty years before, a virulent strain of pertussis—whooping cough—took out a big chunk of the population of South Boston. All those people gone, just because of a cough. A bunch of the people living there tried to get out, but that part of the city was put under quarantine and no one was supposed to enter or leave. Krita sent drones with medicine, but it was too late for most people. There's a rumor that some of the people did break through the quarantine and made it all the way to Old Harmonie, but that would have been a tremendous journey. And even if they had made it here, we couldn't risk letting all those sick people inside our fences.

Dad shrugged on a lightweight coat, which meant he was planning to be out past sunset. "Nothing for you to worry about. I'll be back as soon as I can. Stay inside, okay?"

"Okay," I agreed. Even if I had a choice, there was no way I would go outside during a safe-in-place. Just the thought of it made my stomach plummet.

Distracted, Dad left his phone on the counter. I grabbed it and ran to the front door, but he was already driving away in the KritaCar that had arrived to bring him to Center Harmonie.

When I got back into the kitchen, my friends were staring at one another in silence.

"We're going to be fine," I said, even though I wasn't sure if it was true or not.

"But it's an outbreak, Mori," Benji said.

"They're probably just being cautious. Like when I got that stomach bug."

I was the only one of my friends who had ever been really sick. Benji got the occasional cold, plus his asthma and allergies. Everyone else was perfectly healthy. When I'd started throwing up, they'd taken me in a sealed shuttle straight to the hospital in Center Harmonie. No one was allowed to see me for seven days. I lived in a bubble, cared for by the mechanical arms operated on the other side of a glass wall by nurses who wore masks just the same. I pretended it was all a dream or a scary movie that I couldn't turn off. I told myself it was bad, but it wasn't real, wasn't actually happening to me.

I remember for days my brain was so fuzzy, and all the world seemed terrifying. Just stepping onto the ground when I could finally get out of bed, I imagined all the things that could go wrong—a slip, a trip, the ground disappearing beneath me—and wound up crying and crawling back into bed. The doctors said it was perfectly normal, and my mom said it was because I'd been away from other people so long. I guess they were right, because eventually the fear subsided. I was a lot more cautious after that, though—I never wanted to end up back in the hospital.

I was fine, of course. And I was certain this was going to be something similar. The adults had it under control: that's what our systems and order were for.

"If the lockdown is for all of Old Harmonie, it must be something pretty bad," Julia said. "Something super-contagious."

"There are numerous highly contagious diseases," Ilana said as she contemplated the playing cards.

"Not helpful," Theo told her.

"It's under control. Let's just play the card game." I picked up the deck and tried to shuffle. Several cards fell down onto the table. I scooped them back up. "How many cards should I deal?" I asked Ilana.

"If it were totally under control, we wouldn't be in lockdown," Julia said.

My father's phone buzzed. I glanced over and saw the text message as it scrolled across the screen: *ETA? Third possible case. Confirming diagnosis.*

"Third possible case of what?" Theo asked. He was reading over my shoulder.

"I don't know," I said.

"Well, scroll back through the messages. It might say."

"No," I said.

"Fine. I'll do it," Julia said, and leaned across the table.

"No!" I said again, and grabbed the phone before she could.

"Give me the phone, Mori," she said. I could feel the anger and panic coming off her in waves.

I clutched the phone to my chest with my left hand. I still had the deck of cards in my right hand and I was squeezing them so tightly that I could feel each little edge cutting into my palm. "No."

"This isn't a joke," she said. "Just give me the phone."

Next to me, Benji shifted in his seat. "I know you don't like to break rules and all, but we just need to know. It's the not knowing that's killing us. So just look and it probably is something not so bad, and then we'll all feel better; it'll be fine." His words came fast and he couldn't quite look at me.

"Mori," Theo said. "Benji is right. It's better knowing than not."

"That is generally true," Ilana said. It wasn't exactly a strong agreement. She was sitting in a chair at the head of the table eating an apple from the fruit bowl on our counter.

"Fine," I said, "I'll do it." I moved to put the deck of cards down, and they all flew out of my hands and scattered across the table and on the floor. Kings and queens and aces and spades all staring and pointing at me.

"Fifty-two pickup!" Ilana said merrily.

"What is wrong with you?" Julia asked her.

"Getting agitated isn't going to change the situation," Ilana replied. She took another bite of her apple, then began sweeping the cards toward herself.

"I'm only *agitated* because I don't know what kind of disease is in our community right now and Mori won't tell us."

"I said I would."

But before I could check the phone, Julia lurched forward to grab it. I held tight while she tugged. "Julia, stop! It's my dad's phone!"

"Oh, of course, you want to check it and be the one to tell us. Lord it all over us. Maybe your parents should dampen your selfishness."

"Hey," Benji said, trying to step between us. "That's enough."

Outside, the safe-in-place siren still moaned over and over again. I felt the phone slipping from my hand. Julia's arm flew up and swung back straight toward Benji's head. He ducked, but the phone still caught his ear on its way by.

"Are you okay?" I asked.

He cupped his ear in his hand.

Julia was already across the room, chasing the phone that fell with a resounding thud near the back door. I gasped. My dad was going to kill me, plain and simple. I put my hand on Benji's arm. "Are you okay?" I asked again.

"I'm fine." He lowered his hand and revealed a bright red ear. "Just a little ringing. Nothing so small as a phone can take me down." He forced a laugh.

"It's barely scratched," Julia said, holding the phone up. "It might not even be from the fall. It could have already been there."

"It *wasn't* already there," I said. "And it's not just a little scratch." I could see the crack across the phone's screen even though I was several feet away. I felt my stomach churning. I turned back to Benji. "Want me to get you an ice pack?"

"No." He looked down at the floor. "I want to hear what it is."

"Mumps," Julia said flatly.

"What's that?" I asked.

Ilana cleared her throat, ready to tell us, I supposed, but Julia spoke first. "Are all of those bumps from the bees?" Julia pointed at my arms.

"Yes," I said. But I looked down at my arms, at the faint red bumps that were still there. I didn't know if they were all from the bees. Not really. I wrapped my arms across my chest. "Do mumps even have a rash?"

"I don't know. Why don't we look it up?" She started typing into the phone.

"Give it back, Julia," I said.

She didn't. She focused her eyes on the screen, her expression getting darker and darker, and then she said, "Oh, no."

"What?" Benji asked.

"It says that complications include swelling of the brain or of the tissue surrounding the brain and spinal cord."

"That's meningitis. It's saying this can lead to meningitis," Benji said, his voice cracking. "Do you know how they test for meningitis? A spinal tap. They stick a big needle into your spinal cord and pull out the fluid."

"Benji!" Theo exclaimed. "None of us has mumps."

"How do you know?" Julia demanded. "It says you can be contagious before symptoms even show up, so you could have it and not know it and be spreading it. And it can be two weeks before symptoms even appear."

Theo rubbed his temples. "Wait, we aren't thinking about this logically." He took a notebook and a pencil out of his pocket and began to draw the molecule-like map of Old Harmonie that we were all so familiar with: the center city with spokes coming out leading to each village, then each street. "They have at least three cases, and they can know where those people live and work, so what they have to do is trace where they would go. Like if they live over in Fruitlands and then go to work in Center Harmonie, then they would look at who they work with and where each of those people lived." He squinted his eyes shut. "The lockdown is so that those of us who haven't been exposed won't be. It doesn't mean that the disease has already spread all over—they're doing this so it won't. It might not even be anywhere near us." He circled the villages on the opposite side of Center Harmonie from us.

Julia put her finger down on the circle that represented our village. "But it could be right here. I mean, maybe it was even your mom who brought it in."

"What?" Theo asked.

"Your mom was out there to get your special, perfect cake. Maybe she caught something."

"Julia!" I said.

"Oh, come on," Julia said, tossing a braid over her shoulder. "You all know it's true. If it's something really bad, it had to have come from outside, and Theo's mom was just out there mixing with regular people in their cities just so he could have that stupid cake."

"Statistically, that's not very likely," Ilana said. "There must be a hundred people who go out of Old Harmonie each day to do their work."

"Right," Theo agreed. "Anyone who has been outside, or come in from outside—they could be the patient zero."

Julia sucked on the end of her braid, then let it drop. "What if someone snuck in?" she asked. "Our fences aren't very strong. Someone could be sick and they could've snuck in and are infecting everyone."

"There's no way a stranger could just walk around Old Harmonie infecting people," I said. "And why would someone want to do that, anyway?"

"To try to find medicine, of course!" Julia said.

"Mori's right," Theo said. "If someone did sneak in, they would've been caught right away. Then maybe there would've been one of these lockdowns for an outsider, but it would be over quickly. No, if this came in from the outside, it had to have come in through the gates."

Benji's eyes grew wide. "The gardeners! The ones who were pulling out Mr. Merton's old rhododendron before Ilana moved in. What if they had it and they spread it? We could all be infected!"

"Did you go over and let them sneeze on you?" Theo asked.

"Of course not," Benji said.

"Then how would you be infected?"

"Diseases can change," I said. "They're really smart, actually. They mutate and adapt to take advantage of the human body." I was ready to tell them how the influenza virus was especially good at mutating in order to find new ways to get onto animal cells, but from the looks on their faces, I could see this was not the right time for that story. "Anyway, it's kind of cool, but, then again, not exactly."

"Really not awesome," Benji said. "Maybe we should go to my house. My mom is home. If one of us gets sick I want there to be an adult around. Some diseases can kill you in a matter of hours. They just overtake you and, like, the next thing you know, your skin is falling off." He rubbed his hand gently over his ear.

"It won't do us any good to panic," Theo said. I studied his face, trying to determine if he really was this calm, or if he was just trying to reassure the rest of us. His face was still, but there was a little twitch at the corner of his eye. "Benji already got hurt and we almost broke Mori's dad's phone. This is getting out of hand. We should just play that card game or watch TV or something."

Julia replied as if Theo hadn't spoken: "There are all sorts of workers that come in from outside. Any one of them could have brought the disease. That's why we shouldn't let so many people come in. Or go out. It's not safe out there."

"They're supposed to screen them, aren't they? And the decontamination showers?" Benji asked. He rocked forward. "Just so this sort of thing won't happen?"

It was true that anyone who came in from outside, even just to do a simple job, had to be pre-screened and then got a medical scan each time they came onto the grounds, plus the awful decontamination showers. But like I'd told my friends, diseases are tricky. They want to survive, and so they figure out how. If Krita wasn't aware of a particular disease profile, it might be able to slip past the systems.

"That's why I don't think it was an outsider," Theo said. "They have more intense screening than someone from here who goes in and out all the time."

"Like your mom," Julia said. "Or Mori's dad."

"My dad doesn't have mumps," I told her.

"Whatever. It doesn't matter. If it's been here for two weeks, it could be everywhere. We all could have it. And then what?" Julia asked.

"Most people who get mumps make a full recovery," Ilana said.

"Except Mori just said that diseases can morph or whatever—so maybe this one is more deadly. I want to know who has it, where they work, and what village they live in. They should be sending everyone a message with that information."

"They can't just give out those details," I said.

"Why not?" she shot back. "Anyone who has it should be quarantined and their house needs to be, like, totally cleaned out or whatever. And anyone they came in contact with needs to be told. It's to keep us all safe. That's why we live in here. We follow the rules and we stay safe and we don't end up with a disease taking out half the city."

"But how does it spread so fast out there? Outside the fences?" Ilana asked. She wasn't looking at me; her gaze was still on the cards spread on the table in front of her, but I knew she was talking to me. "When there's an outbreak, don't they have lockdowns, too?"

"I don't know," I said. "They do things differently out there. It's a lot more chaotic. They don't have all the rules and the precautions in place like we do."

"Don't they have vaccines?" she asked.

"Sure, for most things. But some people choose not to get them out there."

Ilana tucked her knees up to her chest. "So they have different rules outside the fences. Can't we help them?"

"This is so not the point right now," Julia said, exasperated.

"We do help them," I said. "We have, like, school supply drives at the beginning of every year. And they get our old textbooks, and—"

"I mean really help them," she said.

"We can't force them to make good choices," Theo said.

Then her voice started to rise. "Do they have the thirty percent enhancement? Or latency?"

We all just looked at Ilana. I'd never seen her lose her cool before, not even with the yellow jackets. Julia tugged on one of her braids, and Benji rubbed his ear again.

"No, I don't think so," I said. "I mean, maybe some of the surgeries—"

"Probably no artificial retinas," she said. Now she did look at me. Right at me and through me so intensely that I thought my heart might explode.

"Ilana," Theo said, his voice calm and adult-sounding. "Krita tries to help the world, but it starts at home, with the Krita families. We can't help others until we protect ourselves."

"It just doesn't seem fair, is all," she said. "They're out there and we're in here."

"That's what Theo is trying to tell you: we're here because our families work for Krita," Julia said.

"Right. Your *families* work for Krita. Your parents or your grandparents."

"People can apply," I said. "People can get in that way. Like your parents, right, Benji?"

"My mom did," he said. "She was working for a different company outside and came up with this patentable idea— don't even ask me to explain it—and she sold the patent to

Krita and part of the payment was moving here. That was before I was born, though."

"So you didn't have to apply," Ilana said. Her eyes were flashing. "None of you did."

"You didn't have to apply, either," Theo said.

"That's true," she said. Her body stilled.

And then none of us said anything.

17

IT WAS BENJI WHO FINALLY broke the silence. He turned the television on and found a special behind-the-scenes program about this celebrity couple, Zane and River. At first it kept getting interrupted by messages telling us that we were in the midst of a safe-in-place—"As if we didn't know," Theo muttered—but the warnings came less and less frequently. It didn't make much difference, though. None of us were really watching. It just gave us something to look at instead of one another.

KritaCars arrived to take my friends home. Mom returned to the house shortly after, but Dad stayed at the central offices. "It's fine," Mom said as she poured herself a glass of lemonade. "Everything is fine."

What choice did I have but to believe her? She told me that mumps wasn't even all that serious.

"So why did we need to be in lockdown?" I asked.

"The vaccinations aren't one hundred percent effective and we want to keep everyone safe."

"What do you mean?"

She pushed a strand of her dark hair out of her face. "What matters is we're taking care of it. Don't worry." But as she spoke, she looked out the picture window toward the street. Flocks of KritaCars were driving around dropping people back at their homes.

A moment later a bot rolled up to our door. "In accordance with Krita Corporation, we are scanning all community members." It blinked its black eyes first at me and then at Mom. "Thank you for your cooperation. You are clear." And then, silent as the wind, it rolled away.

"Does that mean we don't have it?" I asked.

"Yes, honey."

"I need to show you something," I told her. In the kitchen, I took Dad's phone out from under a stack of magazines. "He forgot it and we were looking at it to try to learn more about the mumps and we dropped it and so—I'm sorry."

"Honey, it's okay."

"But we used someone else's tech. That's a basic rule."

"Some days we make exceptions. You all were scared and alone. It's understandable."

Somehow the forgiveness was more frightening than the lockdown itself.

"It's late," Mom said. "I'll clean up. Why don't you go to bed?"

It wasn't really a question or even a suggestion. I gave her a hug and then walked upstairs.

My bed was lofted and had a wide window alongside it so I could look out at the trees. I watched the gray clouds move against the black sky, fast like on TV when they want to show you that time is passing.

I wasn't tired at all. The day kept playing over and over in my head like a broken movie.

I read more from Dr. Varden's notebook. I hoped there might be something about my great-grandmother, like how I wrote about the things my friends and I did in my journal. That night I had resorted to a bulleted list:

- Safe-in-place drill (aka "lockdown"). We were in "the woods" and we all came to my house (WE = Ilana, Julia, Benji, Theo, and me).
- We cracked Dad's phone.
- We were going to play a card game but we never did.
- Mom said not to worry about the mumps. Sometimes when she says not to worry, it makes me worry more.
- I don't think Julia is ever going to forgive me and I don't know if I'll forgive her.

It wasn't a very good entry, but if I ever did lose all my memories, maybe this wasn't even a day I wanted back.

Dr. Varden's journal seemed less concerned with being able to re-create her days. Maybe that wasn't the reason they kept journals back then. I knew that scientists kept research logs, and some people in olden times wrote them just to remember things for themselves or work through their thoughts. I flipped through the notebook to find where I'd left off.

> *Just as a hive works together for the common good, so, too, can people, given the proper training and structure. Education and rewards would be key, perhaps even a lack of knowledge of the system. Humans are, after all, by nature rebellious against tight structures. Perhaps as we have bred Italian bees to be more docile, we could breed our humans to be more cohesive.*

Dr. Varden wrote more about the genetic changes she was trying with the bees in order to keep them alive. And then Baba appeared again:

> *Lucy has an idea that might work. It's a mix of cloned and robotic bees—where the robots teach the clones how to behave. She tells me that Vijay Kumar at the University of Pennsylvania and those working*

on the robobees project at Harvard have had some luck with robotic hives—individual droids that react to the needs of the group. But they are not natural in appearance or essence. They are shadows of the real thing. Which is not to say the logic behind the programming would not be useful.

That was what Ms. Staarsgard had been talking about at the museum: the robobees that could act as one. Still, I wasn't sure if Dr. Varden was talking about the bees or still ruminating on humans. It was wistful, I thought, to want humans to be other than how they were. I mean, you could ache and ache to be different from yourself, but there wasn't much you could do about it. Like how I'd wanted to go into number 9, but was never bold enough to do it until Ilana said she would come with me. I just wasn't a very brave person.

Or the world out there. Ilana said it wasn't fair that we had things that they didn't. It would be great if everyone had the safety and the technological advances we have here. It wasn't just us keeping other people out. Not everyone would buy into the rules. Not everyone wanted to fight the chaos. And Theo was right, you couldn't force them. And that was the nature of human society—chaotic and cruel, unless you had safeguards in place like we did in Old Harmonie. Maybe that's what Dr. Varden was getting at. Old Harmonie is a place where we work for the common good.

I am growing weary—and wary—of all these manipulations, but Lucy says we must try.

I flipped back to the cover of the notebook. The date written in Dr. Varden's neat hand said it was from the year before she left Old Harmonie, which meant that she and Baba had still been friends right up to the end, or close to it. But she also said she was feeling tired of the manipulations they were doing on the bees, the changes that Baba was pushing. It wasn't so different from the latency, I thought, tinkering around and trying to get things just right.

Outside, a cloud passed over the moon, and downstairs, I heard a door open and close as my father came home. My parents spoke to each other in soft tones, too quiet for me to hear the words, though I thought I heard my name. Probably that's when they decided to keep me home for another three days, just in case.

"In case of what?" I asked when they told me in the morning. It was going to be a beautiful day. The sun was already shining and the sky was a gorgeous blue without a single cloud. It would be a perfect day for checking on Oakedge.

"In case one of your friends happened to have been exposed."

"All my friends were here with me. And then the scanners came around to check everyone. If they were sick, they'd be in the hospital."

"I know you think we're being overprotective—" Dad began.

"Yes," I interrupted.

"But you have a history of catching things. Your nose runs like a faucet every winter, and let's not forget that stomach flu."

I shuddered and Mom rubbed my back.

Dad continued, "We have this strain pretty well pinned down, and we're almost done tweaking the new vaccine. Once that's done and you get it, you'll be out in the world."

So I stayed in the house. I worked on my drawings, trying to perfect one of the wild calla (*calla palustris*) that dotted the floor of the forest. This was an important one to get right since it's highly poisonous. It shouldn't have been so hard, even if I didn't have one in front of me: it was just a single leaf, and then a white flower with a thick stamen. Still, each sketch I did was worse than the last, and eventually I gave up, diving back into Dr. Varden's journal, looking at her sketches. Agatha was a much better artist than me. I also noticed that she didn't just draw the plants close up, but also included landscapes, and showed where each plant could be found. The next time I got out to Oakedge, I decided, I would draw the whole kingdom just like she had.

On the third morning, Mom told me I could go outside. "A bus is coming to take you all to get a new vaccination."

Dad explained that the disease wasn't exactly the mumps, but a mutation, and our previous vaccination didn't cover it. "No big deal," my dad said. Theo had been right. It was a resident of Old Harmonie who had picked it up on a trip outside. Only a handful of people were impacted, but Krita wouldn't release their villages or where they worked.

Theo sat next to me on the bus into Center Harmonie, Julia behind us, and Benji and Ilana across the aisle from them. The teenagers sat in the back and DeShawn flicked Theo's shoulder on his way down the aisle. "Still hanging out in the kiddie pool, huh, Staarsgard?"

Theo bristled but didn't say anything.

"Why *don't* you hang out with them?" I asked as the bus began to roll.

"Trying to get rid of me?"

"No." I shook my head. "It's just that you'll be in high school with them now, so—"

"They're stupid," he said. "All they do is sit around talking trash. Trash about girls. Trash about their nonexistent athletic prowess. Trash about their parents and this village and everything."

Julia covered her ears. "I shall hear no evil about DeShawn."

Theo's face had turned a little pink as he spoke, and I decided to drop it. In the back, the teenagers were throwing rolled-up pieces of paper at one another, so I thought maybe he was right—they were just stupid.

Julia popped her head over the seat. "I like your shirt," she said.

"Thanks," I said.

She rubbed her nose. "Things got a little crazy at your house, and—"

"I know," I said. "But my parents said it was okay."

"Really?" Her smile filled her face. "I was so worried, I couldn't even sleep or eat or run or anything. I thought they weren't letting you out because you were grounded for a hundred million years."

"No, it was just them being over-worried. You know how they are."

"Sure," she said. "But I really was afraid we weren't ever going to see you again, and I wouldn't be able to tell you I was sorry, and then maybe I would get the mumps and die. Or you would get it, and you would never know how sorry I was."

"That was never in a million years going to happen," Theo said.

But I said, "Thanks, me too."

"So we've been thinking about going back to number nine, to see what else we can find," she said.

"But we wanted to wait for you," Benji said.

"We were going to come and rescue you today if your parents didn't let you out, and we were all going to go together," Julia said. "But then this came up. But you can come with us tomorrow, right?"

"I think so," I said. My parents were still wary, and a trip to number 9 might be tricky the way they'd been watching me. Which didn't mean I didn't want to get back there. "I had a lot of time to read that notebook of Dr. Varden's. She was really worried about the bees—that's what she wrote about mostly, anyway. But I got the sense that she was worried about this whole place."

"Why?" Benji asked.

"I don't know. She said it was changing—that they were changing it. She even mentioned my great-grandmother."

"What did she say?" Julia asked.

"Just that Baba was pushing for more manipulation of the bees, but she—Agatha—she wasn't so sure."

"Do you think that's why she left?" Julia asked.

I shrugged. I didn't feel quite so angry with Agatha anymore. Reading her journal made me feel close to her, and now I was more worried than mad. "Do you think she asked them to keep her house the same because she planned to come back?"

"I guess it's possible," Julia said.

But Theo said, "Doubtful."

"I just want more of that honey," Benji said. "I think I'm addicted."

"You can't be addicted to honey," Julia said. "Especially not after only eating it once."

"I was speaking metaphorically. My body does not feel like it needs honey to function. It's more like a craving. Like my body is saying, 'Yo! Honey! Get in my belly!' Just like that."

"I think you need to get your head examined," Theo told him.

The whole time we spoke, Ilana stared out the window. "What's with her?" I asked.

Benji shrugged, and Theo said, "The lockdown kind of shook her for some reason. She's been quiet."

"The acquisition of knowledge is our highest calling," Ilana said.

Benji looked over his shoulder at her, and Julia giggled.

"Hmm?" Ilana said.

"What did you just say?" Julia prompted. "About knowledge?"

"I didn't say anything," Ilana said. She turned to look at us. Her face was flat and smooth, like a doll's.

"Sure you did," Benji said. "You said that the acquisition of knowledge is our highest calling."

"I didn't," Ilana said, still expressionless.

"Maybe you were thinking it, but didn't realize you said it out loud?" I said, trying to make my voice kind.

"See? Totally weird," Theo muttered. I elbowed him.

"Maybe," Ilana said. "Anyway, I think we're here."

We lined up from youngest to oldest. Julia had to hold her little brother, Caron. He'd never been very good at getting shots. "We can do it at the same time, maybe," she suggested.

"Mary," the first nurse called to the second one. "Take this one." The first grabbed another syringe before scanning their eyeballs. "Energy a little low?" he asked Julia.

"I feel fine," Julia replied.

"In bed by eight tonight. I'll message your parents."

Julia scowled, but there was nothing she could do about it. The nurses stood on either side of Julia and Caron and pricked them in unison. Julia bit her lip but didn't complain. Caron started crying immediately.

The nurses got through the rest of the little ones, and then it was my turn. The nurse scanned my eyeball and made some notes on her tablet. "Please don't say I have to be in bed by eight o'clock, too," I joked. "I've been cooped up since the lockdown."

"It wasn't a lockdown," the nurse said. Her hair was pulled up so tightly it yanked the edges of her eyes back. "It was simply a precautionary measure."

"Right," I said.

"Your father should have explained it to you," she added.

"He was a little busy."

She looked up from her tablet. "Yes, of course, Mori. Now then." She selected a syringe from a different tray than she had for the others. This one had a blue band around it.

"Um," I began. "Is that—"

"What's the problem, Mori?" she asked.

"It's just that it's different from everyone else's."

The nurse pointed over to Benji, who was about to be pricked by the second nurse. His had a blue band as well. "There are slightly different variations based on individual biology. This is the one you need." Her voice was clipped and sharp and made it perfectly clear that I was being rude.

"Sorry."

It seemed to me that she took a certain pleasure from driving the syringe deep into my arm, where the pain bloomed like a bruise below my skin. I winced, but I wasn't about to let her see me cry. "Thank you."

Next to me, Benji yelled out, "Holy holy he—"

"An ice pack is available," his nurse said, and gestured to a bin.

"I'm good," he whispered.

Next up was Ilana. The nurse scanned her eyeballs and then said, "You're all up-to-date. Must have done it at Calliope."

"Calliope?" Ilana asked. "Back in California?"

"Yes, of course," the nurse said.

"Lucky," Benji said, still rubbing his arm.

Ilana looked at the nurse a moment longer, and then at the tray of syringes.

"This way," I said, and we walked out of the inoculation room together. My arm ached like I'd been stung one last time by a yellow jacket, but all I could think about was how far away Ilana seemed.

18

SOME DAYS START OUT BAD, but that's okay because you have the rest of the day for things to get better. So, sure, we got shots in the morning, but we had the whole afternoon to play and swim and for Ilana and me to check on Oakedge. That's what I was ready for. But then the grown-ups decided that while we were there we ought to do our yearly fitness test. Julia grinned at this news—she always got the top honor—but I scowled. I hated the fitness test.

We were ushered into locker rooms and given our uniforms of shorts and T-shirts. "It seems unfair to do this after vaccinations," I said, rubbing my arm.

"Ah, buck up," Julia said, still smiling. "Anyway, the only thing it will really affect is the pull-ups, and you've never done one of those anyway."

"Gee, thanks. Your support is amazing."

Ilana tightened the laces on her sneakers. "I don't think we had to do this in Calliope."

"What do you mean?" Julia asked. "It's national. They do it at all the Kritopias. I was a top ten finisher last year."

They used to do this fitness test all over the country and called it the President's Challenge. But nothing was standardized. Some kids ran the mile outside, others did loop after loop in a school gym—and even then the measurements were up to the physical education teachers. It's much fairer now.

"I guess I'm just forgetting."

Julia made a looping motion with her finger next to her head.

"Has she really been like this all week?" I whispered.

Julia nodded.

We filed out of the locker room and met the boys who were waiting there. Theo was talking with the teenage boys from the bus, as if they hadn't teased him and he hadn't called them stupid.

"Whoa," Julia said. She grabbed my hand.

The shorts and T-shirts that we were given were tighter than what any of us normally wore, especially the boys. With the teenagers you could see the outlines of the muscles on their chests, stomach, and arms. What was surprising was that Theo, too, had these lines and contours.

"When did that happen?" Julia murmured.

I tried to think back. Even when we went swimming, I hadn't noticed. I felt myself flushing.

"Like, give me your glasses. I think something is wrong with my retina if I'm actually thinking that Theo is attractive."

"Come on," I said, tugging her into line far away from him. None of this was going to help me succeed on the test.

Benji was given an inhaler by one of the trainers and took two long puffs through a spacer. "Just some performance-enhancing drugs," he quipped to us.

Ilana looked confused. "Should I have some, too?"

"No." Benji laughed. "I have asthma. I can't do the run without it. You, I bet, are just fine."

And she was. The girls started on the pull-up bar, where, as predicted, I could not manage even one pull-up. So the trainers timed how long I could hold on. Forty-five seconds. "Better than last year," one said, her voice dry like fall leaves. I looked into her eyes. Sometimes I really wondered if they were replacing the trainers with androids. She blinked. Human. Just an unfeeling human.

Julia grunted through seven. "Same as last year," the trainer said, and marked something on her tablet.

"I can do more," Julia said. "Let me try again."

But Ilana was already up to the bar. She grabbed it and began doing pull-ups, five right in a row before her pace slowed slightly. Six, seven, eight, nine. She kept her knees bent behind her and stared straight ahead. Ten, eleven, twelve. I suppose it shouldn't have been a surprise. Thirteen, fourteen, fifteen. Some of the boys who were waiting to do the shuttle run turned and looked at her. Sixteen, seventeen, eighteen. Next to me Julia kicked at the padded ground. Nineteen, twenty. The trainer held her stylus above the tablet. Even she looked surprised. Twenty-one, twenty-two. And then she dropped. And everybody clapped.

And so it went through the shuttle run, a devious test where you have to run back and forth picking up and dropping off blocks. I imagined my dad did tests like this on the animals in his lab. Ilana did it like it was nothing, bending over to pick up and put down the blocks in smooth, simple motions, like a speed skater going around the track.

The sit-and-reach was my personal strength, probably because Mom and Dad had done yoga with me ever since I was a baby; we named all the poses after animals. But even that, Ilana dominated.

Julia's mood got darker and darker. We headed for the treadmills last. They were arranged in rows and columns, like desks in an old-fashioned classroom. I was in the last row, an empty treadmill next to me. Ilana was right in front of me, with Julia next to her. I saw Julia glance over at Ilana and grit her teeth. This was war.

The trainers started us all at once with a switch on their tablets. Each treadmill measured our stride, heart rate, and more, and also gave updates as to how far we had run.

I had a strategy that I'd developed over the years: First, look at the screen and only at the screen. A little red dot flashed across it. I pretended it was me, jogging across the field in our village, or through Firefly Lane at night when everyone else was sleeping. When I looked at that dot, I could imagine a whole world around me: where I would go, who I would meet, what we would talk about. It didn't make me go any faster, but I didn't get flustered. And anyway, I was never going to be the fastest.

"That's your top speed?" Ilana asked Julia. Her poofy ponytail bounced up and down with each stride.

"Zip it, Ilana," Julia said back. She huffed a little as she spoke, but I noticed her feet were moving faster. "I'm going to set a new record. Again."

"Bring it," Ilana said.

At least Ilana was starting to sound like herself again. I couldn't see her face, but Julia grinned.

My own pace was slowing. I had to concentrate on my screen.

I was building up a whole story about jogging over to Julia's to go for a swim, when, unbidden, my subconscious put Theo next to me. I increased my pace and tried to erase him. "Hey," mind-Theo said. I shook my head and stumbled a little, but I kept my pace. With effort I put Julia next to me. She walked to keep pace with my jogging, and I imagined her telling me a funny story about her brother. Much better. My pace slowed.

A sudden tumbling crash broke me from my reverie. In front of me, Ilana was falling forward. She grabbed the side bars of the treadmill, and righted herself, then began running again. A trainer was upon her in a minute. "I'm fine," Ilana growled. "Just lost concentration."

Beside her, I thought I saw Julia smile.

The trainer made a note on her tablet, but I couldn't see what it said.

Julia's feet started racing faster, and Ilana hurried to keep up. Faster and faster the two girls ran, and I found my own pace quickening as I watched their feet. I checked my progress. Seven-tenths of a mile. They must be nearly done. My heart beat faster, not with the effort, but with anticipation. This was what it felt like to be in a race. It was exhilarating! I pushed my legs harder.

A trainer came to me. "Watch your pace, Mori," she said. "Don't worry about anyone else." I had never heard a trainer speak so kindly.

I was pondering this, and what it meant, when there was first one crash, then another, and another. All the girls in the row in front of me were falling, one after the other. It was like someone had come and pulled their feet out from under them. There were screams and grunts, and one trainer even dropped her tablet as they all ran from different points of the room. I heard someone crying.

"Over here!" a trainer yelled.

"Someone get some ice!"

Julia clutched her knee as she sat on the unmoving treadmill, and Ilana rubbed her head. "What—" I began.

"Keep running," the trainer nearest to me said, back to business as usual. She dropped down next to Julia.

My feet kept moving while I tried to make sense of what was happening. I had never seen anything like it. How on earth did they all fall down at the same time? But there they were, the whole row, sitting on the floor or the edges of their treadmills. One girl who'd been in my class at school and who prided herself on being the toughest kid in the village, she held her elbow while she cried without making a sound.

There was a trainer for every girl in the row. They squatted down in front of the girls, scanned them. They gave them ice and acetaminophen for the pain. And then the trainers helped the girls to their feet and led them from the room while the rest of us thump, thump, thumped along on our treadmills.

Every girl in that row was taken care of. Every girl except Ilana.

When my mile was done, my treadmill beeped a countdown, but no trainer came over. So I stopped, hopping my feet up awkwardly to the side while the treadmill's band still spun. When it stopped, I climbed down and sat next to Ilana. "Are you okay?" I asked.

She looked back at me. Two fat tears streaked down her cheeks. I had never seen her cry before, never even imagined it. "No, Mori, I don't think I am." Then she leaned closer to me, so our bodies were touching all along our sides, and she whispered, "I'm scared, Mori."

"What are you scared of?" I asked.

A trainer appeared then. "Mori Bloom, your test is complete."

"I think there's something wrong with Ilana."

"We're bringing her to the infirmary now."

"Can I go with her?"

The trainer did not even hesitate: "No." Then, as if I had already left, she turned to Ilana and extended a hand. "We'll go get you fixed up now, okay?"

It seemed the longest moment before Ilana spoke, long enough for flowers to grow, but then she said, "Okay."

She didn't say good-bye or look back. She just let the trainer pull her to her feet, and the two of them left through a side door that I had never even noticed before.

19

JULIA AND I SAT ON the grass in her side yard. I had my knees pulled up to my chest, arms wrapped around them. Ilana's house across the street was as still as the summer air around us. "She hasn't been outside for three days," I said.

Julia plucked a dandelion from the lawn and began pulling out its tiny yellow petals, one at a time. "She took a pretty hard fall."

"So did you," I said.

She pushed a smile onto her lips. "Yeah, well, I'm tough."

"So is she," I said.

Julia's smile faltered. "She's not so great."

"I don't understand why you don't like her," I said.

"I never said I didn't like her." Her voice was as flat as dry paint. She plucked three more petals out of the dandelion.

"But you don't," I said.

The plucked-out petals were in a pile on Julia's knee. She brushed them away with the back of her hand. "She's weird, Mori. And she doesn't want to be our friend. She only wants to be with you."

"We could do something together. When she finally comes out of the house. We could do something with just us three girls. Like a sleepover or something."

"Maybe I'm busy. Did you think of that?"

"But I didn't even pick a day yet."

"I still might be busy." She pulled another dandelion from the ground. This time she didn't bother disassembling it: she just popped the flower right off the stem. "Or maybe I just don't want to have a sleepover with her, like, ever."

I turned my body so I was facing her. The toes of our sneakers touched, and she pulled her feet back. "I just don't understand," I said. "She's really nice, if you would just try to get to know her. You have lots in common."

Julia rolled her eyes. "Hardly."

"You're not even trying," I said. "All I'm asking is for you to try."

"You want me to try?" she asked, her voice rising like a roller coaster ready to crest. "Really? You want me to try? How about you? How about you actually try hanging out with the friends you've had your whole life? How about you try to hide that you were so excited to leave us, you jumped all over the first new kid who moved into our neighborhood? How about that?"

"Julia—"

Her gaze snapped back to mine, and now that she was looking at me, I wished she would look away. Her eyes were narrowed and flashing, like slits of fire trained right on me. "You know how Theo calls you dopey—"

"He's only joking with me—"

"Maybe." She shrugged. "But I'm not. You *are* a dope, but I've been your friend anyway, and I've tried to help you out, but if you don't want my help, then fine. Fine by me."

She stood and turned away from me right as Benji coasted up her driveway on his skateboard with Theo right behind. Benji took his helmet off and looked at the two of us. Theo stopped his bike. "Whoa, did the north wind just blow through here or something?"

"It's nothing," Julia said. "Just having a little discussion about our missing neighbor over there."

Theo and Benji looked at me. They weren't stupid, and I was pretty sure they could tell that Julia and I had been fighting. Still, I swallowed hard and said, "We were just wondering when she was going to come back out."

"She took a pretty hard fall, right?" Theo asked.

"That's what I said," Julia replied.

I leaned back and stared up at the clouds that puffed across the sky like smoke from a train in picture books. Once Theo had told me that there weren't really shapes in the clouds, that it was just our brains that were hardwired to see them because we were always trying to make sense of the world around us. "She has to come out today," I said.

"Maybe she's sick," Theo said.

"She's not sick," Benji said. "Maybe she really hurt herself."

"It still doesn't make sense to me," Theo said. He drummed his thumbs on the handlebars of his bike. "She fell down and then the whole row of treadmills lost power?" We had told Benji and Theo about it, several times, but Theo still wanted to go over it again and again.

"She didn't fall. She stumbled and then was running again, and then the treadmills stopped," I told them.

"It was stupid," Julia said. "*She* was stupid. She was trying to keep up with me and she couldn't, so she fell."

"That still doesn't explain why—" Theo began.

"She's just so stinking competitive," Julia said. "Like about everything. She thinks she's so great. So strong. So fast. So pretty."

"She is," Benji said.

I said, "She doesn't think she's pretty."

Julia scoffed and tossed one of her braids over her shoulder.

"Well, she does, but she doesn't think it matters. That's just the way she's constructed, that's what she said to me."

"Constructed to make a mess of everything," Julia said.

A cloud skirted around the sun, and a crow flew above us.

"Hey, maybe Ilana being gone—maybe it's not even because of the fitness test. Her family is all free-spirited, right?" Benji asked. "So maybe they took a spur-of-the-moment vacation or something."

The steady pace of Theo's drumming stilled. "It still doesn't make sense that the treadmills would break during a test. Those trainers must be in some trouble."

"She just sat there afterward," I said. "Everyone else in your row went for ice or whatever, and she stayed, and they left her for last." I didn't tell them that she'd been scared. That something seemed really wrong.

"So you think maybe it was her fault?" Julia asked, a tinge of hope in her voice.

"I don't know," I told them. And I really didn't. All I knew was that she was gone.

"You know, we said we were going to go back to number nine. Why don't we go today?" Benji said.

"I don't know," Julia said.

"To explore. And because, you know, honey."

"Mmm, honey," Theo murmured. "That would probably make us all feel better."

I sat up. I did want to go back. I wanted to read more of Agatha's notebooks, and maybe I could find the gardening stuff that Ilana and I were looking for. Then, when she came back out, we could go right to Oakedge. "Okay, let's go."

Julia sighed. "All right, but I have my painting lesson today, so we can't be in there too long."

We rode around the cul-de-sac to number 9. We took the path around back, then clambered down through the bulkhead door and stopped for warm honey before we climbed upstairs. It was so delicious, I took a jar and slipped it into the backpack my parents had insisted I start carrying around. It had a first-aid kit in it, including an EpiPen, even though I hadn't been allergic to the yellow jacket stings, and a phone that could only dial three numbers: Mom's, Dad's, and the emergency line. It didn't even have a touchscreen, just three big buttons, like a child's toy.

When we emerged from the basement, I stopped short in the bright kitchen. There were cheery yellow curtains and a deep porcelain sink that shone bright white. Along the windowsill were old-looking bottles in varied colors of glass. I felt like I had stepped into a home I had lived in once before. "It's beautiful," I said.

Julia sniffed. "It stinks up here."

"It's been locked up for ages," Theo said.

"We could open a window," I suggested.

Theo just shook his head. "Let's look upstairs," he said. I followed him up to the second floor of the house. There was a narrow hallway with three doors, each a bright white. Theo walked down the hall and opened the door at the far end. It was filled with human limbs.

I stumbled back. "What is this?"

Theo stepped into the room. "They're fake. Early robotics. See?" He picked up an arm and turned it so I could see the metal ball that would go into the socket at the shoulder. Some red and blue wires were laced around it. "Old-school, as Benji would say."

"Robotics or prosthetics?" I asked as I eyed something that had a leg-like shape, but was made from an arched swoop of metal and plastic. I had seen something like it on history videos of the Paralympics: runners with these artificial legs bounded along like cheetahs.

"Look at this," Theo said. His voice was soft. When I turned I saw he held, cupped in both hands, a tiny device, the size of a fat bumblebee and made of yellow-and-black metal. When he split his hands, it dropped for a moment before rising up and buzzing around the room. It bumped against the window. I laughed and clapped my hands over my mouth, and then it turned and headed straight for me. My eyes widened, but it came to a soft landing on my shoulder. "It likes you!"

The robot bee stopped humming and seemed to shut itself off as it perched on my shoulder, but I could still feel its tiny insect legs pinching onto my shirt.

"A robobee!" I exclaimed. "Your mom told me and Ilana about them. And then I read about them in Agatha's notebook."

"You on a first-name basis with her now?"

She did feel like an old friend. "She was working to save the bees; my great-grandmother suggested she clone bees, you know, older bees that had survived, and then use robobees to teach them how to forage and everything."

"It's a pretty good idea, actually," Theo said. "Then once the clones learned, they would pass it on to their descendants. It wouldn't take too long in insects."

"Dr. Varden wasn't convinced," I said.

I started to tell him about how Dr. Varden said she was getting tired of manipulating nature, but then Julia called to us from downstairs: "Hey! You have to see this!"

I tried to remove the robobee, but it was stuck in my shirt. Theo reached over to try, too, the back of his hand brushing at my hair. I saw his cheeks flush a little, and I almost teased him for it, the way he always teased me, but I stopped myself. His fingers tried to loosen the legs, but they stayed firm. "I guess you'll have to, you know, get it from the inside."

"Right," I said as my cheeks grew hot.

"Guess you have a new pet."

"Guys!" Julia called, more urgently.

We clomped back down the stairs, our footsteps echoing in the house. Benji and Julia were in the room off the kitchen where there were several file cabinets and then, pushed back against a corner wall, a computer. Not a new one, not at all, but it was definitely recognizable by its flat monitor and keyboard.

"Boot it up," Theo said.

"That's what I've been saying," Benji agreed.

I scanned it for a power slide. "Will it even work without the right fingerprint?"

"They didn't always use fingerprint scans," Julia said. She pressed down on a button with a circle that had a small hash mark at the top.

Nothing.

"Try some power," Theo said. He picked up a cord that came from the back of the computer and pushed it into an outlet in the wall—another outdated invention we'd learned about. People used to plug electronics into the wall before wireless electricity.

"I doubt there's still power in this pl—" Benji began, but with a groan and a whir, the machine booted up.

"Should we be doing this?" I asked, then answered my own question: "We shouldn't be doing this. It's against the rules. You can't use someone else's technology."

"They aren't rules, they're guidelines," Benji said. "Anyway, those guidelines are for tech devices. This is—" He waved his hand at the machine that was still grinding to life. "Practically an antique. It's history," he said, knowing my soft spot.

When the machine finally turned on, the Krita logo was on the screen. It was surrounded by tiny icons. Some were pictures with a label beneath: WIRELESS PRINTER, VOIP, MUSIC. But others were files: Bee Records, Bee Research, Humanoid, Utopias—History, Calliope, Old Harmonie, Wrightsville, Citroen, and more.

"Where do we start?" Benji asked.

"With us, I guess." Julia clicked on the file marked "Old Harmonie." A window opened up with several more folders: Manual, Operatives, Scuttled, Children.

Julia's cursor huddled over "Children."

"What about the manual?" I asked. None of this felt right to me.

"Boring," Julia said. "'Operatives' sounds intriguing. Are there special secret missions going on here?"

"Doubtful," Theo said.

"Let's look at this one, then." She clicked on the file marked "Scuttled." The window was jam-packed with folders. "I guess they scuttled a lot."

"What does that even mean?" Benji asked.

"Abandoned," Theo told him. "Like that room full of arms and legs. And that." He pointed at the bee on my shoulder.

"Do that one!" Benji said, pointing at a file marked "Artificial Intelligence."

When Julia clicked the file open, it was full of subfolders. She clicked on the first one, "Prince Philip." Inside, there were documents and photos. When she enlarged a photo, I saw my robobee. Then she opened a file called "Specs." It told of the bee's development, its size, its weight, and its purpose:

> To lead honeybees to proper sources of nectar and thereby maintain honey flows.

"Dr. Varden was mad about the bees," I said.

The next line read:

> Further study: record memories of processes and insert into honeybee clones. Expected results: clone bees will more quickly learn their roles. They will learn flight patterns and feeding areas. Drawbacks: will only learn specific route, patterns of android bee. Further work needed to push clone bees to adapt and learn for themselves.

"Whoa," Theo said. "That's a few steps beyond what your great-grandmother suggested."

"Inserting memories?" Benji asked. "Do bees even have memories?"

On my shirt, the android bee flitted its wings. "They're not memories like we're thinking of. It's the procedure. How to do something. So, maybe, how to go out to a flower and remove the pollen and bring it back to the hive. It would be like if someone inserted the memory of how to skateboard into your head," I explained.

"No need, no need," Benji said, grinning widely. "I'm a natural."

"Natural at falling on your butt, maybe," Theo said.

"I wonder where all those cloned bees wound up," Benji said.

"This is the scuttled folder," Theo said.

"So?"

"So scuttled means gone. The clones were killed and if there are any more of these android bees, well, they're probably in the junk heap. They're scrap."

"Oh," Benji said as he pet my bee. "Poor little guys."

Julia closed the first folder. I scanned the names of the other files: Koko II, Phineas, Victoria, Alana, Andromeda, Gage II, Gage III, Bot2000, DARYL, on and on, name after name. "All of these projects were canceled?" I asked. "I wonder if each one is a different android version of an animal?" Then I reread the names. "Koko II! Ilana and I saw that at the museum."

Julia clicked on the Koko II folder, and a picture of the huge robotic gorilla appeared. It looked even more menacing than in person.

"Ilana and I saw your mom at the museum, Theo. That's when she told us about the robobees, and about this gorilla.

She told us that they taught the robot to communicate. They taught it two hundred fifty words, because that's how many words a typical human uses, and then it could have pretty simple conversations."

"I'm pretty sure I use more than two hundred fifty words," Julia said.

"This was what came before chat bots," I explained.

"Animal chat bots?" Benji asked. "So cool. I want a chat bot dog. I would name him Cornelius, and he would talk to me about all the skateboarding stuff you don't want to hear about. It would be so dope."

Julia closed the folder, then opened up "Victoria." When she clicked on the picture, we all rocked back. It wasn't an animal but a human. Sort of. It wasn't exactly right, though it was hard to pinpoint what was wrong. She had white skin, and dark hair pulled back from her face with a bright blue headband that matched her eyes. She smiled. Maybe that was the problem. The smile wasn't quite right.

"Ugh," Julia said as she clicked the photo closed. "Creepy."

Theo reached past her and said, "Click where it says 'Problems.'"

"This is silly," I said. "Learning about all these projects that never went anywhere. They didn't work. We move on, right?"

"Normally you're the one who wants to learn about this stuff," Theo said.

I knew he meant the history, but I thought about what his mom had said, how she was interested in animals and artificial intelligence, and how she thought Ilana would be, too. That's what all these projects were, I realized, more work by Dr. Varden and others on mixing biology with AI. And with this Victoria, it seemed, they were starting to push toward humans. I had a sick, sour feeling in my stomach. Something worse than a hive of wasps was waiting for us in this room.

"Look at this," Julia said. "'While Victoria performed admirably in terms of learning her environment, she was unable to form lasting connections with humans. In fact, child test subjects shunned her, even when they were not informed of her android status. The problem may be what is referred to as the uncanny valley. Her appearance is close to human, but not close enough.'"

"Creepy, just like you said," Benji said.

"Still, it's sad to think of her being abandoned. What do you think they did with her?" I asked.

Theo looked over his shoulder. "You saw that room, Mori. When things didn't work, they took them apart."

Victoria might be in there, in pieces. I shivered. "It's just a robot," I whispered, more to myself than to my friends. Prince Philip buzzed on my shoulder. Then I lifted my head. "But Old Harmonie scientists wouldn't really do that, right? Just ditch a project like this?" But even as I said it, I thought of what Theo's mom had told us: *When a project's outcomes fail to warrant the expenditures, we cancel it.*

Julia's watchu buzzed. "Darn it! I have my art lesson. I have to go."

"Let's just all go back," Benji said. "We can go swimming or play four square or something."

"Right," Julia agreed. "We can come back here another day." She reached out and turned off the computer and the creepy girl faded away.

20

JULIA BOLTED OUT OF THERE at top speed. Late once more and her parents said they'd take away her screen privileges for the whole week, and Zane and River were in the midst of a breakup. Benji said, "I'm off to practice my ollie. Wanna come?"

I shook my head. I thought I'd feel better once we got outside, but my stomach was still churning.

"All right, see you home fries later."

Which just left Theo and me. He picked up his bike.

Scuttled. It was such a strange word. Like a crab crawling across a tile floor. But it meant gone for good, didn't it? They were buried in history unless someone came along and dug them out of the pile like we had rescued the robobee.

Phineas. Andromeda. DARYL. All those names on those files, so many projects gone. I thought again of Ms. Staarsgard in the museum. She had said that science charged forward toward things we couldn't even imagine yet. And that's what scared me. That and one more name that I had seen: Alana. My stomach hitched. I looked back toward the house. My brain was leaping, making a connection I didn't want to make.

Alana only sounds like Ilana, I told myself.

And then I remembered how sad she'd looked sitting on the treadmill while the trainers ignored her.

"There's something I need to look at," I said. "On the computer."

He turned his head over his shoulder to look back at the house. "You shouldn't go alone."

"Come in with me, then."

We retraced our steps. I tried to catch glimpses of him beside me without his noticing. He really was bigger and stronger. His shadow lengthened out like a giant above mine. Maybe his mom had added other changes for him alongside his latency, like medicine to bulk him up. A lot of parents started doing enhancements like that when their kids turned thirteen if they still had their 30 percent left. Other parents only did what was necessary to fix medical problems. Benji's did all the therapies he needed, but hadn't made any enhancements, even if he probably would have liked some

extra coordination for his skateboarding. They never dampened him, either, just like my parents. They didn't think it
was right to mess with temperament like that.

Theo stood next to the bulkhead but didn't bend over to
lift the door. "So what's this all about, anyway?" he asked.

"There's something going on with Ilana," I said. "And I
need to figure it out before something goes really wrong.
And I think the answers are here."

I thought he would say I was being silly again, and chasing daydreams—darker ones than usual, but daydreams just
the same. Instead he said, "Okay. I guess we should get that
clunker running again."

🚲

When it booted, I knew what file I needed to go to, but I
couldn't push the button. The cursor of the mouse just hov-
ered over the file. Finally Theo leaned past me and clicked
on it. All the names were in front of us.

"Alana, right?" he asked.

So he had noticed, too. "Yeah."

He clicked open the folder and there she was: Alana.
Ilana. I felt sick.

Even in the tiny thumbnail picture, I could see her. Not
exactly her, but like her. It wasn't the uncanny valley, though.
No, this girl seemed more real because she wasn't perfect. In
the picture, she smiled crookedly, and her eyes were more

hazel than the green blue of Ilana's. She had a mole on her right cheek. But they looked similar enough for me to know they were connected.

I clicked on the picture and another document opened. "Background."

Alana (Advanced Life Artificial Nuanced Acclimate) represents the forefront of research merging cloning, genetics, robotics, and most importantly, artificial intelligence. Rather than being cloned and raised from a zygote, Alana was born a child, a mix of cloned cells grown in the laboratory, and merged with robotic engineering. Typical nano-enhancements were made. What distinguishes Alana from other bio-robotics is that, for the first time, we have created a silicon consciousness.

I rubbed at my eyes, and the letters danced on the screen. I knew what most of the words meant, but I couldn't piece them together and come up with Ilana. A clone. A clone mixed with a robot. Well, Theo and my parents had both said that cloning was part of reproduction. But clones were babies. This was saying she was born as a child: all of a sudden, she was just there.

Unless it hadn't been all of a sudden. They could clone cells, couldn't they? Skin cells and even brain cells. Those had been grown in labs and used in surgery. Could they have made all the different parts, grown them separately, and then stitched them together?

But this Alana wasn't just a clone. She was robotics, too, like the artificial limbs we had seen—so well-designed, they were even better than what people were born with. And all of this put together, right from the start. They took the cloned parts and the robotics and put it together: that was Alana. One hundred percent designed. The opposite of natural.

We began with memories, recording them using test subjects and androids, and uploaded these wirelessly into her brain, which itself was grown from stem cells harvested from the same child used for other cloning procedures.

"What child?" I murmured.

Theo leaned in closer as he read over my shoulder.

Initial memories were process-based, starting with simple functions like walking. This was deceptively difficult, as it involved not only memories in the brain, but also muscle memory. Slowly, over time, Alana learned to walk, talk, and interact with others. From there, experiments were done with more personal memories, such as a sixth birthday party.

"They put memories in her?" Theo asked.

"But they weren't hers. This girl, Alana, she thought she had a past, but she didn't. She didn't know what she was."

I looked over my shoulder at Theo. He was frowning, his brow furrowed.

We were both thinking about her. Our Ilana.

I shook my head. I needed to learn all I could and then we could make the connections.

I read on about how they were able to give her the memories of a whole life, to give her dreams. It was a big deal when she began to dream on her own. She never left the lab. She didn't have any parents, just the scientists. She was watched all the time, even when she slept or bathed or daydreamed. Her life was not her own in so many ways.

I closed the folder labeled "Background."

"She must have been so lonely," I said.

"That's not Ilana. Not exactly."

"I need to find out why this other Alana was scuttled."

I scrolled through the folders looking for the one titled "Problems," like we had seen with Victoria. A crow cawed outside, followed by a rustling. It sounded big, whatever it was.

"Did you hear that?" I asked Theo.

"You're just skittish," he said.

My heart was racing, beating out a message to me: *Get out, get out, get out.*

But I clicked on the "Problems" file. The screen filled with a document, bullet point after bullet point: *failure to thrive, altercation, social rejection, moodiness, power main-tenance.* My eyes scanned all the terms and landed on the final point:

Conclusion: At this time, the ALANA project must be considered a failure. She is not able to adequately integrate into society. Before that problem can be solved, though, issues of power generation and memory stability must be solved. More importantly, ethical considerations must be fully examined. This project has been put on hold indefinitely.

"Indefinitely until now," Theo said.

I didn't know that words could make me feel this way, that an idea could sink my stomach and my soul until I was twisted into a knot I wasn't sure I would ever be able to untie. "Let's get out of here," I said. I still didn't understand it all, but this idea was starting to crystallize in my brain. An idea I didn't like too much.

🚲

"It doesn't mean anything," I said as much to me as to him. We were sitting on the merry-go-round in the playground. I sat in the middle, and Theo on the edge. His foot hung down and he swung us back and forth, back and forth. "I mean, it might not even be related to our Ilana."

"We both saw the picture, Mori. Ilana could be the next generation. Better technology. Better implementation."

"She's not a robot," I said. I put my head in my hands, my eyes closed: all I could see was Ms. Staarsgard leaning down toward Ilana: *"I've taken a particular interest in Bio-Tech-Intelligence. I presume you have, too, Ilana."* Ms. Staarsgard *knew*. She knew that Ilana was . . . something else.

"Ilana must have created a power surge somehow during the fitness test—when she fell, you know, and that fried the electronics of the treadmills." His voice was growing more excited, like this was one of his complicated puzzles, and he was solving it.

I rubbed my eyes. If it was true, and Ms. Staarsgard knew it, then why would she have wanted us to see the exhibit? Was she trying to tell us the truth? Or was she just so pleased with the developments Krita had made, she couldn't contain herself? No, I told myself. No, I was wrong. I was jumping to conclusions. "She's not glitching or power surging or anything like that. She's a person. She's our friend. She has a body and she has memories—"

"They aren't *her* memories. I bet she wasn't ever in Calliope. She's been here all along."

"Stop it!" I said. But the facts kept piling up in my brain. That's why she couldn't name her flag. It wasn't just that she wasn't from California. She wasn't from anywhere.

Everything from the cells up was manufactured. She had no parents, no heritage to hold on to. She was totally ungrounded.

"Mori, you have to face facts. She's a piece of technology. A really cool, really advanced artificial intelligence development, but technology nonetheless."

I didn't understand how he could be so calm. He was talking about her like she was a homework assignment, something to be figured out. But my mind was untethered from its moorings. All along I'd been convinced she was natural. She was so perfect, so beautiful. But she wasn't natural at all. Everything I'd believed was completely backward.

"Don't talk like that," I said. "Don't even think it. I know the scientists were working on those artificial intelligence projects before, but if what you are saying is true—that's crossing a line. Dr. Varden and Baba had rules and guidelines for things like this. You can't just create a whole new person! That's not right!"

"We have to face facts—" he said again.

"Is that what your puzzle brain is telling you?" I asked. My voice sounded like it was coming from someone else: icy and razor sharp. "Have you figured her all out? Have you solved the riddle?"

"I'm just trying to think rationally," he said.

"Well, don't!" I cried. I stood up. The merry-go-round shifted beneath my feet, and I almost pitched forward onto him. "I shouldn't have trusted you with this," I said. I jumped down from the merry-go-round and started walking away from the playground.

"Mori, wait!"

But I didn't listen to him. I just marched away. I was half-way around the cul-de-sac before I realized I didn't know where I was going. I stopped in the middle of the road, the sun beating down on me. I looked over each shoulder as if the way would suddenly become clear to me. I couldn't tell Julia, because she already hated Ilana. It would overwhelm Benji. I couldn't go to Ilana herself until I knew just what to say to her. I was all alone on Firefly Lane, something I had never been before.

21

USUALLY WORDS HELPED ME, BUT reading Agatha's journal just confused me more. I read it trying to erase what I had learned about Ilana, but all of it kept reminding me. Agatha's bees were failing, succumbing to a wide variety of illnesses. The genetic modifications weren't working, and the cloning wasn't going as well as Baba had hoped, either.

Then Dad tried to be chipper over lunch, but really he was just trying to get back to talking about my latency, and I didn't want to think about that at all. So I ate quickly and then hurried outside.

All along my heart just kept pounding and pounding, and my stomach shriveled to the size of the dates the deliver bot dropped off as a special treat.

On my bike I could feel a little bit freer, like nothing I had learned mattered at all. My head sweated under my helmet, and the wind blew into my eyes, making them tear up, and I could pretend I was a prisoner on the run—an honest kind of prisoner, captured under false pretenses by a corrupt police force. I was making my way to freedom, which meant going round and round the cul-de-sac at an ever faster pace. My retina camera buzzed with trying to keep up with it all.

Finally, dizzy, I slowed, and turned up onto the straight part of the road. My breath came a little fast, and I could feel a drip of sweat going down my neck, and I could almost see why Julia liked running so much.

Ilana was in her driveway, and I cruised my bike up to her. She was crouched over a drawing she was working on with sidewalk chalk. I had seen a movie once about a guy who did sidewalk art that was so real you could actually step into it and go into that other world. Ilana's was that good. It was a whole garden of tangled flowers, each one so detailed and vibrant I could practically smell them.

Because she's a robot. I wish I could say it was Theo's voice in my head, but it was my own.

"That's nice," I said. I hopped off my bike and let it fall onto her lawn.

"Hey, Mori! Thanks!" She wiped her hands on her shorts and stood up. "I'm so glad you came around today."

"Yeah, me too." I looked up the street toward Julia's house.

"I'm fine, by the way." She smiled.

"What?"

"I haven't seen you since I fell on the treadmills."

I kicked my shoe into the ground. "That was so strange," I said. "What even happened?" I wanted to know if Theo was right, if Ilana was robotic and she'd had some sort of power surge—but of course if that was the truth, she wouldn't come out and tell me.

"It was weird, huh? They told me it was a blip in the power field."

"My treadmill was fine. It was just your row."

She shrugged. "You were really cranking."

"So were you. And Julia."

She laughed. "Maybe that was the problem. Julia and I overworked the system."

"Maybe," I said, wondering if perhaps that was getting close to the truth. "I am glad you're okay."

"I know," she said.

"We were wondering when you were going to come back out."

"You know how parents are—cautious, cautious."

I forced a smile and said, "Don't I know it?" But all the while I was thinking, *But they aren't your parents. You don't have parents.* And as I had the thought I realized I was starting to believe Theo's version of things: that Ilana was a new version of Alana. She was a creation of the scientists of Old Harmonie, which meant that everything I had thought about Old Harmonie was a lie, too. I felt dizzy and it seemed like the sun was burning hotter and hotter, melting the road beneath my feet as I stood there.

"Cool. You wanna do some chalk drawings with me?"

I thought of how pale and lifeless my own drawings would be next to hers. "No, thanks." I wished I could unknow what I had learned about her.

"How about hopscotch?" Then her face brightened. "I love hopscotch!" It was like she was just realizing that fact about herself. Maybe she was.

Ilana drew the squares with an orange piece of chalk, a complicated course with a tough mix of singles and doubles. She numbered them all, then grabbed a pebble from the side of her driveway. "Do you want to go first?"

I took the stone from her. "I haven't played hopscotch in forever. Julia and I used to play all the time in second grade." I tossed the pebble and it landed on the three, so I hopped on one foot, one, two, then jumped and landed with my feet strad-dling on the first double. Back onto one foot, then through the rest of the course. I pivoted and started hopping back, but on my second jump, I wobbled and put my other foot down.

"Out!" Ilana exclaimed. Before I could get it for her, she picked up the stone. "My turn!" She tossed the stone and it landed all the way in the right-hand box of the second double. She hopped on one foot like it was nothing, sky-high like a pogo stick, got to the end, pivoted, and returned to the start, scooping up the stone in one easy motion. "One point for me," she said.

"You don't keep score in hopscotch."

"You don't?"

"No. It's just for fun."

"Are you sure?" She handed me the pebble.

I tossed it and it skittered out of the court.

"Tough break." She said it with a smile. "My turn again."

Of course this next round was just as perfect for her.

She gave me the stone. This time I had to jump from a straddle to a single leg, and for some reason I decided to add a spin move, so I stumbled and fell onto my knee. A red patch of blood bloomed up behind the dirt. "You're hurt!" Ilana said.

"I'm fine. It's just a scrape." I handed her the rock. "Your turn."

Another perfect run. And she did a spin with no problem.

"It's not fair," I said.

"What?"

"You're so good at this." I shook my head, but the words echoed in my mind. *Not fair.*

"Maybe if you practiced some more—"

"That's not it." *Not fair. Not fair.* No matter what any of us did, we would never match up to her.

"Is it your eye, then?"

"No. Not *my* eye. Or *my* legs. Or anything to do with me."

Ilana stood up straight and cocked her head to the side.

My knee was still bleeding. I could feel the blood trickling down. "I need to go home. I need to get a Band-Aid."

"We have bandages."

"No. I need to go home." My brain was pounding, and I thought I might explode with all I knew. I would just erupt and be left as a sticky puddle on the ground, and even that would be better than telling her the truth of what I knew.

"See you later? We could go out to Oakedge."

"Sure. Maybe."

"We really should check our garden."

"I said sure."

I grabbed my bike and pushed it instead of riding it. My knee was throbbing in time with my brain. I wish I had never read that file. Because now I couldn't see her the same way. The things that had been so beautiful about her—her strength, her skill, her kindness—all of it was fake. None of it was real.

Ilana was not real.

22

ILANA WAS RIDING HER BIKE up and down the street in front of my house. I saw her after breakfast, when I was headed back toward the stairs to go up and brush my teeth before going out for the day. I had known her secret for two days, and still didn't feel ready to face her. Back and forth, back and forth she rode, slow and easy. But my heart started beating like a mouse on a wheel, faster and faster until it started to pinch my throat. I was frozen midstep. I pivoted, but what would going back into the kitchen do? Instead I hurried up the stairs and into the bathroom.

I watched myself as I brushed my teeth. I looked at my eyes behind my pink-framed glasses. I barely blinked.

I spit into the sink.

It mattered.

I didn't want it to, but it did.

I kept brushing. My little toothbrush clicked off each tooth as I cleaned it, and when I was done with all twenty-eight, I started over and did them again.

When I spit and rinsed, I still stayed in the bathroom. I organized all my toiletries, lining them up like the trees in the woods—neat little rows. Then I looked at myself in the mirror.

"Coward," I whispered.

Traitor, I thought.

I returned to my room and sat down to go over Agatha's journal again as if it might offer me some sort of guidance.

Prince Philip sat beside the notebook as I flipped through it, occasionally buzzing. I reached out and stroked his head, and he flapped his wings slowly. "You like that, huh?" I had never had a pet before. Theo'd had a dog when we were very little, a yippy sort of a thing, and Benji had a hypoallergenic cat that mostly just sat in patches of sun around the house. Now I had Prince Philip.

I sat up on my bed and looked out the window from time to time. Ilana still rode back and forth.

"You are like her. She is like you." I whispered it to Prince Philip, just to see how it sounded. And the words felt true, though they didn't feel right.

"Mori!" Mom called up, and I swear I jumped. When I looked out the window, Ilana was still there, but her bike was stopped.

"Yeah," I called, too softly for Mom to hear.

"Mori!" she yelled again.

I hopped down from my bed and padded to the top of the stairs. Mom was at the bottom, looking up at me.

"What are you even doing up there?"

"Reading," I said.

"Julia's mom sent a text. They want you to come over to make sun prints. I think that's a terrific idea. It's a beautiful day and you should be outside."

"Oh," I said.

"I told her you'd be right over."

"Oh," I said again.

She took a step onto the bottom landing of the stairs. "Is everything okay? Did you and Julia have a fight?"

"Me and Julia?" I tried to look past her out the window, but I couldn't see anything.

"My best friend and I used to get into fights all the time. Huge blowups." She actually smiled like this was a fantastic memory.

"We're not having a fight," I lied.

"Are you feeling okay, then?" The concerned-mother look took over her face.

"Yes!" I said, perhaps too eagerly.

"Then come on down and get your shoes on. Really, it's far too nice to be inside."

"You're inside."

"You know, I'm going to see if it's possible to dampen sass," she said as she turned to go.

I remained at the top of the stairs, but what could I do? I couldn't hide from Ilana forever. So I hopped down the stairs and shoved my feet into my flip-flops.

With a deep breath, I stepped outside. Ilana was there, but I looked at the ground the whole way down our short driveway and onto the road. I thought maybe she was going to let me just slip by.

"Hey, space shot, over here."

I looked up, and she was smiling at me. That big perfect smile with her bright white teeth all in perfect rows, and both halves of her mouth turning up exactly the same amount, and her green-blue eyes shining just so. "Hey."

"I've been riding back and forth forever. Ninety-seven times, actually."

"That's a lot," I said, still walking toward Julia's.

"I was thinking we could go to Oakedge. We really need to check on our plants. Mr. Quist gave me some special plant food that he makes himself."

My gaze flicked up to her. She had her head tilted to the side. I bet in communications classes when they want to teach you how to look engaged and sympathetic, they would tell you to hold your head just like that. I looked back down at my feet, at my uneven toes. "I'm going to Julia's, actually."

"Oh, yeah? Well, that could be fun, too." She hopped off her bike and started walking next to me as she pushed it.

"I don't think you're invited."

All the while, my brain was thinking, *I know, I know, I know—I know all about you.*

"We could ask."

"No," I said. "It's just something for me and Julia. A best friends sort of a thing."

She stopped walking, and I kept going. My stomach felt like it was falling down straight and deep into some pit I didn't even know I had inside of me.

"'Bye, Mori!" she called, her voice hollow as an old bell.

"'Bye," I called back without looking.

I waited for the sound of her getting on her bike and riding off, but I didn't hear it.

🚲

Julia's mom was already out in their side yard. She had on big sunglasses and Capri pants and a brightly patterned apron. "Hey there, Mori! Sun prints await." She'd brought a card table outside, and there was already a tub of water on it. "I'm so glad you could come over. Julia's feeling better now, and she really wanted to see you."

"She was sick?"

"That's why she wasn't out to play the past two days. She had an ear infection."

"Julia never gets sick."

"It's from all the swimming you kids have been doing. The water was down in the ear canal, and well, she was in some serious pain. Swimmer's ear is what they call it."

As I stepped onto the grass, Julia opened the door, clutching the silver folder of sun paper. Julia's mom patted me on the shoulder, then headed toward the house. When she passed by Julia, she kissed her on the head.

"I'm glad you're feeling better," I said.

"Yeah, it was a killer headache."

"Your mom said it was an ear infection."

Julia clutched the folder of sun paper. "Yeah, I mean, that's what it was. An ear infection, but it gave me the worst headache. But I'm better now."

"Good."

"I think I slept most of yesterday. That's why I wasn't outside. It's a bummer, too, because my mom actually said I could watch the Zane and River *We Are in Love* special, but then I just conked out. Maybe it was the medicine they gave me. Did I miss much out here?"

I suppose I could have told her then what Theo and I had learned. Instead I said, "Nah, nothing much. Same old, same old. I actually spent a lot of time inside reading."

"Not hanging out with Ilana?"

I shook my head. "So, anyway, are we going to get started on these sun prints or what?"

"I'm going to make it look like a fishbowl. And the water will be the blue part and the fish will be white with blue spots, and the outline of the fishbowl is going to be so thin. I'm going to do it with yarn," she exclaimed. "What are you going to do?"

I hadn't really thought of it, but I said, "A flower, I guess."

"Like the ones Theo gave you?" she asked with a grin.

"No," I said. "Well, actually, yes, it probably will be a daisy, but only because that seems easy."

"You could do something spotted for the inside, something perforated, I mean, to get the little dots of the—what's the center of a flower called again?"

I wasn't really listening. I looked over my shoulder. Ilana wasn't back at her house, and of course I couldn't see all the way over to my house, but I pictured her there, standing still as a statue while her mind raced to figure out why I was acting so terribly toward her. I clamped my hand onto my stomach. She had to think I was an awful person, an awful friend. And she wouldn't be wrong, even with what I had discovered about her.

"I said, 'You ready?'" Julia asked.

We crouched down in the shade under the table, and Julia carefully pulled two sheets of golden brown paper from the package. She immediately set to work outlining her fishbowl. She had already cut out a fish and punched holes in it. She was all done, but I was still staring at my paper. "Come on, Mori."

Instead of making a flower, I plucked blades of grass from her lawn and arranged them at the top of the paper. Then I found a wide, flat leaf, which I placed below them.

"What's that?" Julia asked as I put it up on top of the table next to her fish.

"You'll see," I said, with more hope than assurance.

"We can make more than one if you want," Julia said.

I shook my head and so she plopped down on the grass.

"I'm so glad you're here. Just you and me," she said.

"Me too," I agreed.

"I'm sorry if I've been a little, you know, a little crabby."

"More than a little crabby," I said.

"Yeah, you're right. I'm sorry. I'm sorry we fought. I never like to fight with you, and now we've done it twice this summer. I don't like it at all. It makes me feel like someone is shaking me up and down until I'm going to puke."

"Me too," I said. I tucked my hair behind my ear.

"I just was feeling—I felt like she was taking you away from me."

"She wasn't, though," I said, looking down at her as she sat in the grass. It wasn't that Ilana had been pulling me: I went to her. I was the one who had left Julia behind, and so Julia had a right to be mad. "I'm sorry, too."

There was a tennis ball close by, and she picked it up and tossed it to me, an easy-to-catch throw. I caught it and sat down across from her. We passed it back and forth a few times, and I realized that this could be the moment where I cut myself free from Ilana. I didn't know how to deal with what I knew, so maybe it was better, instead of twisting myself into knots, to just walk away. So I said, "She's not exactly who I thought she was."

"Oh?" Julia asked. I knew she was being careful, that she didn't want to push me.

"And maybe . . . ," I began. "Maybe things have gotten bad since she got here." I meant the words as I said them, but also wanted to reel them back in. "It's all been so mixed up, you know. The yellow jackets and the treadmills. And the fighting."

Julia nodded.

"I mean, I don't necessarily think it's her fault. Not necessarily. I'm not saying I don't like her. But, I don't know, I guess maybe—"

"No, I understand. She's not a bad person," Julia said.

She's not a person at all.

"She doesn't fit in," Julia continued. "Once school starts, she'll make all sorts of friends and we won't even feel bad about it. It just feels weird now because she's in our neighborhood and the rest of us are so close."

"Right," I agreed.

"She's not a bad person," Julia said again. "She's just not one of us, you know?"

We stood up to check our prints: everything that wasn't covered had turned nearly white. We brushed off our leaves and paper and grass, and then dunked our papers into the water side by side. "The instructions say to leave them there for one to five minutes."

And so we counted. *One thousand one, one thousand two, one thousand three.*

Julia was right. Ilana just didn't fit in with us. That might be the case even if she wasn't a—whatever she was.

One thousand thirty-four, one thousand thirty-five.

And she probably would make friends at school. There was this group of girls who were a little bit odd, and they always hung around together. Not bad odd, just not like us. They were really smart and driven and made jokes that I never quite understood, but Ilana could. Those girls all lived over on Deer Ridge Road, not too far from us. Ilana could even ride her bike there; it would be no problem for her. And they had a brand-new playground.

One thousand fifty-nine, one thousand sixty.

"What do your parents do at Krita?" I asked.

Julia raised her eyebrows. "You okay in there, Mori? You know my dad does some financial thing and my mom works in sustainability research."

"Right. But what do they really *do*? Like, I know what departments my parents work in. My mom is in fertility, but

is she, like, helping people get pregnant or messing around
with their babies or what?"

"Messing around with their babies?" Julia asked. "What
are you talking about?"

"You know what I mean. Is she changing them
somehow—"

"That's not messing around, Mori. That's designing. It's
totally normal. Unlike you today. What's going on?"

"I just think it's weird that our parents go off to work and
we don't even know what they're doing. Krita is, like, the most
powerful corporation in the world, and we assume they're
doing good, but . . ." Julia continued to frown and I let my
voice trail off. We were veering into rocky waters again, and
I didn't want to have another fight right after we had gotten
back together. "I've just been thinking about all of this lately,
about Krita and what all of us are going to do there."

"If you must know, my mom is trying to figure out how
to get more energy out of poop. I kid you not. Poop power is
what my mom does."

I laughed in spite of myself. "Don't let her hear you call
it poop."

"Seriously." Julia grinned. "It's like, 'fecal matter as energy
operative blah blah blah.' You really don't want to go down
that road. There's this other person in her lab who's trying to
figure out a way to use nanotechnology coatings to produce
solar power. That's kind of cool."

"Sure," I agreed.

"And helpful. If that's what you're worried about—being helpful—there's lots of jobs where you could make the world a better place."

"I know." I tried to keep exasperation from edging into my voice.

"And I guess it makes sense that you're thinking about what we're going to be when we grow up because of the latencies and all. But you know you really are just supposed to think about your talents and your testing and all that, and not worry too much about what job you might end up with."

"I wasn't thinking of me or my latency; it was just, like—well, seeing all those projects on the computer at number nine. I guess I didn't realize that we did that sort of thing in Old Harmonie."

"Artificial intelligence?"

"No, like, creating a whole new consciousness. Like that girl, Victoria. You don't think that was crossing a line at all?"

I heard the squeal of a bike braking and wondered if it was Ilana, and if she could see us sitting here all cozy together.

"I don't know, Mori. That's why we have the ethics department, right? To make those decisions."

"I guess."

"Really," she assured me, but she was looking past me, and I figured she was trying to stay patient, too. When she ran the end of her braid over her lips, I knew for sure: she was getting tired of this conversation.

Still, I pushed a little more, "Sometimes people make mistakes, don't you think? They get all caught up in what they're doing and don't see the big picture."

She tugged on the end of her braids. "But that's why Krita has all the systems in place, Mori. Krita takes care of everything. It's what keeps Old Harmonie running and what keeps us safe."

"Yeah, but—"

Julia looked back at me and softened her face. "That's what you should do! For your latency! Something related to ethics. Do you think that would be problem solving or puzzles?"

"I'm not sure."

"Me either," she said with a shrug, and I guess the conversation was over because then she asked, "Do you think that's enough time?"

"Your parents need to dampen your impatience," I said, because it was a whole lot easier—and safer—than trying to talk about these things with her. She didn't see any problem with Krita or Old Harmonie. Me, I was feeling more and more like Agatha Varden—weary and wary.

Julia laughed. "I just had this idea last night, and I really want it to work. I'm going to add some glitter, I think."

"But then it's not really a sun print," I said. "You might as well have just drawn the fishbowl and added some glitter."

Julia thought about that for a minute. "I guess you're right. I do kind of like glitter, though."

"Me too," I agreed. "I bet they're done."

We pulled out our papers. Julia's was perfect. Her fishbowl and fish were crisp and clear. Mine looked like a tree caught in a storm.

"That's nice," she said.

It wasn't, but I thought it was kind of her to lie for me.

"I'm glad we agreed," I said. "About Ilana, I mean."

"Me too."

"It's better this way."

And as long as I told myself that, again and again, I could drown out the voice that was calling me a traitor, the type of person who would abandon a friend just when things got hard.

23

WE MET AT THE PLAYGROUND in the morning. It had been my idea to start doing that, but I hadn't told them why. I bet Theo knew, though, since I first suggested it so soon after he and I found out about Ilana, and we'd been doing it for almost a week. I didn't want her to see us, didn't want her to invite herself over to Julia's or Theo's. It's like I wanted to erase her from my life.

She rode her bike by us a few times the first couple of days, but didn't stop. I saw her go over to the Collinses' and help with the younger twins. They climbed all over her like she was a toy, which, in a way, I supposed she was.

But that first Tuesday in August it was blisteringly hot. "Pool," Julia said. "Must have pool."

I didn't want to risk running into Ilana until I figured out how to talk to her, how to look into her not-really-real eyes, but Julia was right. It was too hot to be anywhere but in her swimming pool.

When we parked our bikes, Julia's mom was across the street, talking to Ilana's mom. Meryl had her hair wrapped in a scarf with threads of silver and gold wound through it. They glittered in the sun, making Julia's mom—always so perfectly dressed—look dowdy in comparison. Julia's mom had her hand up on her forehead, shielding her eyes from the sun. She was nodding, but her body was tense, and turned a bit away from Ilana's mom. Then Ilana's mom leaned over and hugged her, which seemed strange, especially given the heat. Julia's mom crossed the street, heading straight for us.

"Ilana's coming over," she said. "You can go in the pool. I'll make sandwiches."

"Mom—" Julia began. I wondered what she was going to say. *We don't like her anymore. We aren't friends.* But Julia didn't get a chance to say anything else.

Her mom said, "I don't like hearing that you guys are leaving someone out. That's not the way we act in Old Harmonie."

"But—" Julia tried again.

"You know what Steve Jobs believed?" Julia's mom asked, and Julia rolled her eyes. Her mom was always quoting Steve Jobs. "He believed it was the weird ones, the odd ducks, those are the people who changed the world." She looked across the street, and some sort of worry fluttered across her face, but then she trained her gaze right on me. "You should know that better than anyone, Mori."

I felt myself go hot. Was Julia's mom calling me weird? "Uh-huh," I said.

"Dr. Varden and your great-grandmother, back at the beginning, they thought of themselves as odd ducks. The world didn't quite know what to make of them, but this was their place. And they changed the world. They made history."

I looked at the ground.

"So go swim," she said. "Ilana will be over in a minute."

We trudged back to the pool.

"I can't believe her mother talked to mine. What a loser," Julia said.

"I guess maybe she's lonely," Benji said. He hopped from slate tile to slate tile on the path.

"Whatever, I still think it's stupid."

Theo didn't say anything and neither did I. I just felt sick to my stomach. Sick about what Julia's mom had said, and sick about seeing Ilana.

Julia and I tucked into the little pool house. I kept a spare bathing suit there, and shimmied out of my clothes to change into it.

"You think it's stupid, don't you?" Julia asked. "That she had her mom do the talking instead of just coming to see us. We never said she couldn't come with us to the playground. We never left her out. She left herself out."

I yanked the straps of my bathing suit up over my shoulders. "I guess," I said. Then: "Maybe. I don't know."

Julia huffed, but she didn't say anything. She grabbed her goggles from a peg on the wall, and a moment later I heard a splash that I assumed was her diving into the water. I kept my goggles in a special case by the door. I carried them out, took my glasses off, and was pulling on my goggles when Ilana came down the path. She was only wearing her bathing suit, brightly striped in orange and yellow. "Hiya, Mori!" she said. Julia was doing handstands in the water, or I bet Ilana would have said a cheery hello to her, too.

"Hi," I mumbled, then hurried into the pool. The water was sweet relief.

I grabbed a couple of pool noodles and hung on them. Theo and Benji came out of the pool house in their swim trunks. Benji lowered himself down onto the stairs. "Ah," he sighed. "Pool, have I ever told you how much I love you?"

Theo did a cannonball into the deep end that sent little waves the length of the pool. Right after him, Ilana jumped in with a sleek can opener. They traded jumps for a while, each one a bit more elaborate than the last: spins, straddles, backward dives. Then Ilana ran and did a forward flip in the air, diving deep across the water and popping up near me. "Hi, Mori," she said again. She had her huge smile on her face, the one that crinkled her eyes.

My heart felt lighter just to see her, and for a second it was like nothing had changed. I felt myself smiling back at her. "Hi," I said. Maybe nothing had changed. Maybe it was all in my head.

"So," Benji said, leaning back and looking up at the sun. "The 'rents are bugging me about my latency, and I want some idea of what I'm thinking before I go in for my final testing next month." Benji was one of the oldest in our grade. His birthday was in the fall, so he was going to have to make his choice before school started.

"What do you think you want?" I asked.

Benji glanced over at Ilana. "I have many intellectual strengths," he said. "I'm good at designing and building and implementing. Then of course there are mathematics, computer science, and—"

"We get it, Benji," Theo said. "You're amazing. You probably don't even need a latency. Your genius is already wild and running free."

"True that," Benji said. "Still, everyone has a latency, and I plan on picking a good one. I'm really leaning toward the mechanical." He turned back to Ilana. "I designed a skateboard ramp that measures your velocity, the torque on the wheels, the air you got—any measurement you can think of. My parents won't let me build it, but if I did, it would be way coolio."

"It sounds like it," she said. "Way, way coolio."

"And I had this internship in a lab where they put these computer chips into mice—"

"Why?" she interrupted.

"It's a long story, but the point is I realized that there was a hiccup in the system, you know, in relaying the data, and I designed a fix. They practically wanted to hire me on the spot."

"Benji's mother doesn't believe in dampening, or else she definitely would've put the reins on his modesty," Julia said, splashing water at Benji. "It's just so sad how he thinks so poorly of himself."

"He doesn't think poorly of himself," Ilana replied. "In fact, he seems to have a very healthy ego for a small pre-teen boy."

"Joking," Julia said. "And whoa, weirdness."

"And I'm not exactly small," Benji said. "I'm definitely in the average range. The small side of average, but still totally normal."

I did not want this to dissolve into more of Ilana being pushed out of our circle, so I turned to Theo. "What was it like when you got yours?" I hadn't brought it up all sum-mer, not since he'd been so cruel the day after it had been done. I was afraid just mentioning it would relight that angry spark.

"It's like a regular doctor's appointment. You go in, and they scan you. And then you just lie down, and they put you to sleep, and when you wake up, it's done."

"That's it?" I asked.

"I had a terrible headache," he said. He held on to the side of the pool. "And I had weird dreams, I remember that. Like, all of Firefly Lane was being sucked into this big sinkhole. It was bottomless, and the trees were going down it roots and all, and the houses, too, and I knew I had to get out. And I knew I had to find—" He stopped himself. Then he took a deep breath. "I had to find Mori and I had to find Benji."

"What about Julia? Or your mom?" I asked.

"I guess I knew they were okay. It was a dream. It didn't have to make sense."

"Trust me, Theo, only in your dreams would you ever need to rescue me," Julia said.

"And then what about after?" I asked.

"Well, I guess I was a little cranky."

"Just a little?" Julia scoffed.

He ignored her. "And tired. And hungry. Man, I was so hungry, I thought I could eat everything out of the delivery van and let the whole rest of the neighborhood starve. And here's what was really weird: after, they had me solving all these logic puzzles to see how it worked. And my mind would pull one way, and then it was like someone else stepped in and yanked me back the other way. They had to go in and do some adjustments."

"Adjustments?"

"Yeah, just getting the levels right. That's what the doctor said. The latency is really a dampening, you know. They dampen certain areas in the left side of your brain so your right side isn't hindered at all. And sometimes they just make a little error of calculation. That's why I had to go back a couple of times. There were a few more adjustments than normal. It's fine now, but that's why I was so, you know, so—anyway, I'm sorry about that."

"I don't think I need a latency, either," Ilana said.

I coughed into the water. Of course she didn't need a latency. She was already constructed to be perfect, and I bet they could adjust her at any time, probably from some big central command at Krita.

"Sure, Ilana," Julia said.

"Anyway," Theo said. "Benji, did you hear that they might be getting a skate park over in Fruitlands?"

"What? No way. No. Way."

I dunked my head underwater. It was easier than lying. Lying to Benji and Julia about Ilana. Lying to Ilana about what I knew. I felt my hair swirling around my face and shoulders. With both hands, I pushed it away, and opened my eyes. There was Ilana, staring right back at me. Her green-blue eyes were lovely, even underwater, maybe even more so.

And then, like someone turning off a switch, her eyes closed, and she started sinking down. Her arms and her hair drifted up as her body slipped down and down and down. I thought it was a game, like she was trying to scare me, like when she'd jumped off the swing set. But she'd promised me then that she would never frighten me again. Not on purpose. And even with all the things that had changed, I knew she would never break a promise to me.

I swam to her and tugged on her arm. She barely moved.

My own lungs were starting to get tight.

I pushed on her, but she didn't open her eyes, didn't flinch.

My lungs screamed.

I wanted her to open her eyes to look at me, for the light to flash back on, but she just sank lower and lower.

Hooking my arms under hers, I kicked and dragged Ilana to the surface of the water. My fingers pressed into the skin by her shoulders, soft and firm as warm clay. My small fingers barely registered. I was surprised by her weight, the heft of her. It was like pulling a bucket through the water.

When I burst through to the fresh air, I coughed out for help. I'm not sure who pulled her from the water. Julia and Benji, maybe. The light of the sun was so bright in my eyes, and colors danced around the edges of my vision. Theo grabbed me by the wrist and tugged me to the side of the pool. "You okay?" he demanded between heavy breaths.

I didn't answer. I watched as Julia tilted Ilana's chin back. Drops of water spilled from Ilana's hair and onto the pool deck. One clung to the side of her face. "Benji, go get help!" Julia cried. I laughed, I think. It was just like in our first-aid classes. The teacher said you should always designate one person to go for help, or else no one might go, and we had always done it in such an exaggerated fashion. And now, here it was, for real, with Julia's lips forming the words so carefully, and Benji springing to his feet.

"Mori, are you okay?" Theo asked again. I managed to nod. He still had his hand on my arm, and I wasn't sure if it was to stop me from slipping underwater, or to keep me from going over to Ilana.

Julia placed her mouth on Ilana's, and the ends of her braids fell down onto Ilana's face. Did it tickle? Can you feel anything when the breath has gone out of you? Julia blew a stream of air that inflated Ilana's lungs. Pause. Then again. And again.

From the house, I heard a screen door slam shut, and then there was Julia's mom running down the path with Benji right behind, throwing open the fence to the pool.

"Here!" Benji called, and spread his arms wide as if we had created this tableau just for Julia's mother.

"It's Ilana," I said. "She—"

"I'm fine."

I swiveled my head back. Ilana was sitting up on the deck of the pool. The drop of water still clung to her cheek and she brushed it away. Her hair, heavy with water, seemed so much longer than usual, like a dark river going down her back. I raked my own hair out of my face. Next to me, Theo breathed hard. Julia still kneeled beside Ilana.

"What happened?" Julia's mom demanded.

"I'm fine," Ilana said again.

Julia's mom looked at her daughter, then at Ilana, then at me, but none of us said a word.

Ilana didn't want to go home, so I brought her to my house. Mom was sitting outside waiting for us. "Julia's mother told me what happened, Ilana. Are you sure you wouldn't be more comfortable at your house?"

"No, I'm fine. Thanks, though."

"I could run a quick scan."

Ilana cocked her head to the side. "I don't think that's necessary. Do you?"

"No, I suppose not."

We walked upstairs and down the hall. "So this is my room," I said. "I guess you've never been in here before."

She spun around to see it all, then picked up a small trophy on my desk.

"It's for soccer. Everyone got one for something. Mine was for stick-to-it-iveness."

"That's not even a word."

"Julia got MVP."

"Of course. And now that she's had her latency released—"

"No, she hasn't. She's not thirteen yet."

Ilana raised an eyebrow. "Every rule can be flexed, Mori."

She put the trophy down and picked up a thick binder from my desk. It had all my drawings in it, carefully organized by genus and species. She opened it, and her face softened into a smile. "Is this what you were telling me about? How you were cataloging everything in Oakedge?"

I nodded.

"It's really good, Mori."

"No," I said. "The drawings are so shaky. No one but me could even tell what they are."

"I can tell," she said. She turned the book so I could see. "That's a pink lady's-slipper."

"It says it right underneath."

"But I can tell anyway. See how you got the way it bends down toward the ground? It's a humble, beautiful flower, don't you think?"

I had never thought of the flower that way, but when she said it, I knew she was right.

"They almost went extinct, you know," she said. "They take a long time to grow, and they need this special fungus in the soil, so people would dig them up, but then they wouldn't grow, not outside of their natural habitat."

"I didn't know that," I told her.

"So we're lucky that they belong in Oakedge."

"I guess so."

Ilana put down the binder and looked at the holopics I had on a shelf above my desk. There were a lot of me and Julia, of course. My favorite was one we'd taken with Theo and Benji the summer before. We were all on the jungle gym at the playground. Theo stood up at the top with his arms above his head. Benji held on with one hand and had one foot on another bar, while his other arm and leg were stuck out to the side. He said it was like a skateboard trick he was going to learn. Julia hung by her knees so that her braids fell straight down toward the ground. I was sitting in one of the spaces toward the bottom. There'd been a time when I'd loved the top, too, but now the old thing seemed too wobbly and frail to risk it. We all had goofy smiles and it was clear we were as happy as could be.

That was before Ilana.

She looked back over her shoulder. "We need to get a picture of me and you. Maybe out in Oakedge."

"Maybe," I said. I picked up Prince Philip and put him on the windowsill so he could look out.

"We really should get out there tomorrow and check on the garden."

"I'll see if I can."

"Oh wait, shoot."

She sounded just like herself. Her old self. It made my head hurt to think about. "What?" I asked.

"I just remembered I have a doctor's appointment tomorrow. I had it before this even happened. I went last week and they need me to come again this week."

"Why?" I asked.

She shook her head. "I'm not sure. Do you think you could come with me?"

"Would they let me?"

"I don't know. Never mind. It was stupid—"

"No, I want to go. I just never thought of having a friend come to the doctor's office with me. But get me in the morning. I'll go."

"Okay."

"Promise?"

"Promise."

But she didn't come.

Theo found me waiting on her front step. "Hey," he said as he came up the driveway. He looked like he'd just taken a shower, and his hair, for once, was combed out of his eyes.

"Hey," I said back.

"So," he said. "Yesterday was pretty weird, huh?"

"If we had told her, Julia wouldn't have saved her. She'd be dead."

"I don't know if she can really die." He looked up at the house, then held out his hand to help me to my feet. We started walking back to his house. The sun was already beating down on us, and the air felt like molasses. It was going to be another miserable day.

"But Julia gave her mouth-to-mouth. And it saved her. She *breathes*."

"Respiration would be about the easiest thing for the AI people to re-create."

"I pulled her out of the water without thinking. Once my brain caught up, I thought, *This is silly. They'll just reboot her. She'll be better than ever.* If I had thought for even a second, I wouldn't have bothered. I would have let her drown."

"But you didn't, Mori."

"I think we were wrong about her, Theo. Maybe they did create her, but that doesn't mean she isn't real."

"Do you think we should go back to number nine and try to find out more about her? We can't really solve this until we have all the pieces, and there's probably more information in that computer."

Just the thought of booting up that computer made my stomach sour. "I think I'm going to go home, actually," I told him.

"Okay, sure," he said.

I turned, but then he said, "There was something else I wanted to tell you. About yesterday."

I pivoted back around to look at him, but he stared down at his sneakers.

"I don't mean to be so cranky, you know. I asked them to dampen it. My temper. But they said I needed it. They said the temper was tied to quick thinking, and that was part of the problem solving and puzzles."

"*You* asked them?"

"I say things sometimes." As he spoke, his fingers drummed against his leg. "I say them and it's like—" He blushed and looked down.

"What?"

"It's stupid, but it's like I can see the words coming out like speech bubbles in a cartoon, and I want to just cross them out, you know? I don't mean the things I say. Not always." He looked right at me. "I didn't mean the things I said in the playground that day after my latency. I never thought that about you."

I reached out and put my hand on his arm and his fingers stopped drumming. He looked at the hand there, my skinny fingers on his tanned skin.

Then he smiled and said, "Well, except for what I say about Benji. That kid really can be a numb nut."

I checked him lightly with my hip. "Thanks for telling me, Theo."

"I just wanted you to know."

My hand was still on his arm. It felt both strange and natural at the same time. "I'll see you later," I told him.

"Sure, okay."

"And I'm going to try. With Ilana, I'm going to try. I hope you will, too."

He looked up at me, right in the eye. "I will, Mori. I promise."

24

THE NEXT MORNING, THE SKY was bright red. I was up early enough to see the sunrise, and it burned the sky.

I padded down the stairs and into the kitchen. No one was up yet. We had some quinoa-cranberry muffins in the fridge, ready to go into the Jetsonator. I wasn't supposed to use it on my own, but it was just a simple machine. I removed the package of muffins from the refrigerator and read the instructions twice before I put the tray into the side of the oven.

Watching and waiting was boring, and my mind wandered. I wondered if things really had been better before Ilana came, but everything that had happened had been coincidences. She didn't put the yellow jacket nest in the field near number 9. She didn't cause the mumps outbreak. What she had done was be a good friend to me. What she had done was listen to me about the forest, to share that with me, and to create Oakedge.

The Jetsonator kept ticking.

Theo could be right: maybe she hadn't been in Calliope at all. She always had to think for a minute before she could tell you about it, like she was accessing her storage banks to pull out the information. So she had been in the lab. Just this girl alone in the lab. At night, did they turn all the lights off? Did she sleep? Did she know what she was?

I remembered what I had whispered to Prince Philip, that he and Ilana were the same. Both creations. Both programmable. But maybe Ilana had been designed to be more than that. She had been created to be *like* a person. To have ideas and feelings. To dream. She had told me about her dream, the one where she found the clearing in the woods and made friends with the animals. But if she was constructed, were all of those things constructions, too? Did they give her that dream just so she could share it with me and we would become friends? And so what if she had been designed that way? We'd always been told it didn't matter how people were put together—natural or designed—so why should Ilana be any different?

The muffins popped out the other side of the Jetsonator. With a potholder, I tugged the hot metal tray out of the oven.

Once they cooled, I cut one muffin in half and spread cream cheese on both sides, then I sat in the picture window looking out over the lawn while I ate.

Mom came down first. She looked at the muffins on the kitchen counter, then looked over at me. "Mori," she said. My name hung in the air between us. But then her face softened, and she said, "Thanks for making breakfast." She took her coffee mug from the machine on the counter, pre-programmed to be ready when she came downstairs, then sat at the kitchen table.

I moved over to eat with her. "Are you still upset about what happened with Ilana?" she asked.

I was still upset about Ilana, that much was true. But I couldn't tell my mom the whole truth of it. She rubbed at the corner of her eye and then took a sip from her coffee. "Mori, I'm not sure," she began. Then she shook her head.

"What?" I asked.

From upstairs, we heard a *thunk*. Mom said, "Dad fell asleep with a book again. There's going to be a dent in the floor from all those books dropping, eventually."

"What were you going to say?" I asked.

She broke a piece off her muffin and then broke that piece in half. "You're a good friend is all."

"I'm not, though."

"You are. Some people . . ." She took a long sip of her coffee. "Some people are just harder than others—it's a different kind of friendship. Or friendship has its ups and downs. Like you and Julia. You were always together, then this summer you started hanging out with someone else, and now you're spending time together again. It all evens out. It will happen with Ilana, too."

I had no idea what she was trying to tell me, but just then Dad came clomping into the room in his day-off attire.

"Mori made us breakfast," Mom said.

"Oh, yeah?" he asked. He looked at her and looked at me, then back at her as if asking if they really were okay with me using the Jetsonator after all.

"Yep," she said. "Terrific muffins."

"Terrific indeed," Dad said. "Maybe you can make dinner tonight and I'll set up the hammock for a snooze."

"I wouldn't take it that far," Mom said. She stood and kissed both Dad and me on our cheeks, then went upstairs to finish getting ready for the day.

"How's our hero this morning?" he asked. "Plans to rescue anyone today?"

I shook my head, and I guess my face must have looked panicked, because he said, "Oh, hey, I'm just kidding." He took a big bite of his muffin. "These muffins really are good, Mori. You did a great job."

"I didn't make them," I said. "I just put the tray into the machine. It wasn't hard. Anyone could do it."

"I think they taste extra good today."

"You're just saying that."

"No, really, they're lighter than usual. More airy and moist."

"Dad!" I said, standing up. "They're not made by us, by anyone. Every single family that's having these muffins today, they all taste the exact same. The exact flavor. The exact texture. The exact nutritional value."

"Hey there, honey, what's this about?"

I shook my head and said, "Nothing. I need to go." I stomped out the front door, and when I turned to shut it, I saw Mom at the top of the stairs, but I didn't say anything to her. I hadn't meant to blow up at my dad, but he was just making a big stinking deal about those stupid muffins and all I'd done was press a button. I didn't know the first thing about making a muffin. There were cranberries and quinoa, but other than that I didn't have a clue what you would use to make muffin batter. They were little factory-formed nutrition-delivery systems as far as I was concerned.

I had turned right out of my house, heading toward Julia's, but I stopped in front of Ilana's. I had told Theo I was going to try, and that's just what I was going to do. So I marched myself up to the door and rang the bell. As if she'd been waiting for me, she threw open the door and said, "My hero!"

"Don't," I said.

"Okay, but you are. You really are my hero."

"Don't," I said again. How could I tell her that if I had thought for even half a second, she would still be at the bottom of the pool.

"Okay. Want to go to Oakedge?"

I hesitated. "No. Let's just go over to Theo's." I wanted to keep my promise to try, but I wasn't sure I was ready to be alone with her.

Julia and I lay side by side in the grass outside Theo's house. The sun warmed our skin and made us sweat just a little bit. Theo himself was shooting baskets on the driveway with Ilana. Benji was with them, but then trotted over and sat beside us. "This is boring," Benji said. "Let's go swimming or down to the park. I've finally mastered the ollie, and I can show you all."

I was perfectly happy just lying in the sun next to Julia, but she sat up and said, "If I sit still for even one more second, I think all my muscles will turn to mush and you'll have to push me around in a wheelchair for the rest of my days."

Theo sank one more shot, then grabbed his bike, so I guessed that meant we were all going. Ilana dawdled to get ready. The rest of us were astride our bikes, and Benji had already pushed off on his skateboard and was heading around the block.

"You coming?" I asked. Part of me hoped she would say no. Maybe Mom was right and what we needed was a little more time. And then things would smooth over between Ilana and me, and we could pick up where we left off. Eventually I wouldn't feel so weird around her.

"You can wait here, if you want," Julia told her.

Ilana looked at me. "No, it's fine. I'll go."

Benji waited for us in front of number 9. "We need some honey to fortify us," he said, and started down the path.

"Just honey?" I asked. I didn't want Julia and Benji to get back on the computer, especially not with Ilana there.

"Sure," he said, looking over his shoulder. "Unless you want to try some of those pickled eggs."

I wrinkled my nose, and Theo said, "I dare you to eat one, Benji."

"No way, no how," he said.

"I don't know," Ilana said. "It's such a nice day, don't you think? We should stay outside. Enjoy this sunshine."

"In and out," Benji said. He was stopped on the path, waiting for us. "It's a honey extraction mission."

Ilana was right: it was a nice day. There'd been a quick thunderstorm the night before that had broken up the heat and humidity. Now the clouds in the sky were the big, white, puffy ones that looked like cotton candy, placed there so kids would have the game of finding shapes in them, no matter if Theo thought it was just our minds needing to tell a story.

"Come on," Benji said.

We rode our bikes down the driveway of number 9 a bit so they would be less visible from the road. The shutter that had hung precariously for so long had finally given up and now lay on the ground, a black rectangle on the pale green grass.

When I got off my bike, Ilana stepped in front of me. "I'll get you some honey," she told me.

"I just want a little taste," I said.

"I'll bring a jar out for you."

"It's fine, I'll just—"

"I said I'll get it." Ilana's voice dropped at least an octave. "Stay outside."

"I like the house," I told her, which was still true. I just didn't like the robot room, or what we'd found on the computer. "Anyway, I want to grab another one of Agatha's journals. She writes about Baba in them."

Ilana stepped closer to me. "You stay out here. I can get one for you."

"What is your problem?" Julia asked her. "Mori says she wants to go in. Let her go in."

But Ilana reached out and grabbed my arm. Hard. "You shouldn't go in there. It's not safe."

"We've gone in before, Ilana. It's fine," Benji told her.

I tried to pull my arm free, and Ilana's grip tightened. Her fingers were so long, they reached almost all the way around my biceps, and I could feel each one pressing into my flesh. "Ilana."

"You won't go in."

"You're hurting me!" I tugged back again, and she gripped still harder, like those dogs whose jaws lock down the more you pull against them. I could feel tears welling, but I didn't want anyone to see. "Ilana, please."

"No."

Her eyes were different. Darker.

"Ilana," I said softly.

She blinked, but before she could let go, Theo crashed his body into hers, knocking her off me. She stumbled backward, toward Julia and Benji.

"You can't go in there!" Ilana yelled, and moved toward me again, but Julia grabbed her, holding her back.

None of us spoke, but we were not silent. Ilana's breaths came heavy and hard as she struggled against Julia, who grunted with the effort of holding her. Theo's breath, too, was fast, and I swear I could hear his heart beating as he stood just in front of me, blocking Ilana's path to me. Benji had gasped when Julia grabbed Ilana, and now he slowly let his air out. His foot tapped an uneven pattern against the grass. And me, I was crying like the baby I was.

Ilana looked past Theo straight at me. Her whole face softened, and then she yanked herself away from Julia, grabbed her bike, and rode away.

"Ilana!" I yelled after her. "Ilana, wait!"

Ilana left a bruise on my arm that I couldn't hide. It started to form right away. First it was just red marks, but the red gave way to a pale purple, and I knew it would be dark by that night.

"What am I going to tell my parents?" I asked, staring at the finger marks. One, two, three, four thin lines, and one from the thumb underneath.

"The truth," Julia said.

I looked over at Benji, who looked away.

"She didn't mean to do it," I said.

"She didn't mean to grab your arm and squeeze so hard it made you cry?" Julia asked.

"I wasn't crying because of that."

We were sitting out behind number 9, close to the bulkhead, but we hadn't gone in. Above us, the old power line swung back and forth.

"I wonder why she didn't want you to go in," Benji asked. "I mean, there was, like, no way she was going to let you into this house."

"Maybe she beat someone up and hid the body in there." Julia picked up a rock and threw it against the bulkhead door. The metal *clang* rang out around us.

"Not funny," I said.

"You have to tell," Theo said. He was sitting right next to me. He yanked some tufts of grass out of the ground. "I'm sorry, but you have to."

"There was something wrong. I just don't know what it was. But I know she wouldn't hurt me unless she thought it was helping me."

"That is messed up," Julia said. "She's hurting you to protect you? How does that make any sense? You wouldn't even treat an animal that way, let alone your friend."

She was right. I knew that. And yet I couldn't shake the panic I'd seen in Ilana's eyes.

"It wasn't like this before," Benji said softly. "I hate to say it, but it wasn't this crazy before, with people fighting and getting hurt. Before Ilana came, that didn't happen."

He wouldn't look at me.

"It's a coincidence," I said. But even to myself I didn't sound too convincing.

I heard something in the grass behind me. Maybe it was a slithering snake. Maybe it was nothing. I looked straight at Julia. "Have you had your latency yet?"

"What?" she asked. But her face turned red right away. "I'm too young. You know that."

"Was it one of the spatials? Mind-body awareness, is that what it is? I know it has to be sports related."

"I haven't done it yet."

"Just tell me the truth," I said.

She looked down. "We aren't talking about me right now."

"Otherwise you wouldn't have been able to grab her and hold her, I don't think."

"It's not strength. That's not a latency."

"No, but still—" I began.

"So what if she has?" Theo asked. "She's right. The problem here is Ilana."

"No, the problem is how everyone is reacting to her. She's a better athlete than Julia, so Julia's parents let her get her latency done early. That's against the rules. Order, remember. We have to have order."

"It's just a couple of months early," Julia said. "I was on track to be one of the first anyway, since I'm so tall and already started puberty."

"TMI, Julia. Like totally," Benji said, trying to lighten the mood. It didn't work.

"It wasn't because of Ilana. After the fitness test, the trainers said I was ready."

"After the fitness test. When Ilana was beating you."

"Until she made us all crash," Julia said. "Another example of how she's just ruining everything."

"She's not ruining everything," Benji said. "I feel a little bad for her, actually. I mean, she came to this new neighborhood all the way from Calliope. Everything's new and different for her. She's having some trouble adjusting."

Theo took my hand and lifted my arm. "This is not trouble adjusting," he said. Then he turned to me. "If you're not going to tell your parents, I will."

Everyone looked at me, but what could I say? My parents would see the finger marks. If I lied, I would only be implicating someone else, someone innocent. It's not like I could say I'd done it to myself.

"I'm getting more journals," I said. "So if you could help me open the door, Theo, that would be great."

"Sure, Mori," he said. "Of course."

We lifted the bulkhead together. It was at an angle since he had most of the weight. When we put it down, he offered me a hand to go down the stairs, but I didn't take it. I went down into the deep of the basement, the cool air surrounding me and cutting me off from the heat above. *Put the door back on*, I wanted to call up. They could just put the top on and leave me there. I could live in that house all by myself, just like Agatha had. I'd shut the door to the creepy room with all the old robot parts and make a home for myself in the rest of the house.

"Mori," Theo called down. "You okay?"

"Fine," I called back. It was a lie.

25

BENJI CAME WITH ME TO tell my parents. We hung out
at his house until my mom got home from work. I wore one
of his sweatshirts, and his sister said, "Don't you know it's
summer?" Benji told her to shut up.

"It was an accident," I assured them as I slipped my arm
from my sleeve. Dad's eyes grew wide and Mom put her hand
on her lips.

"Ilana?" she said.

I don't know how they knew. Julia would have been
strong enough to do it. Or Theo. Or any of the adults on our
cul-de-sac, for that matter.

"We were going to go back into number nine, and she
stopped me."

"Number nine?" Dad asked.

"You've been going there?" Mom asked. "For fun?"

"Just exploring, you know. Being curious?"

"There's honey there," Benji said. "Delicious, delicious honey."

She clapped her hands over her mouth. "Is that where you were? When you were stung?"

I lowered my head. "Yellow jackets don't make honey."

"Mori, you lied to us?" She seemed confused by it.

"I didn't lie. I just—"

"Went along with what your friends said." She bit her lip.

Benji lowered his head. "I'm sorry," he mumbled.

Mom stood up and paced the floor in front of our mantel. Her sake set looked a little off-kilter. "Mori, you can't lie to us. Or hide the truth. We need to— It's part of keeping you safe, you know?"

"Okay," I said slowly. "I just, by the time I got to talk to you, you already thought I'd been in the woods. And anyway, we don't go by the yellow jackets anymore. We know where they are."

"What about the snakes?"

"There's a path through the grass." I didn't tell her how Theo and I had almost stepped on one.

"You can't go there ever again."

I hesitated.

"Mori."

Dad cleared his throat. "So Ilana grabbed you?" he asked, getting back to the first of the awful subjects.

"I really don't think she meant to grab me so hard. Something's happened to her. I really think she was trying to protect me."

"It was all kind of crazy," Benji said. "But we were there with her, and Ilana let her go."

"And then did you go into the house?"

I shook my head. Lie by body gesture.

They didn't say anything else about it. They just sat there for a little while, as if the information was sinking through their skin and into their brains. Finally Mom said, "Why don't you two go outside and enjoy the sunshine. It's a beautiful day."

"Sure," Benji said for both of us. "That sounds like fun."

But all we did was sit on the lawn and pick buttercups. Benji held one under my chin, but I wasn't up for games. I said, "You know, in beehives, there are guard bees, and they stand at the door of the hive, and they use smell to know which bees belong there and which bees don't."

Benji leaned over and sniffed me. "You belong."

I sniffed him back. "You, too."

I wanted to sleep in my tent, but my parents said no, and I didn't argue that it was the perfect night for tent sleeping—

the Perseids meteor showers would even be starting. I was sick of arguing and fighting, and I knew they wouldn't change their minds, not after the day we'd had.

So instead I lay in my bed on my stomach and looked out my window. I took Prince Philip out of the box I kept him in and put him on the sill so he could look with me. He gave a little buzz. "Today was just . . . confusing."

He batted his wings as if agreeing with me.

The moon was full, and it rained its light down over our whole block.

I hadn't written about the day in my journal. I didn't know what to say, didn't have the words to describe it.

And this was definitely a day that I would be happy to lose.

My arm still hurt, a throbbing reminder of what had happened. Not that I needed it. When I closed my eyes, all I could see was Ilana staring back at me. What was it that she didn't want me to see in there? What did she think would happen to me?

I put my chin on my fists. Prince Philip buzzed closer to me. "Do you miss your friends?" I asked him. At one time, there had been hundreds of these robobees built in the Krita labs. "Do you even remember you had friends?"

Outside, something moved and caught my eye. A fox? We had those sometimes, prowling around the edges of the neighborhood. But no, it was much bigger. A bear? Once these woods had been full of them. But no, it was much smaller than a bear, I thought.

I stared out into the shadows and silver light. Then I saw her. Ilana. Making her way down the street in fits and starts as she raced through the light to the shadows.

What's she doing out there?

What's she up to?

But who was I to be suspicious? I liked a nighttime walk. Maybe she just wanted to go out to the woods to the fence, too. Or somewhere else. Somewhere all her own.

"I could follow her," I said to Prince Philip. He didn't respond. "Or not."

I ought to let her be, I thought. Let her figure out what she needs to figure out. I was glad to see her, though. I was glad to see she was okay. But I couldn't follow her and I probably couldn't be her friend anymore, not after what she had done to me. It was time to let her go.

26

"THOSE ARE FUNNY CLOUDS," BENJI said. He and Theo and I were walking back to our houses for lunch after a swim at Julia's. Benji was right about the clouds. They looked like a stack of blankets, one on top of the other, each a slightly different shade of gray.

"Storm coming," I guessed. "I love a good thunderstorm."

Theo glanced over at me. "Really? I would've figured they scared you."

"I'm no fraidy cat," I said, my voice sharp.

"Hey, sorry," he said.

We were passing in front of his house when we heard the *woo-woo* of the alarm siren. I felt my eyes go wide. We had thunderstorms all the time with no alarms. "It has to be a drill," I said.

Theo grabbed Benji and me and dragged us into his house, where he finally said, "Why would we have a drill so soon after the real thing?"

"Maybe this storm is worse than it looks," Benji said. "Or maybe another outbreak?"

"Ugh, I'll be stuck inside for another week." I moaned.

The rain started coming down in heavy sheets, and we watched as it turned over to hail, thumping against the ground and the roof and even against the windows of his house. There was a sharp sound, and then a crack appeared in the glass of his front door.

I stumbled back as the hail kept coming, pelting the house.

"What's wrong with you lot?" Theo's nanny, Clara, called. "It's a bad storm! Down to the basement with you."

She held the door open for us, and we hurried down the stairs. "Tornado?" I asked when we were settled onto the big old leather couch in front of the television that flashed colored bars and the word "STORM, STORM, STORM" over and over.

"I don't think so," Theo said.

"Maybe a hurricane?"

"They were saying something about high winds and flash floods," Clara said, shaking her head so her red curls bounced. "And the three of you outside up there watching it like it was a movie."

"We weren't outside," Theo grumbled.

"You know, I was trying to get these fools to safety," Benji said. "It's often said that I'm the brains of this group."

"Who says that?" Theo asked.

The television crackled, then was silent.

"Is it over?" Benji asked.

"Stay put," Clara told him. "All of you." She started up the basement stairs.

The lights flickered.

"It's still going—" she called down.

And then the lights went out. We were in darkness. Absolute darkness. I could even hear the little camera on my glasses buzzing as it tried to make sense of it. I reached up and turned the camera off. What did I need it for now?

"Mori?" Theo called.

"Uh-huh."

"Benji?"

"Right here, chief."

Their voices sounded both closer and farther away. Like we were swimming in a swirling cauldron.

"There are flashlights down here somewhere," Clara said. Then a few unmentionable words. And then there was a faint glow of a light. I turned my glasses back on.

Clara handed each of us a flashlight and we set them up on the table to make something like a central light, but it was uneven and frail.

"We've never lost power before," Benji said.

Clara shook her head but didn't say anything.

"They'll be out to fix it as soon as they can," I told him. "The maintenance workers are very efficient."

"My brother's on the crew," Clara said.

"But I thought they were all droids," Benji said.

"Droids with a human captain for each crew."

"And someone from outside can be the captain?" I asked.

"You think a baby from Old Harmonie is going to grow up and do it?" she snapped back.

"I'm sorry," I said. I glanced at Theo, but he was looking away from me. It wasn't entirely out of the question that someone from Old Harmonie would be on the maintenance crew. Even with our interventions, some kids were more inclined toward that kind of work, less for the intellectual work of the Krita Corporation. Krita found a place for everyone.

Clara smoothed out her skirt. "Storms make me nervous is all. And I don't like to think of him being out in it."

I thought about Julia and my parents; they were all probably safe, either at home or in an office. But what about Ilana? I still hadn't seen her since the day she'd hurt me. Was she safe? Was this type of thing even a danger to her?

"You cold?" Theo asked.

"No," I said, shaking my head. "Just hoping everyone is okay."

🚲

The lights stayed off, and we stayed in Theo's basement. Eventually I fell asleep on the sofa, and someone put a blanket on me. I woke up and saw Benji sleeping on a beanbag chair. Clara was on the floor. I didn't see Theo anywhere.

With my blanket still wrapped around me, I took a flashlight and headed up the stairs. Theo was back standing by the front door, which he had opened. The rain had stopped, and the moon shone through breaks in the clouds. A huge tree had fallen and lay across his lawn and driveway.

There were more trees down all along the street.

"It's going to take them ages to clean it up," he said. "Don't you think?"

I nodded. "You okay?"

"I don't know where my mom is."

"She probably stayed in Center Harmonie."

He rubbed his head. "But maybe it was worse there."

My house was on the other side of the cul-de-sac from Theo's, through the woods. I squinted, but of course I couldn't see any lights, if there were any lights to see.

"I can walk you home if you want," he said.

"Should you tell Clara?"

"She's sleeping."

I shrugged the blanket off and left it in a ball by the door, and we stepped out together. It was even quieter than my usual nighttime walks. The hum of electricity was gone. But after a moment I heard other noises. The chirping of crickets, and the hoot of an owl. A bat swooped down above us before disappearing back into the clouds.

The houses were darker, too, and it was easy to imagine that they were empty, that every other person on Firefly Lane had been sucked up by the storm and that we were all alone.

I peered across the street to Ilana's house. It was as dark as all the rest. Was she in there? I hoped she was. I hoped she was sleeping soundly.

But part of me also hoped that the storm had picked her up and blown her away someplace—someplace where she belonged.

Theo and I walked along the street with the two yellow circles of light from our flashlights in front of us. They bounced together and then apart, and then together again. Each time we stepped, our feet made a slapping noise as the soles of our shoes hit the still-wet street.

A large tree, full of summer leaves, had fallen across the road. It was so big it didn't seem like we could go under or over it. We both stopped. "We should just go through the woods," I said. So we cut between the Grays' and the Darlings' houses—both dark—and entered the woods at the center of the cul-de-sac. These woods were not as wild as the ones around the outside of the neighborhood. The trees had all been planted at once, in even lines, and though there were a few new trees starting to sprout up, we could still walk down the aisles between the old trees with little problem.

The ferns were all curled up, and the leaves beneath our feet were slick with water. I took a deep breath.

"You really like it out here, huh?" he asked.

"Yeah." I sighed.

His foot snapped a stick.

"I like the other woods better, though. The ones around the neighborhood. It's not so orderly. And there are still some things from before. Like once I found part of an old stone wall, all covered with moss." I stopped myself. I was talking too much. Too loud.

He held up a branch, and I walked under it. The leaves gave up their raindrops, and they dripped down on me.

"Sorry," he said.

"It's okay."

Another bat swooped low near us, as if it wasn't quite sure we were real. I wasn't quite sure we were, either. That's how strange the night felt.

"Maybe when I grow up, I'll build a cottage right out here in the middle of the cul-de-sac, and I'll have a little dirt road that leads out to it. It will have a green front door with a curved top." I stopped my description and asked him, "Where do you want to live?"

"I don't know. I guess Nashoba is as nice as any of the other villages."

"You don't think about it more than that?"

"Why bother? It's not like you get a choice."

"Everyone gets some choice. And you, with your mother, I'll bet you'll get a big choice."

He snorted. "She'd send me down to Citroen if she could. Heck, I bet she'd even send me to one of the Kritopias in India or China."

"No way."

"When we went for my latency, she asked the doctor if it was too late to change it to something 'more inclined toward leadership.' Those were her exact words. 'More inclined toward leadership.'"

"But you are a leader," I said.

"Maybe I won't live in a Kritopia at all."

"Very funny, Theo."

"Why? Aren't you curious about what it's like out there?"

"Of course I'm curious. I'd like to go out there sometime to see it. Sometimes I—" I stopped myself from telling him how I liked to go out to the fence and look toward the lights and wonder what it was like in the city. He would probably get all nervous, though, like Julia had when I mentioned that I thought the town where the gardeners came from—Somerville—sounded pretty.

"Sometimes what?"

"You know how in high school some of the kids actually get to bring the supplies they gather out to the city, and they get to meet the little kids there and play with them for a bit? I think I would like to do that."

Theo smiled.

"What?" I asked.

"That doesn't surprise me, that's all." The wind rustled a tree, sending a shower of rain drops from the leaves down onto us. He pushed his damp hair out of his eyes. "But you wouldn't want to leave here. Not ever?"

I hesitated. "No," I said. But the word didn't sound quite true, even to me. There was a time when there would have been no doubt in my mind. But things had changed.

Another branch blocked our way. He held it way up above us, and I passed under his arm. "So this cottage," he said. "What's it like on the inside?"

"Well, it will have a cozy living room with a stone fireplace. And the kitchen will be all yellow, like in number nine. And my bedroom will be right off the kitchen so I can get midnight snacks easily. And I'll have a big feather bed with a canopy." I hadn't ever seen that type of bed, but I liked the idea of it. I'd read about it in books. "And a dog," I added. "And a cat. She'll like to sleep in front of the fireplace."

"Sounds nice," he said.

"Yes," I said. And I supposed I would be perfectly happy there, away from everyone else. "The truth," I told him, "is that I really want to live in number nine."

"To feed your honey fix?"

"No. I mean, well, sure. I'd have to fight Benji for it. But I want to fix that house up back the way Agatha had it. I'd get all that junk out of there and make it a home again. Mr. Quist and I can keep bees back there, and I'll have gardens and keep chickens and—"

"They'll never let you move in there," he said.

We were nearly out of the woods now. I could see the outline of my house in front of us. "Why not? It's just sitting there."

"They just won't. It's not like the other houses."

"So?"

"Having the houses all the same makes things easier."

We stepped out onto my lawn, which squished underneath my feet. "I guess we'll just have to wait and see."

"Sure thing, Mori. We'll just wait and see."

"You're going to be okay getting home?"

He smiled more at the ground than at me. "Yeah, Mori. I'll be okay. Good night."

"Good night."

He started walking away.

"Hey, Theo?"

"Yeah?"

"I like this version of you. This midnight version. Even if you do tell me I can't have my dreams."

Maybe each of us had a midnight version of ourselves, I thought, one without dampening or latencies or enhancements or therapies. Maybe that's why I'd always liked going walking at night.

"Too bad it's only the midnight version," he said. And then he disappeared into the trees.

I'd had every intention of going right inside and telling my parents I was home, but I wasn't ready to let go of the feeling of this night. I was afraid it would slip away and I would never have it again. Clara had sent them a text message letting them know I was okay, and as far as they knew, I was still at Theo's. So I walked around to the sidewalk out front and made my way around the lower half of the cul-de-sac.

I passed number 9, which was as dark as always, and walked past the houses of my neighbors.

The woods on this side were eerie, too. The wind had knocked down a string of trees, and they offered up their roots like a lady lifting her skirt to reveal not legs, but a mess of snakes.

I didn't go out toward Oakedge. I was afraid of what I would find. Instead, I walked on, right up the fence.

A tree had fallen here, too. It bent the fence and then reached out over the stream. The leafy top rested on the far side of the gully.

If I wanted to, I could climb right up on the tree, walk across it like a balance beam, and go all the way to the other side of the gully. And from there—who knew?

A bat swooped above my head and I nearly dropped my flashlight. I reached out and touched the tree trunk. It was wet, but not too slippery. Tucking the flashlight under my arm, I clambered up onto the trunk, first on my knees and then onto my feet. My heart and my brain were going a mile a minute, telling me this was a bad idea. It was hard to breathe. But I slid my feet along, moving forward until I was right above the fence. Then I slid a little bit more.

For the first time in my life, I was outside the fence.

I held my arms out wide and looked up at the gray night sky, a smile spreading across my lips. I knew I was not going to tell anyone about this breach. It didn't matter. After all, it's not the fences that keep us safe. It's us.

27

ONCE I FINALLY GOT INTO bed, I slept till almost noon. I checked on my trees, which had made it through the storm okay, and then helped Mr. Quist clean up his garden. Most of the vegetable plants had been trampled down by the rain, but a few survived and we retied them to their stakes. He sent me home with a tomato the size of my two fists.

That night my parents sent me to bed early. My watchu had checked my status, and some blip told them I was tired. Or maybe it was just the dark half-moons under my eyes. I picked up Prince Philip and stared into his black digital eyes. He buzzed, then settled in on my hand. "I'm not tired," I told him, since I had no one else to tell.

I stayed in bed for a while, flipping through Agatha's bee book. Her bees were not doing well. Each day she found more bee carcasses in the snow.

Lucy says I'm being too hard on myself, but it's safe to say this experiment with modified and cloned bees has failed. What's odd is that what I feel is not the curiosity I used to feel when an experiment failed to yield the results I'd hoped for—no curiosity, no drive to reboot. Instead what I feel is akin to homesickness. And there, too, is something strange. When I lived in Cambridge, all I ever thought about was Old Harmonie—getting out here for the weekend, escaping the city. My heart was here. Now, though, say the word "home," and I think about my lab at MIT. This place is not mine anymore. Perhaps it's time for a homecoming.

So there it was, the answer I had been seeking: she left because Old Harmonie didn't feel like her home anymore. It had changed, or she had changed, or both, maybe, and she wanted to return to her lab.

It still didn't explain, though, how she had left her best friend behind.

Thirsty, I climbed from my bed and edged down the hall toward the bathroom. My parents were in the living room, and their voices danced up the stairs to me.

"So what are we supposed to tell her?"

"The truth."

I crouched down at the top of the stairs so I could hear them better.

"Really. So it would go something like, 'Oh, honey, sorry to tell you, but your new best friend, she's a top-level project and she's being recalled.'"

I could feel my heart beating faster and faster. Ilana. They were talking about Ilana.

This was not news. Theo and I had figured it out. But the way they were talking . . . What did "recall" mean?

"Nothing is definite yet. Maybe they can solve—"

"And if they can't?"

"Then we'll just say they moved back to California."

Dad made a noise that sounded like a cross between a sigh and a grunt. "Will she believe it?"

"I'm not sure they're even that close anymore. Anyway, Ilana showed up out of the blue, and she'll leave just the same."

I thought of that day she had emerged from the car, how perfect she had seemed. Now everything was upside down.

"If I had realized there was any chance of this project being scuttled, I wouldn't have been in favor of bringing her onto Firefly Lane," Mom said.

Scuttled. The files on the computer flashed before my eyes. And then that room, that horrible room with all the pieces of old projects. I squeezed my eyes shut, but the awful sight was in my brain: Ilana falling down into that pile of parts.

"I was never in favor," Dad said.

"It's easy for us to sit here—"

"I know. Other people have struggled. But we have limits here, guidelines. And this project pushed those limits. Bold new directions," Dad said. "Your grandmother would be rolling over in her grave."

I tried to force myself to take deep breaths. This couldn't really be happening, could it? They weren't really talking about getting rid of Ilana?

"Maybe," Mom said. "But haven't there been days? Like after the yellow jackets—haven't you wanted to just up Mori's resistances?"

"Her common sense, maybe," Dad said. "We let free her curiosity, and I thought we'd dampened down her bravery enough."

Every bit of me froze.

My body, my breath, even my heart. Stopped cold.

They'd always told me they'd never dampened me. But they had. I wrapped my arms around my stomach.

I twisted my hair around my fingers. How could they have done this without my knowing? It was an easy proce-dure, but you still needed to go to a doctor—

As soon as I thought it, I knew. I knew when they had done it: it was a few years ago, when I'd been in the hospital with the stomach flu. The fear I had felt when I got out of bed, it wasn't just because I had been so sick, or the trauma of being in the hospital so long—they'd dampened my bravery too much, so everything was terrifying. Then they'd fixed it, adjusted the levels like Theo had said.

My parents had lied to me.

"Fine. Tell me you didn't want to bring the mumps vaccine straight home to her, and not risk her getting on that bus and going into the center."

Dad didn't reply.

My body shook. They had *lied* to me. Not only that, they had stolen something from me.

"The point is, I understand what Meryl Naughton did. Ilana might not have been a real girl, but she was like a daughter to Meryl. And now we know it wasn't successful, and that's good knowledge to have. I just wish it wasn't our kids who were caught in the middle."

My head spun.

"Nothing's been settled yet," Dad said. "Maybe they will be able to figure her out."

There was a shifting sound, and I imagined my mother nestling into my father. They didn't speak anymore, or at least not loud enough for me to hear.

I tiptoed back to my room with my hand against the wall to steady myself. What, exactly, were they thinking of doing to Ilana? They couldn't possibly scuttle her, I told myself.

They were probably just going to bring her back to the lab. They would keep working on her programming, keep training her so she acted right.

The way my parents had messed with me.

I stopped at the bathroom. With the light off, I leaned over the sink and scooped water into my mouth. My hands looked silver in the darkness. Like they belonged to someone else. I turned off the water and stared at my fingers. Ilana's were so long, and when she tended to the plants in Oakedge they curled gently around the stems. My own hands were small, with narrow fingers that never seemed to work quite the way I wanted them to. Had my parents chosen these hands for me? Or had they been a mistake?

Ilana's hands were perfect. They had probably come out precisely the way they were designed. It was the behavior that they were still trying to program just right.

Tears pooled at the bottom of my eyes.

None of this was her fault. She hadn't asked for any of it. She'd been lied to just like my parents lied to me. That bad dream I'd felt like I couldn't wake up from—that was because of them. What must this life feel like to her with constant adjustments? Every time she wakes, she could be different. She could be kind or she could find herself attacking her best friend all because of adjustments and manipulations she had no say over: how unsteadying that must be!

I closed my eyes to wipe away the tears, and when I did I saw that room full of parts again. Arms and legs and torsos. And on top of the whole big pile, I saw Ilana, her eyes closed as she sank down, down, down into the pit just as she had sunk in the water.

And that, I realized, that was the lie. She was not just a container to be filled and refilled, shaped and reshaped. She was Ilana, and Ilana was my friend.

28

I WIPED MY EYES ONE more time and took a deep breath. Crying would not fix anything. It never did. The air cooler was circulating cold air into my room, but it still felt stifling. I needed to clear my head, and there was only one place that I could do that. I needed to get outside. I thought about that night of the storm, when Theo and I had gone walking. Everything had been still and quiet and new. And I remembered how it had felt to be on that tree trunk, standing on the outside of the fence. I had told Theo I would never want to leave, but now I could imagine walking on that trunk, marching right out of here. That would serve my parents right.

My stomach hitched at the thought of it.

Still, even if I didn't go out the fences, I knew I couldn't stay inside the house with those—those traitors. Not a moment longer.

Maybe I could go back to the center of the cul-de-sac. Maybe it would still be peaceful.

And so I did something I had never done: I slipped out of the house and wandered through my neighborhood. I had been out alone many a night, but somehow it felt more deceptive leaving through the sliding door in our kitchen than unzipping the door of my tent.

I stepped outside and my nose filled immediately: smoke.

It plumed up from the bottom of the cul-de-sac. I knew which house it was, but still I ran around the bend and toward the driveway to number 9. Smoke drifted up from behind the house.

Down the driveway, and then around back.

There were the flames licking against the back wall of the white house and turning them black. The fire was reflected back in the windows, making them look like demon eyes. I felt a hitch in my throat, like I was going to throw up, at the same time as tears welled in my eyes. Agatha Varden's house was always supposed to be there. Number 9 was never supposed to change. It was our house. My house. And now it was burning to the ground.

I sprinted all the way home.

The smell of smoke followed me.

I would tell my parents as soon as I got home, that's what I told myself.

But I didn't.

What I did was let myself in the sliding door, slip down the hall to my bedroom, change back into my pajamas, and then lie awake the rest of the night because everything—everything—in my world had changed.

The smoke still drifted up and over Firefly Lane the next morning, acrid and harsh. We followed it down around to the bottom of the cul-de-sac, and I tried to pretend I was as surprised as everyone else when we stopped in front of number 9, or what was left of it: a black, smoldering pile.

"What I don't understand is how it caught fire *after* the storm," Theo said. "If it had been hit by lightning during the storm, then that would make sense. But this was a day later, so how did a fire just start?"

"Maybe it was an electrical thing," Julia said. "It still had that old electricity. Maybe something got knocked loose and no one even knew."

I looked over at Theo. He was holding Benji's skateboard, running his hands against the wheels to make them *whirrrr*.

"Just as long as we don't have another lockdown," Benji said. "Although if we do, and we could be with your nanny again, Theo, that would be rad. She's pretty cute."

I expected Theo to make some snide comment about Benji or his nanny, but he said, "Yeah, that was all right."

The firefighters tromped over the ashes, poking it with rakes and shovels.

"I'm sure they'll figure out what happened," Julia said. "It's probably for the best anyway. Now they can build a new house there like all the rest, cut down the grass, get rid of the yellow jackets and snakes."

"We're definitely safer without it, but man am I going to miss that honey," Benji said.

We kept silent after that and watched the firefighters do their work, poking and poking, turning over red bits of wood and metal.

Eventually Julia and Benji rode away, and it was just Theo and me in front of the house.

"You okay?" he asked.

This had been her house. Her home. Not just another building made by Krita, but one she had lived in and made her own before everyone's house was the same. There was something much more personal about it. Baba had been there. Destroying the house was like cutting her and Dr. Varden out of our history.

My voice came out cracked, dried from the smoky, dusty air of the fire: "I guess so." It wasn't even a house anymore, really, just a pile of black and red, like coals in the barbecue. The heat still came off it, though, washing over us in waves that turned our cheeks pink and brought beads of sweat to our temples. Poking up through the ashes were pieces of twisted metal of various sizes. Some of them were probably the robot parts we had found.

I turned so I was facing him. His profile was strong against the smoke-gray sky, and I got the sense that he was changing before my eyes, slowly enough that it was barely perceptible, but surely, all the same, he was morphing into something stronger and sturdier than he had been.

"I'm not a very good person," I said.

"Mori." His voice cracked. "Did you start this fire?"

"What? No! Why would I do that?"

"To cover up for Ilana. To make sure no one else found out."

"They all know," I said.

"What do you mean?"

"We were right about Ilana. You were right. She's a project. An advanced project. Your mom knew right from the start. All of our parents did. And I guess she's not working the way they expected. They want to recall her. To scuttle her."

"Wait, what? Who told you that?"

"I heard my parents talking last night. They said they never would have let her come to Firefly Lane if they thought the project would ever be canceled."

"They said they were going to scuttle her?"

I thought back to my parents' conversation. "Not definitely, but they seem to think it's a real possibility. They said something about pushing limits. About bold new directions."

Theo tugged on his hair. "I don't think that's what my mom meant," he said.

"But it is!" I cried. "Remember the first day the family came? Your mom stayed home. After already missing two days for your latency, she stayed home *again*. She *never* stays home. And then she marched us all over there and was so excited for us to be Ilana's playmates. Not our friend, our playmate! She was so excited for this project, and for you and all the rest of us kids on Firefly Lane to be a part of it."

"Maybe," he said. Then he took a deep breath. "They didn't say they were for sure going to scuttle her, right? So that's good. It means it's just a possibility."

"How is that good?"

"It means they're going to figure it out. The adults will fix it," he said, but he wouldn't look at me.

"That's what I was thinking, too. That they would take care of it, that it wasn't my problem. But now I'm not so sure we can trust them to do that. Every time they try to fix things, they mess it up."

"Mori—"

"No, Theo. You should know this better than anyone. When she grabbed my arm—that wasn't her hurting me.

It was whatever they did to her after she almost drowned. Remember she went to the doctor? They adjusted her but they overdid it or something, and that's why she grabbed me. It was just like you after your latency, how mean you were."

"I said I was sorry." He looked down at his scuffed sneakers.

"I know, Theo. And I forgive you. And I forgive Ilana, too. She didn't cause this. None of us did. But it *is* my problem. That's what I meant about not being a good person. She was my friend and once I learned what she really was, I abandoned her. Part of me was relieved when I heard my parents say that the adults were going to take care of her. But that's not right, is it?"

"Mori, you can't take this all on yourself."

"I have to," I said. "I'm her only friend. What kind of person abandons her friend?"

"You're just trying to keep yourself safe. We all are."

"Ilana's the one I need to keep safe. The answers were in that house, and we missed our chance to go in and it's all my fault. My parents—I told them how we'd been there, and now the house is gone."

"You don't think your parents burned the house down?"

"Of course not. But I think they took it up the line, to your mom . . ." I paused. Something else Ms. Staarsgard had said to the Naughtons came back to me: *If there are ever any problems, you will call me. Immediately.* Maybe my parents hadn't realized that stopping the Ilana project was a possibility, but Ms. Staarsgard had.

"No," he said. "She wouldn't have called for that, or authorized it or anything. All that information? And all that equipment? No way."

He was right. We didn't waste anything here. Waste and secrets and destroying evidence—that wasn't the way things were done in Old Harmonie.

One of the firefighters called out to another, and then together they lifted a huge beam and dragged it from the wreckage.

Theo said, "You are a good person. I know that much. I think we're just getting all mixed up. It's been a crazy couple of days."

"It's like I can't get enough air," I said.

He turned and put his hand on my shoulder. "Is it the smoke? Do you need me to—"

"No, I mean that's what it feels like. Ever since I heard my parents talking about Ilana and how they might scrap her. I can't get a full breath."

"Mori, we really don't know if that's what they're going to do."

"If she doesn't get better, they are going to get rid of her. How can they do that? How can they create a person and then get rid of her? That's not what Old Harmonie was supposed to be about. Failure is just supposed to be a chance to do it again. To do it better." That's what they had done, I realized, they had tried to create Alana again. Only they had ignored the note in the problems file: they hadn't considered the ethics of creating a person, of giving her friends, and then taking her away.

"She's not a person," Theo said.

"She *is*."

"But not to Krita."

And once again, his mother's words came back to me: *When a project's outcomes fail to warrant the expenditures, we cancel it.* Krita would show Ilana the same lack of mercy they had shown to any other project that had failed. Only she wouldn't get a chance at a second life as some sort of museum exhibit.

The smoke was drifting high up into the sky and out over the rest of Old Harmonie.

"Can I show you something?"

We rode over to the park and left our bikes by the empty tennis courts. He slowed down, but I kept walking right into the woods. At the pointy rock, I took a left. I could have walked this path in my sleep. Straight to the tree with the crook in it. A large branch had fallen on the path, and I bent over to lift it up. Theo crouched down next to me and together we got it out of the way.

He didn't say anything, and I led him right to Oakedge.

The plants were doing wonderfully. The chard had thick, full leaves, and the mustard greens danced up perkily.

"This was our garden," I said to Theo. "Mine and Ilana's." I reached out and picked two of the pea pods—one for him and one for me. They were the kind you could eat pod and all, and were as sweet as could be. "She's been taking care of it. I gave up on it, but she never did."

We both looked out over the garden. It was so easy to picture Ilana coming out here all alone, humming to herself as she tended the plants. "She helped me name Oakedge and make it real. Before, it was just some place I liked to come to, but it didn't mean anything. We were going to have our own rules. No physical problems. No latencies. Just us kids."

"Wouldn't that mean there would be no Ilana either?"

"In Oakedge, she's just a regular girl," I explained. If only it could be true. If only you could build a place and have it be just exactly the way you had wanted it to be. I guess that's what Agatha had wanted for Old Harmonie, Agatha and Baba both, but it hadn't worked out for them and it hadn't worked out for us, either. Agatha had left because this wasn't her place anymore, but Oakedge could still be for me and Ilana.

I sat on the damp earth and patted the soil around some of the chard. Theo dropped to his knees beside me, and together we weeded the whole patch and smoothed out the dirt behind us. Maybe she would come back and see it, I thought. It would be like a message to her. Maybe she would come back and see it and then we could both believe that everything really would be okay.

29

FOR TWO DAYS IT SEEMED like Theo was right, that Ilana would go back to normal and it would all blow over. She didn't come out to play with us, but we saw her around the neighborhood. I saw her with Mrs. Collins and the twins one morning, and I saw her out running with her mom. Things were almost normal.

Maybe everyone had forgotten about it all. About her glitches and how she'd grabbed my arm. Maybe they had figured out the programming or whatever it was that was giving her troubles. Maybe she'd be all right.

That morning I put on my denim shorts and the red T-shirt I knew she liked. I was going to have to see for myself. I was going to go see her.

It was Dad's day at home, and he was out front sweeping off the walk. He wore a large brimmed hat that covered the bald spot that was starting to grow on the back of his head, and he had a special towel around his neck that was supposed to keep him cool.

"One for the record books today," he said, and wiped at his brow. "Eighty-seven degrees already and it's not even nine o'clock. They've issued an air-quality warning, too, so once you get wherever you're going, you make sure you stay inside."

"Okay," I said.

"And if Benji even tries to leave the air-cooling, you tackle him. His lungs definitely can't handle the ozone."

"I don't know if I'll see him today. I'm going to go over to Ilana's."

Dad stopped sweeping. "Ilana's?"

"Yeah. It's been a little while since I've seen her. I wanted—I just want to see her."

"I don't know if today is the best day for that." He took the towel off from around his neck and wiped his face.

"Why not?"

"Oh, Mori," he said. He looked at me with the saddest eyes.

"What?"

"I'll tell you what, you go over to one of your other friends' houses. And then later this afternoon maybe you and I can go over to Ilana's house together."

My dad wasn't normally so weird about things, and I wondered what was going on. But part of me was relieved to have an excuse to put off seeing Ilana. "I guess I'll just go to Julia's, then."

"Good!" He grinned. "And, remember, stay inside."

"I promise," I agreed.

The air was hot and heavy, and I decided to walk instead of putting on my helmet to ride my bike. Even the tar of the road seemed soft, like it was squishing under each of my footsteps.

I came around the bend of the cul-de-sac at the exact time a white van drove by on the street. I froze. It had no windows in the back, and tinted ones up front. No markings at all, not even a license plate. It slowed and I thought perhaps there was a driver—one who I couldn't see—and he was going to roll down the window and talk to me, but instead it pulled into Ilana's driveway. The van's battery switched off, but no one got out. It just sat there, ominous as storm clouds.

I started running. My legs pumped and my glasses bounced on my face. When I arrived at Theo's door, my breath was coming in heavy puffs. "What's wrong?" he demanded.

"It's happening," I managed to croak out.

"What's happening?" I could see the panic in his eyes, but I could barely pull in a breath.

"Ilana," I finally said. "Look."

From his house, we could see the van. The side door opened, and two people got out. They were wearing white jumpsuits. It was just like Julia had told me about with Mr. Merton, the way the men in the jumpsuits had come with a van to take his body. One of them carried a large silver case.

"They're going to scuttle her!" I said. "She'll be like those parts we found."

"No." He shook his head.

"They are." My breathing was more even now. "My dad didn't want me to go over there, and this was why. They're doing something to her. They could be taking her apart right now. They'll throw her in the trash heap."

"They won't just throw her away," he said. His voice was flat, and his face drawn. "She's biological, too. I don't know what they would do about those parts, but you know they'll reuse some of the tech."

"Don't talk like that. She's our friend!"

"What do you want me to say? I think you're right. I think they're going to scrap her."

"Theo, we can't let that happen."

He pressed his palms into his eyes as if he had a sudden and fierce headache. "I know," he said. Then he shook his head. "If it's happening right now, there's nothing we can do about it. But if this is just the first phase, then maybe we still have time."

"First phase? What do you mean?"

"They're probably still figuring it all out, how to shut down a project like that. That van and those guys, maybe they were just getting her parents ready. Or maybe they'll like—you know, like with a hospital patient, at the end, when they turn the systems off, the breathing tube and the feeding system and all of that. Maybe they are going to start turning off her systems, and just let her—"

"Die."

"Just let her go. Let her shut down naturally."

"We have to get her out of here."

Ilana's front door opened again, and the two people exited. They didn't have the case. Ilana's parents stepped onto the front walk, and the four adults spoke for a while. Ilana's mom nodded a lot, then wiped at her eyes. Then the two people in white got back into the van and it pulled away.

"They don't have her," I said. "She's still in there. We have to get her."

"You figure out where we need to take her. I'll figure out how to make it happen. In the meantime, we can't tell anyone. We'll go tonight."

These were the things Theo and I had settled on:

We would have to leave at night.

We would tell no one else.

We would tell Ilana at the last possible moment.

We would find Agatha.

It wasn't much of a plan. But we knew that we had to move quickly. Even waiting as long as we did seemed risky.

I felt certain that Dr. Varden would help us, especially when I told her that Lucy Morioka was my great-grandmother. Theo had wondered if she was even still alive, but I figured if she had died, people at Krita would have known, and we would have celebrated her. "She's alive," I told him.

"Okay," he said. "Then let's do this."

We had to live that day as if it was normal. So we went over to Julia's house and played in her pool. Julia sat on a deck chair at the edge of the pool watching me and Theo as if she could tell something was up.

"Hey, do you drain your pool in the fall?" Benji asked Julia.

She shook her head. "Just partially, then you put a special cover on. Why?"

"It would be so dope to skateboard in there."

"I think my mother would personally break your skateboard into bits."

Benji laughed. "Come on, guys, that's funny. Can you picture Julia's mom breaking anything into bits."

I tried to force a laugh, but Theo just let himself submerge underwater, the bubbles coming up around his head.

"What's up with you two?" Julia asked as Theo burst out of the water.

"Nothing."

"Yeah, right."

Theo wiped the water from his eyes and looked at Julia. "What are you staring at?"

"Nothing. I'm staring at a whole lot of nothing." Then she turned back to me. "My mom wants to know if you can have a sleepover tonight."

I glanced at Theo. He frowned. I was being too obvious. "I can't tonight."

The water in the pool felt cold, and I shivered. There were little goose bumps rising up on my arm like tiny ant-hills blooming.

"What are you doing?" Julia asked.

"Swimming," I replied.

She frowned. "Tonight? What are you doing tonight?"

"Ilana's coming over. Actually." Not that I'd spoken to her yet, but that was the plan.

Julia blinked her eyes, and I knew she was remembering what I had said, that it was better without Ilana. But then she narrowed her gaze. "Actually," Julia mimicked.

"I miss her," Benji said. "The old Ilana, I mean. Not the off-her-rocker-do-that-to-your-arm Ilana."

"There is no old Ilana or new Ilana. There's just the same girl," I said.

"Exactly." Julia lowered her sunglasses over her eyes. "There's only ever been one Ilana."

I dove under the water, sick of these circular conversations, and sick of Julia pushing and prodding.

Maybe I should have handled things differently from the start. I should have brought Ilana over to Julia's pool instead of going out into the woods with her. We could have all been friends, and Julia never would have gotten so jealous, and then maybe—just maybe—all of the other pieces would have fallen differently. But that would mean I wouldn't have had Oakedge with her. Or the day she came to get me and take me to the museum. She was so excited about everything, then, and so was I. Now, just thinking of her felt like a weight dragging me down.

How had things changed so quickly?

I saw Theo moving toward me, his body fuzzy; the receptor chip still had trouble when I sank underwater; it couldn't quite recognize the images sent by the camera in my goggles. When his wavy foot was near mine, I popped out of the water, startling him. "They're going to scuttle her," I said to Julia as she came into focus. "They're going to scrap her and I'm not going to let it happen."

And so I told them everything I had discovered. We'd gotten out of the pool and were wrapped in towels as we sat around the table on the deck. I told them what Theo and I had found in number 9 and what I had heard my parents say. "She's Agatha's project," I said. "Or at least an offshoot of it. We're going to bring her back."

"Take her back where?"

Clara had said that home was home. Well, Agatha's house had just been burned to the ground, but she'd left it long before to go back to her real home. "She's back at MIT. At her old lab."

"MIT?" Julia asked. "In Cambridge? You know that's practically Boston, right? There's only a river between them. You can't go to Boston."

"We have to get her out of here," I said.

"This wasn't our plan, Mori," Theo said. "We weren't going to get everyone else involved."

"You should've stuck to your plan," Julia said, sucking the water from the end of one of her braids.

"No. You can't leave us out of this," Benji said. He cleared his throat. "It's the same as her dying, isn't it? If they scrap her?"

"If they made her once, they can make her again," Julia said.

"Julia," I said, as if just saying her name could mend the broken thread between us.

"Put aside all the awful things she's done, all the things she's ruined—we're not even talking about a real person. She's a step up from a droid, maybe two steps up from a helper bot. Not to mention the fact that she assaulted you—"

"That wasn't her. It was a—"

"Glitch," Theo finished for me.

"Right. Because she's a project. A *thing*. Don't you get it? What you're talking about, it's theft. It's the same as walking into a lab and taking an experiment—someone's work. That's the kind of thing that could get a family kicked out of Old Harmonie."

I glanced over at Theo, who looked straight ahead. Benji rubbed the space above his lip.

"Not that you have anything to worry about, Theo," Julia added. "The Staarsgards aren't going anywhere, but we don't all have moms who run this place. Our parents need these jobs."

"This wasn't Theo's idea," I said.

Julia turned to me, her braid *thwap*ping against the deck chair and her eyes flashing. "Oh, I know whose idea this was. Trust me. But tell me, Mori, would you do the same for me? Or Benji?"

"Of course, but I would never need—" And then I stopped myself and looked down at my hands in my lap.

"That's right. You would never need to do something like this for us," Julia said. "You wouldn't have to because we're people. We're your actual human friends, and she's—"

I lifted my eyes and looked at Julia. Her nose was perfectly straight between her two perfectly shaped and evenly shaded brown eyes. Had her parents chosen that precise shade of brown? Had they planned a girl with long hair that they could put into two braids each day? And her strength? Her early latency? "If she's a thing, so are you."

"Well, that's just perfect."

I pushed my glasses back up my nose. "And so am I. All of us. It's a matter of degree."

Julia tightened her towel around herself. "You're not making any sense."

"Think about it. Our parents can dampen us and we have our latencies. And the enhancements. We can say it's okay to alter up to thirty percent of a person, but why thirty? Why not ten? Or nothing? Or ninety-nine point nine nine nine. It's arbitrary."

"It's not arbitrary," Julia said.

The phone rang inside Julia's house, and a moment later, her father's heavy laugh drifted down to us.

"But Ilana wasn't changed," Theo said. "She was created from the ground up. That's different."

"Why? Our parents have been fiddling with us since before we were born, trying to get us just the way they want us to be. And when we don't measure up, they bring us in to get fixed."

"I think they're just looking out for us, Mori," Benji said. Which was easy for him to say, considering his parents had never lied to him like mine had to me.

"I'm supposed to be braver. Don't you remember? I used to be brave. Remember how we used to fly off the swings, Julia? I was brave and it scared my parents, so they dampened it so I wouldn't get hurt. 'Just curious enough,' that's what they always said, like they were so proud of me. But it wasn't me. And it wasn't my choice."

"Your parents were trying to protect you," Julia said.

"And so are Ilana's. Or they were."

Julia didn't have a response to that. So all we could do was try to look anywhere but at each other as the truth settled in: every single one of us was a creation.

"I bet out there the parents don't mess around with kids like that," I said.

"That's because they don't know how," Julia said.

"Maybe they don't know how because they didn't want to figure it out. Because they know it's wrong," I said, speaking into my towel. "Our parents and all the adults here say they're improving us—keeping us healthy and safe and making sure we reach our full potential. But what are they really doing?"

Julia bit her lip and shook her head. "You're not making any sense, Mori. I know you're upset—like, really, really upset—and I get it, but you need to take a step back."

"I understand what you mean," Theo said.

"Really, Theo? Not helping," Julia said.

"All that stuff you've said about my mom, you were right," he said to Julia. "She has controlled and manipulated the system in order to get me to what she considers my rightful position. She has this vision of who I should be, and she's doing whatever she can to make it happen."

"Because she loves you," Julia said.

"Maybe," Theo said with a shrug. "What I'm trying to say is, I could always see it. I knew what she was doing. But Mori's right—all of your parents have been doing it, too. They've just been keeping it under wraps."

Benji pulled on a loose string from his towel. He'd been quiet a good long time while we talked. "I just can't believe that this is happening. This isn't— I mean, we have these rules in place to protect us. Old Harmonie is about discovery, not secrets. Are you sure you heard right? Do they really want to scuttle her?" Benji asked.

"Yes! And that's why we have to help her. I *would* help you, Julia. I would. If your parents wanted to make you more competitive, so they dampened your kindness—I would help you."

Julia tugged on her towel. Her eyes went soft, but then she looked away from me. "I can't help you," she said. "But I won't tell."

I looked at her, at the way her eyelashes were still wet, and the thin set of her lips, and I knew that was about the best I could hope for.

30

IT WAS A STRAIGHT SHOT across the street to Ilana's from Julia's, but I might as well have been running up a mountain in a hurricane. My feet dragged and the walk seemed to take forever, her house looming large in front of me. My finger even hesitated on her doorbell, like it couldn't quite be convinced to ring it.

Her mother answered, and I let the breath from my lungs like a balloon deflating. She stood in the half-open doorway. "Why, hello, Mori. You haven't been around much lately."

"I know. I'm sorry. Is Ilana home?"

"She's resting." Meryl stepped outside and shut the door behind her.

"Is she okay?"

"She's just fine." Her grace unnerved me. She put a hand on my shoulder. "I've been meaning to thank you for your help with Ilana."

"Help?"

"The other day, that little moment in the pool."

It had been more than a moment. It had felt like an eternity. I looked down at the cement stairs and twisted my foot back and forth. "She helped me when I was in trouble."

"She did, didn't she?" Her voice sounded like she was floating on one of those puffy clouds, far, far away, the clouds that were just stories in our minds.

"That's what friends do," I continued. "They help each other. No matter what." I bit my lip.

She let her hand drop off of my shoulder. "Sometimes problems are too big for children to solve on their own, wouldn't you say?"

"Krita doesn't think so."

I looked up at her and she looked back at me with eyebrows raised.

"Krita says that kids are the community's most important asset," I said.

"The children are our future—"

"No, I mean, well, yes, but when we visited the Idea Box, the people working there said that the thing that set them apart is that they still thought like kids. Without limits."

"That's what they tell you, dear. It's one of the things I've never agreed with about the Kritopias. Always telling the kids that they are so precious and so rare. In the end it's only setting you up for disappointment."

"What do you mean?"

"You can't all be precious, can you? How is it rare if there are so many of you perfect little children running around?" She clasped her hands in front of her chest. "I'm sorry, Mori, I shouldn't have said that." Then she kind of laughed to herself. "It's been a trying week, wouldn't you say? I'm feeling a bit raw."

"Oh," I said. And then because I could think of nothing else to say, I added, "Well."

"Well indeed."

"When she wakes up, maybe you could send her over?"

"If she's up to it."

I wanted to ask her more questions. I wanted to know how much they had known, how much they had done—and how much they could control about what happened to Ilana. But I kept my mouth shut.

I turned to go and saw Julia standing outside her house just staring at me. I waved, but she didn't wave back. Then her mom came out, put her arm around Julia's shoulder, and guided Julia back into the house. And I got a sinking feeling in my stomach.

ᗑᗌ

"If we have any chance of making this work, we have to do some planning," Benji said when he arrived on my doorstep later that afternoon. Theo stood beyond him on my driveway. "Let's go over to the playground."

We sat underneath the climbing structure, and Theo took out a map that was starting to tear at the creases. "Mr. Quist keeps these old things. I kind of liberated it from his garage."

"You stole it?" I asked.

"I guess I didn't think he would mind," Theo said. He spread it out on the woodchips. "So this is where we are," he said, pointing to a green swath of land. "And this is where we need to go." He pointed with his other index finger. It seemed a huge distance to cross. "This here," he said, running his finger along a hashed line, "is an old train line from when people used to commute into the city. The trains don't run anymore, but we can walk along it. It's a little bit more out in the open than I would like, but it will take us directly into Cambridge." He moved his finger again to a place shaded yellow.

"Where is MIT compared to that?"

"It's on the opposite side of town, but I think . . ." He paused and rubbed his nose. "I think that once we get to Cambridge, things might get a little easier. We can ask for directions or take a bus or something."

"Just four out-of-town kids all alone in a city?" I asked.

He shrugged. "I'm still working some things out."

One of the Collins twins came racing across the playground, right past us, and leapt into the sandbox. His mother was right behind, dragging the other twin. When they passed, I said, "Remember she had that doctor's appointment? She was scared. She couldn't tell me why. She was just scared. And I think they did something to her. I think that's why she hurt me."

"Why would they send Ilana out to hurt you?" Benji asked.

"I don't think it's like that. I'm not sure they know what they're doing."

"We don't even know who 'they' are."

"Her parents," Theo said flatly.

"No—" I said, thinking of how kind Meryl and Greg had been to me. But then, her dad worked in materials and her mom in AI, two of the departments that would be essential for this type of project. I thought of how strangely her mother had acted that afternoon. They might not just be two people chosen to be her surrogate parents: they were both probably on the team that developed her.

"It's not just them, though," Theo said. "They would need more people, whole teams of people with all different kinds of skills. That's a whole lot of people with a whole lot at stake."

Benji dug a notebook out of his tote bag. "Here's the thing. We can't just walk out of here with her. She'll be tracked."

"What?" I asked. "How?"

"It could be something as simple as RFID, you know, a radio frequency ID. Or it could be something more. And then we have these." He held up his wrist to show his watchu. It fit him precisely with its blue rubberized band, just like my pink one and Theo's green one.

"Our watchus?" I asked.

"You sure are naive," Theo said, shaking his head, and I wondered if he was thinking of backing out, too.

"What are you talking about?"

"They have tracking devices," Theo said. "In case anyone tries to kidnap us or something. That's why you can't take them off."

I looked over at Benji. He said, "I think I can deactivate them and then we can take them off. If Ilana only has the one in her watchu, then great. But if she has something else, something implanted—well, that will be harder, because we don't know where it is on her body. But if I can get a phone, I can hack an app to scan for it."

I put my hands over my face. "This is crazy. We can't—"

"We can't, but we have to," Benji said.

"*You* don't have to," I said.

"If I can't deactivate it, I'm going to have to cut it out," Benji said, as if I hadn't spoken. During Benji's sixth-grade internship in the animal lab, they'd taught him how to slice mice open to insert tiny computers. I'd never really been clear on what they were testing. Mostly I'd felt bad for the mice, but now I was glad for the skill he had learned there. Maybe a few mice dying so that Ilana could be free—well, it didn't seem like there was any real arithmetic to measure such trade-offs, but it felt like perhaps things had balanced out.

"No. I mean, it's clear we need your help to get out of here, but once that's done, you can stay. Both of you. I'll take her."

"I'm going," Theo said. I looked over at him. He didn't look too happy about this statement, but he also didn't look like he'd be dissuaded. As if he could sense my hesitation, he said, "I've already charted the most likely obstacles and plotted alternate routes should they arise." He pulled a crumpled piece of paper from his pocket. He'd drawn a grid on it, and then filled it in with notes in handwriting too small for me to read. Arrows connected boxes, and there was a big question mark in the lower right-hand corner. "I mean, think about my latency, Mori—all of this is one big puzzle. I've practically been designed for this mission."

"Fine. But no one else."

"Oh, we're all going," Benji said. "Theo may be the puzzle master, but I'm the tech genius. The all-around genius, actually. You need me."

"Benji—" I began.

He held up his hands. "We're the Firefly Five, aren't we?"

"Minus one," I said.

"Listen, Mori," Benji said, still writing notes to himself on his pad of paper, "Julia's just . . ."

"Just what?"

He sighed. "She's practical. Things are either good or not good."

"And this is not good?"

"This is in between. I think that's hard for her."

"Do you think she'll change her mind and come?"

"I'm more worried she's going to change her mind and tell someone," Theo said.

Benji shook his head. "No, she's good. She'll keep her word." But then, after a moment, he added, "At least I think she will."

I convinced my parents to let Ilana and me have a sleepover in the tent. When I asked, they did a lot of their eye talking, and at this point I could practically hear their words: *One last time before they take Ilana away. One last time.*

The sleepover not only provided cover, it also meant we'd have the tent and sleeping bags. I told Theo about the fence out beyond the tennis court, and how the tree that had fallen on it would be easy to climb over. That was going to be our meeting place, at midnight.

In the meantime, Ilana and I sat scrunched up in our sleeping bags in the tent. It was my job to tell her, but I didn't know how. She had a comic book, a thick one, that she was bent over, her headlamp shining on the pages.

"Have you ever, you know, thought you were different from everyone else?" I asked.

"Everyone thinks they are different from everyone else."

I shifted and my sleeping bag rustled loudly. "No, I mean really different."

She put the comic book down and looked straight at me. I thought maybe she *did* know, and was about to confess. But then she said, "Just because you're not super sporty like Julia and Theo and me, that doesn't mean you're totally different."

My cheeks grew hot. "That's not what I mean. It's more like—well, I used to think that the more perfect something was, the more natural it was, because nature has had time to work things out and nature doesn't make mistakes. But I guess nature does make mistakes, and that's how things change. It learns from its mistakes."

"Nature isn't something that can learn."

"But our genes can, and the systems can—anyway, that's not the point. The point is, I was wrong about you. I thought you were natural, but you're not."

"So I'm designed. Big whoop."

"I think you may be more than designed."

She put the book down, then sunk deeper into the sleeping bag. Her headlight shone up onto the roof of the tent. It seemed like she was going to just go right to sleep, but then she said, "Yes, I'm different."

"You know?"

She shook her head. "I don't know. I just feel. And sometimes I don't feel. And sometimes I remember. And sometimes I don't. And then sometimes memories and feelings just appear, like an app loading on a device, and . . ." She shook her head again. "My mom calls it an existential crisis."

"I don't know what that is."

"It's stupid. She says it's the human condition."

"I don't think you're human." The words burst out of me like a bubble popping.

"Sometimes I think that, too."

"I mean, not entirely," I added. "Something in between. Something else."

"Something," she echoed.

Her usual perpetual motion had stilled. She had no ball to bounce, nowhere to run, no pool to swim through.

"We have to go," I told her.

"*I* have to go. You don't." She reached out and put her hand on my arm. I didn't mean to flinch, but I did, so she let her fingers slip off my skin. "This is your home. You have your friends here, and your family and your trees. You have Oakedge. This is your place."

"Oakedge doesn't mean anything without you."

"Mori—"

I shook my head to stop her from talking. "Agatha thought this was her place, too. But then things changed. I think she started to see it differently."

"What are you saying?"

"I'm leaving because we're the Firefly Five. You're one of us and I want to help you. But I'm also leaving because I'm not sure Old Harmonie is the place I thought it was."

Ilana looked down at her lap. I reached over and slipped my hand into hers, and she turned to face me. "If you're sure—"

"I'm sure."

We waited as the dark crept deeper over us. Clouds were blowing in from the west, and they covered the moon. I checked my watchu over and over and over again. At 11:45, I said, "Now."

31

THE MOON WAS NEARLY FULL, like a drawing done by a little child who walked away with a few crayon strokes remaining. Its bright light made the night seem safer, like it wasn't night at all, but early in the morning. This is what I told myself as we edged around the cul-de-sac.

As we made our way toward the tennis courts, I let her know our plan. We were going to leave Old Harmonie by the fence, then walk to the train tracks. The tracks would lead us into Cambridge, where we would have to navigate to the MIT neighborhood. From there, it was fuzzier. Somehow we would find Agatha. She would help Ilana.

"That last bit is a little rough," Ilana said.

"I know," I admitted. "Theo is doing some more research. I've seen the map—the train tracks really do go right into Cambridge. We just need to follow them. It'll be okay."

"Until we get to Cambridge," Ilana said.

"Well, then maybe we can take a bus or something to MIT. Everyone must know Dr. Varden there."

"Why do you think she'll even help us?"

I knew Ilana had started as one of Agatha's projects, and a scientist always sees a project through to the end, but I said, "Because she owes me one. She owes Baba."

"I see," Ilana said.

"I have her notebooks, so I think I know where her lab is. Theo was going to do some research, too. To see if she still had a page on the MIT site or anything."

"Theo," she said. "Why him? He thinks I'm a danger to you."

"But he likes you, too. He helped me get this started. We just started talking, after the fire. I'm not very good at keeping things in."

"I set the fire."

My feet stopped. An owl hooted.

Finally, I managed to speak. "But why?"

"You're not the only one who saw this coming."

"You overheard your parents talking?"

She huffed at the word "parents." "No. I just sort of knew. And I guess I knew there was something about me in that place. The same reason I didn't want you to go in there. It was a compulsion."

A compulsion. Something she had to do. Which before would have been a simple concept. We all have things we feel we have to do. Like how I felt I needed to get Ilana out of there. But with her, those feelings, were they even her own? "Was it like a voice telling you?"

Ilana started walking again with strides so long, it was hard for me to keep up. "No, doofus. I just knew it was what I had to do."

"We were thinking that maybe it had something to do with your doctor's appointment. What did they do?"

"I don't know. I got there and then I must have fallen asleep or they put me under, because I don't remember any of it. Then I woke up and it was all done. I just felt lethargic, you know? Like I could barely move and didn't even really want to. All I remember is hearing them say something about dampening."

"They must have pulled back on one of your qualities. But it made you act overly concerned instead."

"I never meant to hurt you, Mori."

"I know."

"But I did hurt you. In my mind I was protecting you. What if it happens again? While we're trying to get away, what if I can't let you go over that fence?"

"Don't worry about it."

The thought had never even occurred to me. What else hadn't I considered?

"My parents dampened me once," I told her. "They told me they never had, but I overheard them say that they made me less brave. That's why I'm afraid of everything now."

"You're not afraid of everything."

I shook my head. "I am. It's okay. Because now I know. I know that it isn't really me to be so afraid, that somewhere in me the bravery is still there." The latency digs deep and finds something that's buried within you and ready to come out. When my parents had dampened me, they'd done the opposite: they pushed the bravery down inside of me so I couldn't feel it anymore. But it was still there.

We made it to the tennis courts and eased between the fence and the overhanging trees. Not that anyone was up and looking out their windows, but it still seemed the safer course of action. My backpack caught on a branch, and Ilana loosened it for me.

Once we were deeper into the woods, I put my headlamp onto my head and flicked the switch. Ilana veered to the left, away from the fence, but I knew just where she was going. Oakedge was bathed in moonlight, looking more magical than ever before: silver and cool. If a fairy or a fawn had stepped out into the clearing, it wouldn't have surprised me one bit.

I looked up at our oak. It's funny, I never named that tree. How can you name something that's older than you?

I never tried to draw it, either. I pushed my glasses back up onto my face and thought about the first time I'd brought her out here, when I had told her that maybe I wouldn't get a latency. I hadn't meant it then, not really, but now the idea seemed more plausible.

Ilana dropped to her knees in front of our garden and began carefully pulling out the plants. She wrapped them and put them into her backpack.

If I did choose a latency, I wanted to be sure I'd pick something that wouldn't change me too much. Dad's latency let him play out how a certain course of action would go, what the domino effects would be. That would be terrifying: if I could think through how this escape with Ilana was going to go, I probably would be too frightened to do it.

I crouched down beside her and began pulling peas off their vines. "I never thought we'd really need the things we grew," I said.

"I wish Oakedge were real," she said. "I wish we'd built a house and we could come here and live."

"I know," I said. "Me too."

"All of us," she said. "You and me and Theo and Benji and Julia. We'd be okay."

"We would," I agreed. "We will." I wanted a latency that would make my words true, that would mean my friends and I could always be together. But maybe true friendship was something bigger than our science could understand.

Ilana got to her feet. "Come on, before it's too late or I change my mind."

"You can't."

"Maybe it's not really mine to change or not."

As we approached the fence, I heard voices, low and whispered. I stopped and reached out to get Ilana to slow, too. I flicked off my headlamp, but not before I saw two silhouettes. "It's us," Theo called out. "You're all clear."

We came up to the fence with only the moon to light our way. They were standing in the shelter of the snakelike tree roots.

Benji held up a phone, probably his father's, judging by the faux-wood case it had on it. He swiped around until he found the app, then ran it over my watchu, which beeped a quick digital melody, then faded.

Theo had a knife. The blade was cool against my skin, but he cut through the band with ease, and my watchu fell to the ground. My wrist felt strange without the slight, constant pressure of the wristband. Theo scooped it up and dropped it into a bag. "I'm going to run this stuff back to the playground so they don't know where we left from. But we need to get going soon."

Ilana held out her wrist. "I have a watchu, too."

Benji deactivated her watchu, and Theo cut it off her as he explained, "We're guessing they've marked you internally. Benji has an app that can scan for the tracker."

"I developed it myself," he said. "It was meant to check for hidden tracking devices. I was way into spies when I was little. I just hope my deactivation app works on the tracker."

"And if it doesn't?" I asked.

We all looked at Benji. "I'll have to cut it out."

Ilana's eyes grew wide.

"It's okay," I told her.

"Listen," he said, "I'm not just a skateboarding genius. I also happened to ace every test they gave me at the animal lab. Remember, you and me, we don't need latencies, right?"

Ilana nodded. "I'm pretty sure that was already taken care of when I was created."

"Well, home fry, not only do I have many intellectual geniuses, I also happen to have a very steady hand. If we can find the device, it's just a quick slice. But first, let me scan you."

Theo paced away from us. He looked up at the moon, then peered back through the woods.

Benji ran the phone up and down Ilana's body. At her ankle, it started to vibrate in Benji's hand.

Ilana rubbed her ankle.

"You feel anything?" Benji asked.

"I don't know. Maybe."

"It's worth a shot." Benji typed into the phone and scanned Ilana's ankle. He bit his lip and tried again. He shook his head. "It's not working."

Ilana sat down and put her leg up on a rock. "Okay, Benji, let's do this. Something tells me it's gonna be gnarly." She tilted her head back and closed her eyes.

🚲

I bandaged her ankle as best I could. Benji had brought gauze and tape, and then we wrapped an Ace bandage around it, too, just to be sure.

"We have to leave," Theo said.

Benji looked down at his phone. "I feel like we should leave a message or something for our parents."

"We don't have time."

"I'll do it. Quickly. I promise." I took the phone from Benji and began typing into the notes application:

To our parents, our neighbors, our teachers, and friends:

We did not make this decision easily or lightly. We did not do it to defy you. You have raised us to believe that we are all the same, the designed and the naturals. You have raised us to look out for one another. We

think you made a mistake when you wrote the core
values. Creativity, ingenuity, experimentation, and order
are essential, but the founders left out Community.
Community is what we are. Community is how we
function. Community is how we survive. And so we
made the choice to save our friend. We hope you
understand.

Sincerely,
The Firefly Four

As I was passing the phone back to Benji, we heard a
crashing noise. Theo dropped to the ground and pulled me
with him.

The crashing grew closer, and it breathed heavily.

Theo was right. We should have just gone. We'd been
missed already, and now we'd be stopped before we even
started.

"I'm here."

It was Julia.

My heart danced in my chest. "You came!"

"Miss this? Are you crazy? We're the Firefly Five, aren't
we?"

32

I STEPPED UP ONTO THE tree that lay across the fence while my friends stood on the ground behind me. The moon shone through the trees on their faces like they were each under a spotlight, the stars of my universe.

My legs were shaking, and my heart, and all of me. Still, deep in the center, I could feel it. Calm or strength— something to hold on to and pull out. I could do this. My parents had pushed my bravery down, that was true. They had hidden it inside of me, but I didn't need a procedure like a latency to get it out. I had to find it myself. I had to search inside of myself and find that bravery and pull it to the surface. I could do it because I had to. Because Ilana needed me.

I looked over my shoulder and saw Theo coming back through the woods. He had gone to toss our watchus and the phone by the playground. He jumped up beside me, shaking the tree. I put my hand on his arm to steady myself. "This is the midnight version of all of us," I said. "The midnight version of the Firefly Five."

"What's the midnight version of you, Mori?" he asked.

"Brave," I answered. As I said the word, I started to feel it: a hardening in my chest and my stomach. I took a step forward.

Theo and I walked along the top of the tree like it was a balance beam. I heard our friends get on behind us. First Benji, then Julia, then, after a moment's hesitation, Ilana.

The gully was deeper than I had thought, and I swayed a little. Theo put his hand on my shoulder and we walked the rest of the way, right into the leaves that should have been sky-high. Maybe that's the root of our bravery: each other.

The woods on the outside of the fence didn't seem much different from the woods on the inside of the fence. The trees grew tall and strong, and the bats and a lone owl flew over the fence like it was nothing to them.

Theo had a digital compass, and he used it to guide us through the woods. We walked in a single-file line, dodging tree stumps and puddles as best we could. We held the branches out of the way for one another. It almost felt like the hikes we had taken when we were younger as part of our nature studies unit. We'd even done one at night and our teacher had shown us glowworms, which were really lightning bug larvae, and also that if you snap a mint Life Saver candy in your mouth, it will spark.

But this time we stumbled through the dark. Ilana and I had our headlamps, and we all had glow sticks and flashlights, too, but we didn't use them. Not that anyone knew we were missing yet. We just didn't want to draw attention, I guess. Didn't want to announce our presence.

We were beyond the fence. Well beyond it. In the wild, confused world. The one where chaos reigned.

"It's quiet out here," Benji said. "I didn't expect it to be so quiet."

"Just because it's quiet doesn't mean it's safe," Julia said.

"It's not safe," I said. "None of this is. But we still have to go." I knew what I said was true. That was something else they had left out of our core values: kindness. Because what did all the others matter—the creativity, ingenuity, experimentation, and order—if you weren't willing to help a friend who needed it?

Ilana smiled at me and squeezed my hand. "Mori the night-walker," she said. "My hero."

I tried to smile back at her, but it was hard. I managed to say, "Forever sisters, right?"

"Come on," Theo said. "We have to keep moving."

We came out of the woods into the bright light of the moon. Ahead of us was another forest, but down a ravine were the train tracks that we would walk along to bring Ilana back. To bring her home. And maybe, I thought, maybe I would find where I belonged, too.

Theo scrambled down first, half running and half sliding over the rocks and leaves that lined the ravine. He looked back up at us, and we followed down after him. Benji, Julia, then me. We waited at the bottom for Ilana. She stood up on top of the ravine, bathed in moonlight. It outlined her sharp profile, the smooth lines of her strong body. It made her hair and skin glow. She was like us, but not. For certain, though, she was one of us.

She ran down the hill in three graceful strides, then stood next to me. We were all on the train tracks now, facing east.

The tracks stretched out straight ahead of us, a clear path of where we needed to go. We'd done the hard part— we'd left Old Harmonie. Now all we needed to do was walk toward the lights of the city.

They were the same lights I'd seen from the other side of the fence hundreds and hundreds of times, but they did seem different from this side. Brighter. More steady. Or so I hoped.

I turned to Ilana. "Come on," I said. "It's time to go home."

ACKNOWLEDGMENTS

IN FEBRUARY OF 2014, MY family was visiting Florida, and my husband and I snuck out for a walk into town. Over fried oysters, I started telling him about this idea I was working on for a new book. *It's a utopia*, I told him. *But something goes wrong.* I laid out the key points of the book, and we kept talking about it as we walked home on a beautiful, warm evening. Thank you, Nathan, for being the first person to believe in this story.

My agent, Sara Crowe, let me know I was on the right track and encouraged me to keep building this story and this world. Sashi Kaufman also read an early draft and helped me to focus my themes. Maria Albrecht's creative writing students at the Clinton School for Writers and Artists

340 ACKNOWLEDGMENTS

gave me honest feedback on the opening, and answered my questions about characters and world building.

Once I had a sturdy enough draft, I sent it on to my editor at Bloomsbury, Mary Kate Castellani. Words cannot express how smart an editor she is: she crystallizes for me what I am trying to do and asks just the right questions so I can make it work. The entire team at Bloomsbury is wonderful. Thank you to Erica Barmash, John Candell, Beth Eller, Melissa Kavonic, Cindy Loh, Cristina Gilbert, Kerry Johnson, Linette Kim, Donna Mark, Lizzy Mason, Catherine Onder, Emily Ritter, Claire Stetzer, Ilana Worrell, and Regina Castillo.

Writing itself takes support, and I am grateful to my family: Eileen Frazer, Joseph Frazer and Susan Tananbaum, Ed and Audrey Blakemore, and that aforementioned husband, Nathan. Thanks also to Meg and Brendan Parkhurst for providing a second home for my kids—not to mention the delicious meals!

And finally, and perhaps most of all, thank you to all of the readers—those who have just read *The Firefly Code*, and those who have read the books before. It's an honor to share my worlds with you.

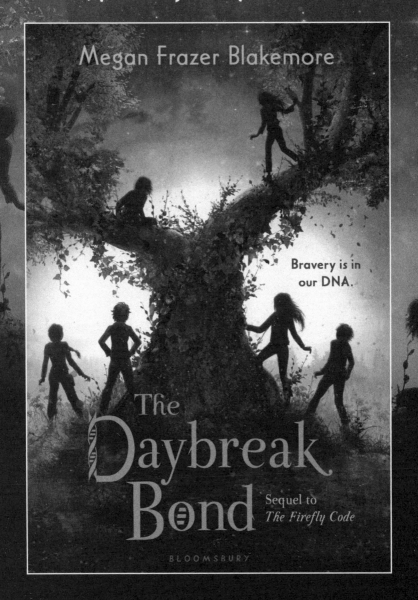

Megan Frazer Blakemore

Bravery is in
our DNA.

The
Daybreak
Bond
Sequel to
The Firefly Code

BLOOMSBURY

Read on for a glimpse at the thought-provoking sequel to
The Firefly Code, where Mori and her friends leave their
community and embark on an adventure that will change

OUR VOICES DANCED UP INTO the sky like fireflies escaping a jar. We tramped through the woods away from Old Harmonie, giddy and edgy and loud. Theo had given up on keeping us quiet, and sometimes he even joined in with our singing.

The trees out here grew wild and magnificent, like something I thought only existed in fairy tales or my imagination. Thick-trunked hemlocks and pines with boughs that hung low and brushed our shoulders. Creeping bunchberry flowers sparkled over the ground, and moss cocooned the rocks. I still couldn't quite believe it was real. We were outside the fences of Old Harmonie. The plan to leave had been hasty and shaky, but here we were *outside*. Theo had lifted a map from Mr. Quist, and it had led us right to the train tracks that went into Cambridge. We were on our way.

"The Firefly Five!" I yelled into the night.

"The Firefly Five!" my friends called back.

That's what we called ourselves: Ilana, Julia, Theo, Benji, and me. We'd never been outside the fences of our town before. But Ilana was in trouble, so we went out to the wild world. Her ankle had a bandage wrapped around it from where Benji had cut out what we hoped was her only tracking device. She was something other than human—more than or less than, I still wasn't sure. She was a project of Krita, the corporation that ran the community where we lived. They wanted to scuttle her and we weren't going to let them. She was our friend.

It sounds much simpler than it felt.

But I couldn't let the confusion and sorrow weigh me down. I climbed onto a small boulder next to the tracks and watched my friends marching in a line.

A mosquito buzzed around my ear, then drifted down my body and landed on my ankle. I smacked at it, but it got away. The bugs out here were bad, and that was worrisome—insects carry many diseases—but as long as we kept moving, only a few of them landed on us.

I leaped from the boulder and landed clumsily, but for a moment it had felt like soaring.

"Okay, guys, so, this is the coolest, right?" Benji asked as he hopped along the tracks. "Here we are, out in the world, saving our friends. We're superheroes!" He ran and jumped with his hands out in front of him, trying to look like a flying hero. He tripped, though, and rolled forward with a soft *oof*. "Benji!" I cried out.

He held up both hands. "No biggie. I've taken way worse diggers on my board."

Ilana walked over and reached out her hand to him. "Nice tumble," she said as she pulled him to his feet.

"It was a pretty great flip, right? I mean, if you're gonna fall, it's best to do it with style." He brushed himself off with his hands.

We made a single-file line and started marching toward the orange-green lights of the city. The tracks were set on railroad ties: thick, square slabs of wood that had grayed in the sunlight. Some still had their original brown color, and these oozed tar the way a sugar maple oozed sap. The smell was pungent and unfamiliar and gave me a headache. Between the metal cross-tracks were stones, most no bigger than a super bounce ball, but still big enough to roll your ankle. The tracks held down the growth enough to make the walking easier.

"The city looks close," I said.

"It's an illusion," Theo replied.

"Twenty-four point eight miles. Just a little bit less than a marathon. People run that in like three hours," Ilana said.

Then she glanced over at me and smiled. "But don't worry. You won't need to run it."

"Well, good," I said. "Because I would smoke you all. Even you, Julia!"

"Watch out," Benji said. "Mori Bloom is fired up!"

And I was. A week before, I never would've believed this was possible.

Ilana straddled tracks and walked with one foot on each rail. She stepped right over a tiny white starflower. I thought she hadn't noticed, but then she turned around and whispered to me, "Star light, star bright, first star I see tonight."

She didn't need to finish. We were all wishing for the same thing: Ilana's safety.

We walked on toward the glow of the city.

"All those lights," Julia said. "It's like a million people. At least."

"Two point seven million," Ilana said.

I shuddered. Nothing we had ever heard about the city was good. Fortunately, we didn't have to go into Boston proper. We were headed for Cambridge, a city just on the other side of the Charles River. Close enough to Boston. Dangerous enough. Scary enough. My mouth went dry as a garden before the rain.

Benji brushed against me as he caught up with Ilana. "I was wondering, what do you remember about Calliope?"

"Why?" Ilana asked.

"She wasn't actually there, you know," Julia said.

"Yeah, but she remembers it, and that's pretty cool. I was just wondering how detailed those memories were."

Ilana tugged at a curl. "I remember the cafeteria at my school."

"Was the food good?" Benji asked.

Theo punched him in the arm. "She didn't eat it. She wasn't there."

"I remember how it smelled. Like eggs. Fried eggs. But we never had breakfast there. Isn't that weird?"

"Your brain must have created a false connection," I said. "That smell probably goes back to something at the lab where you—" I stopped myself, but Ilana looked at me expectantly, almost hopefully. "Where you were born."

Ilana pivoted to face me. I tilted my head back to look up into her green-blue eyes, which flashed with anger. "I wasn't born. That's the whole problem. That's why we're out here on this silly walk."

I rocked back, surprised by her sudden anger. Theo stepped up between us. "Hey." His voice was low. "Mori's just trying to help you."

I knew what he was thinking. We all did. The truth was, we didn't really know what she was capable of, and whether or not something might glitch up her programming.

Ilana looked down at her orange canvas sneakers, the toes scuffed black from the tracks. "Sure. Whatever. Sorry."

I bit my lip. What if Ilana's functioning was somehow tied to Old Harmonie? We thought we'd gotten her tracker out, sure, but what if there was some deeper connection between her and the lab back at KritaCorp? It was possible, I imagined, that her whole operating system was linked to their servers and as we got farther away and the connection weakened, she might face more problems.

Theo brushed his hand through his hair. "We just can't do this right now, Ilana." We all knew what he meant by *this*. If Ilana glitched, we were done for.

If she *was* glitching, it could be related to the programming they'd given to her. They'd never seemed to get it quite right. I rubbed my arm. The bruise she had given me was mostly gone, but of course I still remembered her grip tightening around my biceps. The truth was, whoever had designed Ilana was smart. Really smart. And even they hadn't fully understood her. How could I expect to?

Stop, I told myself. The way my thoughts were spiraling, that wasn't really me, I had to remember that. That was the fear that came from being dampened. My parents had been trying to protect me, and so they'd taken away my bravery and made me afraid of everything. Just thinking about it started a red, angry feeling all over my body. I could feel it in my stomach and my head and the tight set of my lips. Who were they to change who I was? I had been bold and wild and that scared them, so they had made me fearful. I kicked at a rock. Angry was better than nervous, I decided. Anger pushed me forward.

"It's okay," I said. "We're back on track now. Let's just keep going."

"Good one, Mori." Benji laughed. "Back on track."

Theo grimaced. "We should be able to do it in less than twelve hours, so even with some breaks, we should get there by the afternoon. And then we find MIT and Dr. Varden."

"I still say that's a pretty weak final stage of the plan," Julia said. She was wearing a sweatshirt with reflective strips down the arms, and every once in a while they would catch the faint moonlight and gleam.

"Dr. Varden is still listed as a member of the lab. Professor emerita, whatever that means. It's in the Stata Center," Theo said. "Getting there will probably be the easy part."

"We'll find her," Benji agreed.

"She'll know what to do," I said. "She'll help us. She has to."

"That's the shaky part of the plan," Ilana said.

But I knew Ilana was wrong. Dr. Agatha Varden had founded Old Harmonie. She'd helped to design the ALANA project—the predecessor to the project that had created Ilana. But more than that, she'd been my great-grandmother's best friend. That's how I knew she'd help us.

"You cold?" Ilana asked me. "You can have my sweatshirt. I'm pretty warm, actually."

"I just want to get you there and get you safe," I told Ilana.

Ilana looked up at the sky. Her jaw was set in a hard line.

"She will help you, Ilana," I said. "I promise."

"You can't make a promise for someone else."

"I just know she will, that's all."

"She was Mori's baba's best friend. That matters," Julia told Ilana, with a bit of edge in her voice.

Ilana stopped walking. She pushed her fingers into her temples.

"What's wrong?" I asked.

Theo and Benji turned back to look at us. "You okay, Ilana?" Benji asked.

Ilana didn't answer. She closed her eyes.

I remembered the day in the pool when she had just shut down. "Ilana," I cried. "Ilana!" I grabbed her by the arms. "Don't do this again!"

She blinked her eyes open. "It's a headache. That's all."

I glanced over my shoulder at Benji. I wished I could telegraph my question right to his brain: *What if they had programmed her to stop? What if she can't go any farther?*

"THE NICENESS OF THE OUTSIDE world is actually a little disappointing," Benji said. "Like, I was expecting plagues of locusts and mind-sucking zombies and all that stuff."

"They might not be locusts, but these bugs *are* awful!" Julia punctuated her sentence with a hard slap against her calf. "Ha! Got you!" She held up her hand smeared with her own blood. "I am the slayer of beasts. If there were mind-sucking zombies, I'd save your life."

"I'm sure you would," Benji said.

"When I was little, and I'd hear about the bogeyman or monsters or whatever, I'd think it was someone from outside," I said.

"I used to have nightmares my parents brought me out

here and left me here," Julia confessed. "It was like this dark, burned-down landscape. No trees, no houses, nothing."

"But you could see the forest from Old Harmonie," Ilana said.

"But we couldn't really see beyond it," Julia said. "I'd have one of those nightmares and I could hardly sleep for weeks."

"And now here it is—all big, pretty trees and cool night air," Benji said, holding his arms wide. "Nothing scary at all."

"Except the bugs," Julia said.

"Except the bugs," Benji agreed. "Where's the danger? You can't have an adventure without danger."

"You'd better stop talking like that, Benji," I said.

"What?" he asked.

"I'm serious. If you jinx us—"

"There's no such thing as jinxes, Mori," Theo said.

"That's true," Ilana agreed. "If you see something as bad luck, that's just your way of seeing it. The universe doesn't care."

But not five minutes later, we ran right into our first big obstacle.

"What is that?" Julia asked. We all stopped short.

We'd come around a bend and then up a slight hill that had blocked our view of the city lights. We'd crested the top and now saw something hazy and pink shimmering in front of us.

"This makes no sense," Theo said.

"Beautiful things usually don't," I heard myself reply.

It was a lake. The rising sun was reflected across the flat surface of the water, so it seemed like we were being swallowed in a golden pink-and-red haze. I felt my breath go shallow at the beauty of the lake that appeared out of nowhere.

"This makes no sense," Theo said again in a low, quiet voice.

I knew he wasn't thinking about the sunrise or the steam off the water or the way it made me feel full of awe to the point I thought I might actually start crying. He was talking about how the train tracks ran right into the water, which lazily lapped at the rails.

"It's not on the map?" Benji asked.

Theo shook his head.

"How old is the map?" Ilana asked.

Theo spread out the creased paper and we all peered at it. "See, we're right here. There's no water anywhere. Just that river off to the west a bit." His voice sounded hollow.

Julia sighed. "See the copyright? This map is decades old."

Theo's face turned ashen, even in the pinkish light. "We can't," he began. Then he turned to Ilana, who was crouched down beside him. "I'm sorry. I didn't even think about how it might be out-of-date. I'm just used to maps that are always updated. I wasn't even thinking."

"It's okay," she said. She smoothed out the map with the palm of her hand.

"But now we have no idea—"

Ilana cut Theo off: "In a situation like this, there are always three choices: over, around, or through."

"Or back," Julia said.

I blinked. "No."

"Mori, just look at this lake: it's huge. We can't see where it ends. And without a map, we have no way of knowing how big it is. If we walk around, it could be miles and miles and who even knows where we would end up."

"I guess it's over or through, then," I said. I held my body as still and tall as I could, as if standing strong would make me feel strong.

"Are you honestly suggesting we swim? Or, what, build a boat?"

"We could build a raft," Benji offered.

"I'm saying that if we've come this far, we ought to at least look around before we give up entirely."

"Mori's right," Theo said. "Maybe there's another way across. Let's just split up and walk along the edge in each direction and see what we can find. Fifteen minutes out and back. That's it."

"Then we make a decision?" Julia asked.

"Exactly. An informed decision," Theo replied.

Julia twirled her braid. "Fine. But to be clear, building a raft is not actually an option."

"It wouldn't be that hard," Benji said. "We have access to plenty of wood. We'd just need to find something to hold it all together. Maybe some vines or—"

Julia narrowed her eyes at him.

"Mori, you can come with me," Theo said. "Benji, Ilana, and Julia, you go that way."

Ilana and Julia both hesitated, but then they headed off in the southerly direction, while Theo and I went north. We had only walked about five minutes when we saw a granite post with a plaque on it:

ALCOTT RESERVOIR
Drinking water area.
No swimming, boating, or fishing allowed.
No trespassing.

Underneath, the words "KritaCorp" were stamped in firm, capital letters.

"This is where our water comes from," I said.

"Of course," Theo said, and pushed his bangs from his forehead.

"But if this is our reservoir—" I began.

Theo interrupted me. "I knew the reservoir was east of Old Harmonie. What was I thinking?"

"It's not your fault. None of us thought of it either. None of us even thought to get a map."

"I'm guessing there's a lot we didn't think of."

He was right, of course. We'd barely had a shadow of a plan when we set out, so no wonder it was falling apart.

The bright sunrise was over, but the sky was still a dusty pink. My eyes were drawn to a shape by the shore: dull brown and arched toward the water. A tree that had toppled? Or could it be a rock?

Then the shape stood up.

I grabbed Theo's arm and pulled him to the ground. Perhaps it was the sheer shock of my forcefulness that kept him quiet. My glasses jostled off my face, but we were close enough, our cheeks against rough sand, that I could see his wide eyes. "Outsider," I whispered.

Megan Frazer Blakemore is the author of *The Daybreak Bond*, *The Firefly Code*, *The Friendship Riddle*, *The Spy Catchers of Maple Hill*, and *The Water Castle*, which was listed as a *Kirkus Reviews* Best Book of the Year, a Bank Street Best Book of the Year, and a New York Public Library Best Book for Reading and Sharing. She is also the author of the young adult novels *Secrets of Truth & Beauty*, *Very in Pieces*, and *Good and Gone*. A part-time school librarian, Megan lives in Maine with her family.

www.meganfrazer.com
@meganbfrazer

From **sweet** friendships
to **high-stakes** adventure
to **unexpected** magic,
there's a lot to love
from Kate Messner!

www.bloomsbury.com
Twitter: BloomsburyKids
Facebook: KidsBloomsbury

Get swept away by these stories from
Megan Frazer Blakemore!

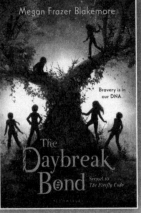